Praise for *The Cloud St...*

The Cloud Strike Prop... fiction. David wrote the novel to inform the reader about radical Islam while introducing the gospel in the context of the narrative. His novel fulfills both aims with remarkable success.

As a student of Islam and radical Muslims, I can attest to the truthfulness of his information and description. Jihadists are the greatest threat Western culture has ever faced. His novel explains their beliefs and exposes their vision for national and global conquest.

His plot is compelling and believable. David demonstrates a strong grasp of Jewish history and culture (he's led more than 20 study tours of the Holy Land), and sets his characters and narrative within a fascinating Hebrew context. The strategy he describes for a jihadist attack on Americans is chillingly realistic. I've read everything Tom Clancy and Robert Ludlum wrote and found David's novel to be in their league as a thriller.

While engaging the reader with a powerful story, he presents the gospel clearly through his narrative. The reader never feels that the Christian faith is forced on the plot, but encounters the love of God as the characters experience it. I will be giving the novel to non-believers I know, confident that they will enjoy the book and will understand God's grace more fully.

The Cloud Strike Prophecy is a work of fiction, but the issues it addresses are not. Nor is the good news it offers the world.

James C. Denison, Ph.D.
President, Denison Forum on Truth and Culture

1

Wadi Qumran
Northwestern Shore of the Dead Sea

It was much too pretty a day for the end of the world—as the Teacher of Righteousness had predicted. Judah ben Simon paused from his climb up the steep rock face and wiped the sweat from his eyes. He glanced back over his shoulder at the azure water of the Dead Sea. Though the sky was cloudless, the colors shifted and changed throughout the day and now it was the deepest blue he could remember seeing.

He shifted the weight of his burden to his other shoulder and allowed his eyes to gaze westward over the Judean mountains. Thirteen miles due west, Jerusalem was under attack. A thick cloud of black smoke rose and covered the horizon. The prevailing wind carried the pungent smell of charred buildings and trees.

Groups of Jews fleeing the Roman attack reported that the Holy Temple had been overrun and the soldiers of General Titus had set fire to the entire complex. Roman swords were stained with the blood of thousands of Jews who had desperately clung

5

to the Temple in the misplaced belief that Yahweh would come at the last moment and rescue them. But heaven was silent. Surely this was the final event that the Teacher had promised would come to end the age.

All but a few members of the Yahad Community at Qumran had already fled. Only Judah and three master scribes, too old to travel, remained. The scribes had spent the last ten sleepless days quickly and carefully preserving over 600 of the Holy Scrolls. The scrolls contained the words of Scripture, the rules of the Community, and the Teacher's predictions about the Messiah and the Final War between the Sons of Light and the Sons of Darkness.

The master scribes lovingly coiled the scrolls and sealed them with beeswax before placing them inside linen bags. The tops of the bags were tied with cords of woven palm leaves and then sealed again with more beeswax. Finally, the sacks were inserted into tall clay jars specifically made for this purpose. A lid was added that fit perfectly over the opening and was then sealed with a double layer of the beeswax. A prayer for preservation was recited over each jar.

As an apprentice, Judah's job was to carry the jars, three at a time, into the caves dotting the limestone hills rising from the Dead Sea. Two other apprentices had been helping him for the past three weeks, but they had both disappeared, joining the frightened mob fleeing the Romans.

Judah felt as if he had been climbing this same mountain forever. He was hungry and frightened but mostly exhausted. The Teacher of Righteousness had left specific instructions to hide the scrolls in twelve caves, representing the twelve tribes of Israel. The master scribes had chosen the caves from the compound below and pointed them out to Judah. They watched as he scaled the cliff.

This final climb was different. He was carrying only two scrolls. One was a special copper scroll. The other, the War Scroll, was inside the largest jar he had seen. He had overheard two members of the Community mention in hushed tones about how the War Scroll was the most sacred, but Judah didn't care about that by now. He was just happy to be nearing the end of his task.

When he asked the master scribes what was so special about these two scrolls, they refused to answer a lowly apprentice like Judah. His only instruction was to carry these last two scrolls to the highest and smallest cave, one that couldn't even be seen from the foot of the mountain. After climbing over the final ridge, Judah carefully deposited the last jars. When he returned to the compound, it was deserted. He wondered where the master scribes had gone, but he wasn't going to try to find out. Grabbing his small pack, he joined the ranks of Jews fleeing Jerusalem for Masada.

2

November 21, 1946
Wadi Qumran, Northwestern Shore of the Dead Sea
4:38pm

Khalil was terrified. He grabbed for a toehold on the steep, limestone rock face, but his thin sandals kept slipping. His fingers were starting to cramp from the strain, so he kicked off his sandals, freeing his toes to dig into the cliff. He watched them fall over 300 meters to the rocky floor beneath the cliff. Curling his toes over a small ridge, he gained traction and held on. His cousins Muhammed and Ju'ma laughed from below, taunting him.

"Come on, mountain goat! Are you afraid? That climb should be easy for a stinking goat like you!"

Their insults strengthened his resolve and Khalil managed to scale up onto a narrow ledge. He was no goat. But he was trying to herd some goats with a streak of rebellion in them. He looked up to see three of his bearded charge calmly munching a rare sprig of grass growing on a ledge 20 meters above him.

He couldn't lose the goats or his uncle would beat him without mercy.

There was no way he could climb up to them, so he grabbed a nearby stone and took careful aim. If he could throw the rock above the skittish animals, he might scare them down the mountain. The rock flew over the goats and disappeared. Khalil heard a distinctive "clunk" when the rock landed, which the goats promptly ignored. His trained ear recognized the sound of breaking pottery.

His uncle had told stories of hidden treasure in the mountains. Could this be a hidden treasure trove?

Curiosity and greed drove him upward. Carefully gaining footholds and handholds, Khalil eventually reached the ridge where the goats were feeding. He peered into a shallow cave that had not been visible below. As his eyes adjusted to the darkness, he saw over forty dusty clay jars. One was cracked open from his errant throw.

Climbing down into the cave, Khalil's heart hammered inside his chest. Would he find gold or jewels inside these tall clay pots? He was already thinking about ways to spend the riches that would soon be his.

Removing the lid of the broken jar, he extracted the contents. The remains of an old straw bag fell apart in his hands. He brushed away the powdery remnants to examine his treasure. Excitement quickly turned to disappointment as he realized that his "treasure" was just a worthless, old scroll. He broke the dried wax seal and stared at the strange writing. Khalil had never learned to read in any language, so he didn't recognize the Hebrew characters visible on the scroll.

Khalil broke open the lids of six other jars, hoping to find something of value. But each jar contained the same useless old scrolls. He stuffed all seven scrolls into his shirt and climbed out of the cave. After driving the goats down the mountainside, he started the long, slow descent to the foot of the mountain where his Bedouin cousins were waiting.

Khalil didn't realize that the scrolls he had discovered near the Dead Sea were indeed priceless. Mere fragments would eventually be worth billions of dollars and change the course of history—and the future.

3

MARCH 26
Alpharetta, Georgia
1:38am

Regan noticed the dark windows of her townhome as she pulled her silver Mercedes C250 into her designated parking space. Digging in her purse for her keys, she got out of the car and made her way to the front door, pulling her large Louis Vuitton suitcase behind her in an exhausted daze. Somewhere on her block of identical-looking redbrick townhomes a dog barked, annoyed with her late arrival.

After finding the right key, she entered the front door and fumbled for the light switch in the entryway. Nothing. She flicked the switch up and down. Still nothing. Making her way down the short hall to the living room, she tried another light switch and confirmed her suspicion. Her power was off. Again. She had forgotten to pay the electric bill. Again. This identical scenario had played out late one evening only two months ago. But then again, she hadn't been home for two months either.

"Come on," she complained aloud to no one in particular, letting her luggage fall awkwardly to the floor. In the darkness, she felt her way along the wall to her bedroom and climbed onto the top of her bed wearing the same clothes she'd had on since about 17 hours ago when she'd left her Paris flat for Charles de Gaulle Airport.

She didn't even have the patience to stay awake long enough to dig out her pajamas or wash her face. She didn't care—morning would be here soon enough. Fortunately, it was a pleasant evening this time of year, early spring in Georgia. Had this happened a month later, sleep would have been impossible without air-conditioning.

It was difficult to keep up with her life in two places. By now, she had a separate wardrobe, bank account, commuter route and favorite restaurant in Paris and Georgia where she split her time. Paying taxes in both countries was another bonus to her dual lifestyle—one she could do without. But she was paid well, all things considered. Besides, what was she going to change? There wasn't anything she could do except quit her job and that was out of the question. First principle of wing walking: Never let go of what you've got until you've got hold of something else. What that something else could be, Regan had no idea. But sometimes she felt as if it might be out there looking for her— whatever it was—a new career, a place in the country, maybe a boyfriend. Or at least a date. That would be nice. Was that too much to ask? She threw a leg over her pillow, but before she drifted off to sleep, she remembered something. Something important.

Regan sat up in bed so fast that it made her dizzy for a

moment. She tried to get her tired mind to review the events of the day. She recalled frantically packing for her trip in her Paris apartment in the Marais district earlier that day. She remembered nervously watching the clock, afraid she would miss her flight home again. Regan was brilliant in many fields, but she sometimes had a difficult time reasoning time and distance. As she threw her remaining clothes in her suitcase, the bell in her Paris apartment began ringing incessantly. She answered her door and saw a girl standing there with a sheepish grin on her face.

Bridget worked at the same financial consulting firm with Regan and they had become acquaintances, although not friends, over the past two months. Bridget's beautiful, dark eyes shone out from under the cover of her hijab, a head covering worn by all conservative Muslim women. Bridget spoke French and Arabic fluently but struggled with English.

"Pardon moi, Miss Regan. I mean to gave you this gift at office. But you leave before I have chance. I am sorry."

She held out a gift wrapped in shiny gold paper. It was the size and weight of a college textbook.

Regan said, "Oh, Bridget. You didn't have to buy me a gift! I'm not leaving. I'll be back in a few weeks."

Bridget smiled but she seemed nervous as she explained, "Oh. This gift, please, is to my sister, which is living in Atlanta. Can you be as kind to take to her? Here is card with her address. Please, may you take it for her soon after you arrive?"

Regan had been anxious for Bridget to leave so she could complete her packing and grab a taxi to the Charles de Gaulle airport.

"Certainly, Bridget. I'll be glad to help." Bridget thanked her and left.

Regan stuffed the card in her purse and tossed the gift into her already-full suitcase. Zipping it up, she pulled it to the street to hail a cab.

Ninety minutes later, after chewing one of her fingernails to the quick because of the Paris traffic, she arrived at the Delta check-in counter. She got her boarding pass and checked her bag to ATL. When she arrived at the security checkpoint, an officer asked her, "Did anyone give you any packages or gifts to carry in your luggage?" Regan thought momentarily about Bridget's last-minute gift, but she was running late. So she smiled and said, "No, officer." After security, she hurried to her gate. Just as she arrived, her flight started boarding.

With a deep sigh, Regan settled into her Delta Business Elite seat near the front of the aircraft. Although she paid an exorbitant price for this seat, she didn't mind. Money was the least of her worries. Since graduating with an MBA from Harvard, Regan had honed her skills in predicting the global commodities markets. She based her calculations on proprietary software developed by one of her fellow Harvard students. The executives of Global Wealth Advisors, or GWA, considered her a near wizard at predicting the fluctuations in the futures prices of copper, coffee, and sugar. Her recommendations had paid off in a profit of hundreds of millions of dollars for the big-hitters in the commodities market. GWA paid her an obscene salary, which included an extravagant travel expense account to commute between their two headquarters in France and the United States.

As she fluffed her thick pillow in her oversized seat, she smiled. She considered the comfort, quiet, and amenities of this class to be well worth every dollar.

After the flight attendant cleared away her dessert dish, Regan pushed a button on the armrest and her seat reclined to a fully lie-flat bed. She had already slipped into her flannel pajamas and slippers provided to first class passengers. With two layers of duvets and an extra pillow, the bed looked inviting, but once she placed the soft eye mask over her face, she found it difficult to sleep. A multitude of thoughts competing for her attention made her rest fitfully.

Eleven hours later, after landing at Hartsfield Jackson International in Atlanta, she cleared passport control quickly. As a frequent traveler, she was a Trusted Traveler in the Global Entry program offered by the T.S.A., which allowed her to speed through a special line reserved only for passengers with this standing.

She walked straight to the Global Entry kiosk, inserted her passport into the slot and within fifteen seconds she had received her print-out to proceed to baggage claim. Within minutes, she was passing through customs and aboard the shuttle bus to claim her car in remote parking. Since it was after midnight, the Atlanta traffic was sparse. She made it to her home in only 45 minutes. She should have known things were running a bit too smoothly.

Regan hadn't given Bridget's gift any thought until now. As she sat up in her bed, she remembered the package. She barely knew Bridget, and the few times that they had talked, she seemed to be a kind person. Regan didn't recall telling Bridget where she was from, but that must have come up in some conversation.

"Why are you so paranoid?" she asked herself. "It's probably just a harmless gift—maybe a book."

Unable to return to sleep, Regan slipped out of bed and used a flashlight app on her almost-dead iPhone to illuminate her suitcase as she zipped it open. There was the mysterious package. She picked it up and examined it. Should she open it and examine the contents before she delivered it to Bridget's sister? No, she decided, that would not be right. After all, it was a gift and Bridget was a nice girl. Still, she wondered why Bridget had waited until the last minute to give it to her and even made a special trip over to her Paris apartment.

"Stop driving yourself crazy," Regan said to herself. "It's just a gift." She padded into the foyer and laid the package on the entryway table beside her purse. That way she would be reminded to deliver it tomorrow.

Regan's head fell heavy against her pillow once more when she made it back to her bed. She was definitely not going to figure out anything else tonight, which was actually now Saturday morning. Sleep soon overcame her weary mind and she drifted into her dreams.

4

6:15am

Daylight was streaming into her bedroom windows. Regan stretched, smoothed her hair off her forehead and decided to dress and go out for coffee since there was nothing to eat in the house. She headed to grab her purse off the entryway table and a flash of something small and dark caught her eye. It was a cricket. *How did that get in here?* Regan wondered. She scooped it up and was about to open the front door to release it when she noticed the open window in her dining room. At once, she turned and saw that her purse, which contained her keys and her phone, was gone. And so was the package.

Regan was confused. Did she leave the window open?

But within seconds, her thoughts began to crystallize around a horrible realization. She didn't leave the window open, and she always left her purse in the same spot.

"Someone has broken in my house!" she cried.

She felt nauseated at the thought of someone violating her personal space. Fear gripped her mind with an iron fist as she considered the possibility that the intruder might still be inside.

She thought about her alarm system and wondered why it

hadn't alerted her before she remembered that her electricity was off. She didn't have a gun in her house. When her friends had told her she needed a firearm to protect herself, she had been the first to laugh and say that the only thing she would do with a gun is shoot her own foot. But now she chided herself for not being armed.

Regan tiptoed over to the fireplace and grabbed the first thing that might serve as a weapon, a metal poker with a sharp point. The fireplace set was only for decoration since the gas logs were ceramic. The handle of the poker felt flimsy and cheap, but it gave her a small sense of security.

She slowly moved from room to room, fully expecting a dark figure to jump out and grab her at any moment. The toughest task was opening each closet door and looking into the darkness to try to find evidence of an intruder.

Tired of slinking around her own home, she was finally convinced that she was alone. She didn't see anything else missing.

She sat down heavily on her favorite ottoman and tried to collect her thoughts amid a jet-lagged mind.

Okay, what do I need to do? she wondered. *Maybe I should call 911 now.*

Regan didn't have a landline since she conducted all her business online or with her smart phone. She got up and walked to the table in the entryway to retrieve her iPhone, which she kept in a special pocket in her purse. Her brain was so mushed by now that she thought, *Now where did I leave my purse?... Oh, yeah. Right. It's gone. Girl, you really are losing it.*

She felt the first flood of emotion coming over her. Her

eyes swelled and filled with tears. She knew her only solution was to visit a neighbor to ask for help. But she didn't know any of her neighbors. This was strictly a place where she slept and worked. She didn't really consider it home and had intentionally refrained from making friends. Her mom lived hundreds of miles away in Alabama.

She stormed out her front door and halfway down her short sidewalk, the tears coming in a fresh flood of frustration. Angry at her weakness, she gritted her teeth and muttered, "I am *not* going to cry!"

As she sniffed loudly and defiantly wiped the tears away, she looked up to see a tall man at the end of the sidewalk of the neighboring townhome. Standing only ten feet away, he had just retrieved his newspaper. He was holding a cup of coffee and staring at her with a sly grin on his face. A second of awkward silence passed. Then he spoke in a deep voice cast with a hint of humor, "Hey, as the song says, 'It's your party and you can cry if you want to...'"

Regan was speechless.

"Uh, sorry," the man said, his smile faded. "Are you okay?"

Regan was at a loss for words, which was unusual for her. She wiped her nose as she stared at this stranger who apparently lived next to her. He was well over six feet tall, slender, with a head-full of salt and pepper hair still unruly from sleep. He was dressed in pajamas, slippers, and a robe. With a coffee cup in one hand and his paper in the other, he looked relaxed and handsome.

Regan had a silly thought that almost had her blubbering with inappropriate laughter. And she was the queen of inappropriate laughter. She thought, *If only he had a pipe in his hand, I would think that Hugh Hefner, Jr. was my neighbor!*

But no words came out of her mouth. She brushed her hair from her face and thought about how she hadn't taken the time to fix her hair or apply make-up. She imagined he must think she was a crazy homeless woman.

Before she could come up with an explanation, he held out a hand and said, "Hi. My name is Tyler Kensington. I don't think we've ever met."

5

TWO YEARS EARLIER

JANUARY 5, 2011
12,000 feet above Wadi Marib, Yemen

It was just after dawn as the CIA-controlled RQ-1A Predator Drone cruised above the desert sands of Yemen making hardly more noise than a commercial weed eater. The pilotless craft was under the control of a twenty-six-year-old operative sitting in air-conditioned safety 200 miles away aboard the USS George H.W. Bush in the Arabian Sea. Bush, a Nimitz-class super carrier, contained metal in her hull manufactured from re-forged steel from the World Trade Center wreckage.

The pilot, along with two sensor operators, didn't resemble the typical hotshot fighter pilot. Each was chosen for this specific job because of his ability to control a remote aircraft with a joystick while watching a computer screen. This skill had been honed by thousands of hours spent gaming as teenagers.

But this was no game.

"Tracking the SUV now," reported the pilot into his mouthpiece.

"Roger that," replied CIA officer Tony Parker.

The conversation was occurring real-time, but Tony was 7,000 miles away at CIA headquarters in Langley, Virginia. Parker was a 30-year veteran of the CIA and had climbed to what he assumed was the top rung of his career ladder as the Chief of the MENA Office (Middle East and North Africa Analysis).

The drone's camera was focused on a white Toyota Land Cruiser raising a rooster tail of dust as it sped across the desert. Local human Intel had confirmed that Anwar al-Rimi, a senior Al-Qaeda leader, was in the SUV. Al-Rimi had planned the attack on a U.S. run hospital in the Marib province three years earlier where three American medical workers were killed. Recent chatter indicated that he was planning another upcoming attack on an American oil company office.

"Locked on target," the pilot reported. The beeping tone in his headset and the green indicator on his screen verified that the Hellfire missile was locked on the moving SUV. Parker glanced at the three assistants watching the same image. "Any objections to launch?" he asked.

All three shook their heads no. The SUV was quickly approaching the outskirts of the village of Wadi Marib, which contained about a dozen buildings. It was now or never.

"Permission to fire on target," Parker commanded.

"Permission to fire on target confirmed. Missile away."

With practiced ease, the young pilot raised a protective cover on the right side of his joystick and flicked a switch into firing position and depressed it. The sound in his headset changed to a constant tone and the propellant of the 100-pound Hellfire briefly obscured the image on his screen as it launched toward its target reaching a speed of Mach 1.3.

In less than five seconds, the missile tracked toward the vehicle, trailing a stream of white smoke. On the screen, the SUV swerved violently off the road trying to avoid the missile at the last second, but it was a futile effort. The rocket slammed into the truck at almost 1,000 mph and detonated at the same moment. None of the occupants could survive such a blast.

As smoke and fire erupted from the SUV, the momentum of the blazing truck carried the inferno another 100 feet until it slammed into one of the houses on the outskirts of Wadi Marib. The building was quickly engulfed in the fiery conflagration.

Parker turned to his assistants and said, "I think we got the bad guy. But let's hope there weren't any civilians in that building."

***

Bridget, whose real name was Ameera Saad, awoke at once at the sound of the massive explosion near the front of her home. At first she was confused and tried to remember where she was. In a split second it became clear. This wasn't her apartment in Paris. No, she remembered that she was home on holiday and her proud parents had spent the last days hosting their friends and beaming with joy about how successful Ameera had become in her job at a global financial firm in Paris.

But all that was forgotten as Ameera jumped out of bed and ran terrified toward the front of the house. She couldn't make it past the kitchen because there were flames spreading everywhere and gasoline covering the floor. She could hear screaming from the front room, but there was no way she could help. The flames and smoke were already robbing her of precious oxygen. Unable to breathe, she knew that if she fell there she would die. With her last ounce of strength, she lunged for the back door and fell hard onto the dirt. Her final thought before passing out was of fire and smoke, and she briefly wondered if she was already dead and in hell.

When Ameera opened her eyes, she realized she was lying on crisp sheets in a white room with a brilliant light shining into her face. *Is this Paradise?* she wondered for a moment. But the dull ache in her shoulder reminded her that she still had the ability to feel pain. And she felt pinpricks and pressure on her right thigh as if someone were sewing her skin together.

She tried to speak through her cracked lips and all she could utter was, "Where...?" At once, she recognized the face of her father as he moved over her with a small cup of water.

"Here, my princess. Don't speak. Just drink."

The cool water tasted delicious and after the first cup, she gulped down two more. Her parched mouth finally had enough moisture to ask, "Where am I?"

"In a hospital," her father began. Her eyes welled up with tears at this news.

"No, no," her father shushed, touching her arm. "Just a bruise to your shoulder, and your leg has a wound from when you fell on a sharp rock. The doctor is sewing up your leg now."

Her father's smoke-darkened face came into focus. She noticed dirty tracks of tears running down the crevices on his weathered cheek.

"What happened, Father?" she asked.

His shoulders now shook with unabashed sorrow. "They're gone!" he managed between sobs. "Your mother and Akmed are dead."

***

Dr. Hakeem Saad left his daughter's side at the hospital with a heavy mixture of deep sorrow and barely controlled rage. His world had just changed. Military Investigators had already determined that the fire that robbed him of his wife of forty-two years and his thirty-year-old son had been caused by a rocket attack from a drone aimed at an SUV that had crashed into the front of his home. Dr. Saad knew that the Americans flew the Predator drones over Yemen.

He had left his house before dawn that morning after bowing on his prayer mat toward Mecca and saying the Fajr. The drive to his job would take an hour. As Head of the Biotechnology department at the University of Science and Technology in Sana'a, Dr. Saad was scheduled to lead the faculty meeting later that morning.

The meeting never happened. A frantic neighbor had been the one to call his cell phone and tell him that his house was engulfed in flames.

He had driven like a madman back to Wadi Marib. When he saw the smoking ruins of what had been his house, he knew there would be no survivors. The remaining shell appeared to have been bombed. He fell to his knees in shock as he viewed the charred remains of his life, certain his wife, son, and daughter had been in the house.

Just then, the leader of the local volunteer fire department delivered the sad news that two bodies had been discovered in the remains.

"Two?" he had asked. "But there were three people in my home. Who survived?"

"We found your daughter, Ameera, in the alley. She was unconscious and injured, so we sent her in an ambulance to the hospital in Sana'a.

Now as he drove back to his office on campus, he realized that he could very easily be dead himself. He praised Allah for sparing his life.

For the first time in many years, he thought back to his work in Iraq before he had escaped after the First Gulf War. Here in Yemen he was known as a science professor. Nobody knew what kind of work he had done as part of Saddam Hussein's evil regime. A plan now began to formulate in his mind. He made a silent vow to Allah that he would extract vengeance on the Great Satan, the United States, for what they had done to his family.

6

JANUARY 19, 2011
Hajjah, Yemen
11:52pm

Dr. Saad glanced at his watch and wondered for the twentieth time tonight if this was a smart move or not. He had been standing outside an abandoned bunker for the past hour waiting for someone to meet him. The instructions indicated that he should be there at 11:30pm. It was now almost midnight.

This is crazy, Dr. Saad thought. *I should probably just forget it and go back home.* But he no longer had a home. The American devils had destroyed it on the morning they murdered his wife and son. After Ameera was released from the hospital, some relatives took them in.

He had thought it would be relatively easy to contact a member of a jihadi group in Yemen. Yemen was a hotbed for terrorist organizations, but he had discovered that they didn't take out ads in the newspaper or host a website enlisting soldiers. The Americans had spies everywhere and nobody could be trusted.

He had finally received a lead through a former science

professor who had been fired for seditious activities. This professor had given Dr. Saad a phone number to call.

When the call was answered a voice said, "Hang up immediately. You will be called back at this number."

Dr. Saad had done exactly as they asked, but nobody called back that day. On the next day, his phone rang at 5:00am. He rubbed the sleep out of his eyes and said, "Hello."

A strange voice said, "Dr. Saad? That is your name, correct?"

"Yes it is. Who are you?" Dr. Saad replied.

"I'll ask the questions," the voice seethed. "Now, convince me why an old science professor thinks he can help in our holy jihad."

"The American infidels killed my wife and son two weeks ago," Dr. Saad shouted passionately into the receiver. "I have pledged to Allah that I will punish them for this act of murder, or I will die trying."

There was silence.

"Hello, are you there?" Dr. Saad asked.

Click. The other party hung up.

An hour later, his phone rang again. Another voice told him, "Meet us tonight in front of the abandoned bunker on the N5 highway four kilometers southwest of Hajjah. Park your car and walk a hundred paces toward the bunker. Be there at 11:30pm and come alone."

The caller hung up before he could ask any questions.

Now, alone in the total darkness, he had waited in front of the said bunker almost thirty minutes and hadn't seen another vehicle. He was ready to turn and walk back toward his car when the brilliant light from four car headlights suddenly cut through the darkness. The headlights silhouetted him in a milky white glow and he held up his hand to shade his eyes.

A calm but authoritative voice spoke, "Dr. Saad, turn around. Place your hands behind your head and get on your knees."

A cold bead of sweat started down the side of his forehead as he did as they instructed. He heard footsteps crunching on the pavement as two men approached him from behind.

Without warning, a thick, black cloth bag was placed over his head. He couldn't see anything and could barely breathe.

"Is this necessary?" Dr. Saad mumbled.

"Silence!" the voice answered. Then the man roughly pushed him forward onto his face. Dr. Saad barely had time to put his hands out to catch his fall, preventing his head from smashing to the pavement.

Then one of the men roughly grabbed his hands and pulled them behind his back. He clipped them together using plastic ties to bind them.

"Ouch, that's too tight," Dr. Saad protested. "Hey, I'm not the enemy."

"We'll be the judge of that," one of the other men said.

Each man grabbed a shoulder and hoisted him to his feet. One of them frisked him to make sure he wasn't armed. When he was satisfied he commanded, "Walk with us."

The two men stood on each side and guided him for what seemed like 300 meters. They left the pavement and walked through sand. Finally, they came to a stop. Dr. Saad was breathing hard from the exertion and the lack of air in the suffocating bag.

Without warning, they tossed him into the back of an SUV.

The door slammed and the truck pulled onto the highway. For the next hour and a half, Dr. Saad felt every bump and hole in the road. Finally, he sensed that the truck slowed down and made a turn. He could tell they were climbing slowly over a rough road. After ten minutes, they stopped.

The back door opened and the two men collected Dr. Saad and led him inside a building before shoving him into a chair. The two men then left the room.

His patience exhausted, he was ready to yell out for help. But before he could form the words, a door opened. He heard someone approach him from behind and was relieved when the plastic ties around his wrists were snipped. Dr. Saad brought his arms around to the front of his body and rubbed them, trying to get the blood flowing again. Then the hood was removed from his head.

He looked around and found that he was sitting in a small, nicely decorated room. It was spartan but clean. There were rugs and pillows on the floors amid maps and boxes of ammo. Different kinds of rifles and RPGs were stacked behind the ammo boxes. To his left, he saw that an entire wall was taken up with high-tech computers and monitors.

A tall man with a long beard held a small cup of steaming coffee. He said, "Salaam alaikum, Dr. Saad. I apologize for the unkind way you were treated, but we are at war and we can't be too careful. There are spies and traitors everywhere and we had to be certain you weren't working for our enemy."

He handed the cup to Dr. Saad and said, "Here, please accept this Turkish coffee. I understand it's your favorite. And two lumps of sugar, I believe?"

Dr. Saad gratefully accepted the coffee and sipped it. It was delicious—hot and very sweet. He looked up and said, "That's right. How did you know?"

"Oh, we've done a great deal of research into your background over the past few days," the man said.

"By the way, pardon me for not introducing myself. I am Amar al-Fasad. After the American invaders brutally assassinated our leader, Anwar al-Rimi—may Allah receive him into Paradise—I have been promoted to the leader of Al-Qaeda in Yemen."

"Al-Rimi was killed in the same attack that killed my wife and son," Dr. Saad replied.

"We verified that," al-Fasad said. "And we've also become aware of your training and background in bioweapons. You created quite a stockpile for Saddam Hussein, did you not?"

Dr. Saad smiled and said with pride, "I did. It was the largest array of bioweapons on the planet."

"What happened to all those chemical weapons?" al-Fasad asked, setting down his cup.

"I believe the Americans destroyed them in the First Gulf War. They had smart bombs and their jets targeted both the lab and the storage facility."

"If you had access to a lab, could you manufacture more of those bioweapons?"

"Absolutely. But the World Health Organization maintains microscopic scrutiny of all labs handling those chemicals."

Al-Fasad smiled. "This lab will be in a secret location and it will be under the radar of WHO and any other government organization."

"Of course," Dr. Saad said.

"Our supreme leader, Osama Bin Laden, may Allah honor him, has devised a plan for another massive attack on the Great Satan. He says it will be even more glorious than the attack of the blessed martyrs on September 11, 2001. We already have teams embedded in the United States to carry it out. Your skill in creating a particular toxin is the final piece of the puzzle. Are you willing to be a soldier for Allah?"

"I am," Dr. Saad affirmed.

"Are you willing to kill and even die for the glory of Islam?" al-Fasad asked.

"Yes! I am ready to kill the infidels and even die for the cause of Islam!" Dr. Saad shouted.

Al-Fasad embraced him and kissed both of his cheeks. "Welcome to the holy jihad, my brother."

7

PRESENT DAY

MARCH 26
Southern Israel in the Negev Desert
6:15am

Solomon Rubin, or Solly as his friends called him, stared out across the desert outside the city of Dimona, Israel. The morning sun was just peeking over the mountains of Jordan. As he sipped his first travel mug of strong coffee, Solly wondered how many times his forefathers Abraham, Isaac, and Jacob had watched the same sun rise over the same mountains.

Then he gazed in the direction of the massive Negev Nuclear Research Center nearby. For all official purposes, the facility didn't actually exist. The Israeli government acknowledged its presence, but they refused to confirm or deny that its suspected purpose was to enrich plutonium for nuclear warheads. When the facility was under construction in the early 1960s, the Israeli government reported to the IAEA (International Atomic

Energy Agency) that the largest of the reactor components were part of a massive desalination plant to be sold to Latin America.

But Solly knew that this facility was the main reason Israel still survived as a nation. Enough plutonium had been enriched by now to provide 150 nuclear weapons, creating a stockpile of arms that kept the howling war wolves of their neighbors at bay. As a longtime undercover agent for Mossad, Israel's premier intelligence agency, Solly knew that those who longed to see Israel destroyed were aware of their nuclear capability.

Solly was an unforgettable character. In his mid-sixties, he was still fit enough to run up the snake trail at Masada as he had done as a young man in the Israeli Defense Force. He had a quick smile and an even quicker wit and exuded a vibrant energy that was contagious. With a full beard, now more gray than brown, and his long, braided hair hanging down from the back of his leather Aussie hat, he looked the part of an outdoor hunting guide. However, his cover job wasn't to hunt animals; instead, he led archeological tours to hunt for buried treasures in Israel's varied and vast landscape. History marched through Israel and it was often said that anywhere you dug in Israel, you were bound to find archaeological treasures.

As Solly inhaled the morning air, he thought about the unusual circumstances that had first brought him to this land of promise. Solly had grown up in Australia, his parents nominally involved in Judaism. They enjoyed a Sabbath meal every Friday evening and observed the Jewish holidays. They even attended the synagogue occasionally, but Solly grew up with little interest in God or his Jewish heritage. To him, being Jewish was like being left-handed—some people were, but most weren't. And this was definitely a world that favored right-handers—and Gentiles. As a teenager, Solly had developed a pronounced irritation about his Jewish family. A typical junior high kid, he didn't like being different from his other Aussie friends.

Solly had always been a fast talker with a keen mind who could circle a topic and then dive in with the accuracy of a spear gun. By the time he was in college, he learned that he had a gift for debate. He seldom lost.

One of his debate opponents, Calvin, befriended him and began to ask him many questions about his Jewish family. Soon this friend began to plant doubts in Solly's mind about the Jewish people. Being several years older than Solly, Calvin decided it was his job to educate him about the disadvantages of being Jewish. He and his group of friends began to convince Solly that Jews were to blame for most of the problems in the world and that a handful of Jews ruthlessly controlled most of the global economy.

When Solly asked one day, "Well, what about the Holocaust?" Calvin merely laughed and said, "It never happened. It's all a lie that the Jews have spread to create sympathy for themselves. There were no death camps or even Jewish prisoners...it was all a grand hoax."

Solly had never heard this and it angered him that he had been deceived all these years. Calvin closed the argument by handing him a copy of *The Protocols of the Elders of Zion.*

As Solly read the words, he was shocked at first. Then he was furious at his parents and grandparents for supporting this lie. The book, supposedly written by a handful of powerful Jews, revealed their plan for world domination.

Solly was also confused. All of his relatives seemed to be happy, productive people. They didn't seem to be part of a huge conspiracy to take over the world.

Not long after reading the spurious ramblings in the controversial book, Solly was taken by his parents to meet the new Rabbi who had come to their local synagogue in Sydney.

Solly had long since lost any interest in Judaism and had no desire to meet another Rabbi. His previous Rabbi had been an old, boring man who smelled strangely of mothballs.

But this new Rabbi was young. Solly's parents insisted he attend a reception to welcome him. After milling around and speaking politely to a few of the old people, Solly was ready to escape.

Just then he felt a firm hand on his shoulder and turned to the see the young Rabbi who didn't seem to be much older than Solly.

"How do you do, Solly?" the Rabbi said with a broad smile. "My name is Neal Allen. Your parents have told me that you've been asking them some questions about our Jewish heritage."

All of Solly's bitterness and frustration bubbled to the surface as he said with a great deal of control, "The only trouble I have is that this is all a lie. We're not a special people, and I know for a fact now that the Holocaust never even happened."

Instead of reprimanding him or being drawn into a debate, Neal simply asked, "So where did you learn that there was no Holocaust?"

"I have my sources," Solly beamed. "And there's no proof that the Holocaust ever took place."

Neal took Solly by the arm and gently led him to an old lady who was sitting in a chair sipping tea.

"Our young friend here is convinced that there is no proof of the Holocaust," Neal said. "Emma, do you have anything you'd like to show him?"

Without a word, Emma rolled up the sleeve to her sweater, and Solly saw a blurred blue line of numbers tattooed on her thin forearm.

"I got this tattoo at Auschwitz," Emma said quietly. "I survived, but the other six members of my family were led into showers which were actually gas chambers. I later saw their bodies stacked outside the shower building."

Solly was reeling as reality began to sink into his youthful, arrogant mind. Neal led him to four other elderly people at the reception who revealed the same blue tattoo on their forearms.

Solly's world was rocked as he realized he had been intentionally duped by Calvin. The next day, Solly found Calvin and his friends and confronted them. Calvin smiled and said, "Oh, we just wanted to see how long it would take the little Jew-boy to see that you're no better than the other liars and thieves. All Jews are pigs— the scum of the earth and that includes you."

Solly clenched his fists and considered rushing Calvin. But he knew he was far outnumbered. Calvin continued to torment him.

"If you love the Jews so much, what are you doing here in Australia? Why don't you run home to Israel? We don't want you here."

As Solly walked away, he thought about what Calvin had said. He was in his early twenties now, but he couldn't see a future in Australia. He had never been to Israel, and his aunt who lived and worked in a kibbutz outside Haifa had invited him many times to visit.

Why not? he thought. *I need a change of scenery. It can't hurt.*

Solly's parents were both surprised and pleased with his interest in visiting Israel. They bought him a round trip ticket from Sydney with an open return date. When Solly walked down the stairs from the El Al jet at Tel Aviv airport in Lod, he had the strangest feeling that he was coming home instead of visiting an aunt. He never used the return portion of the ticket.

Solly smiled at that forty-year-old memory as he stretched and poured out the remaining lukewarm coffee. He headed back toward the compound of tents. There he met one of the visiting archeology students and said with a big smile, "Good morning, Mike! How did you sleep?" Solly still spoke English with a melodious Australian accent, but his Hebrew and Arabic had no trace of his being from "down under."

"Not so well," Mike said. "It's too blasted quiet here in the desert!" Solly just nodded—these newbies to the field had a lot to learn about the solace of a place like the Israeli desert.

Back inside his tent, Solly opened his MacBook Air and connected to the secure Wi-Fi network provided by a satellite uplink outside.

The people on his archeology tour had no idea that their guide was really a recruiter for Mossad. The full name of the Israeli intelligence service was *HaMossad leModi'in ule Tafkidim Meyuhadim.* The English translation is, "Institute of Intelligence and Special Operations."

Solly logged on to one of fifteen different email accounts

he utilized and noticed there was a message in the drafts folder. That could mean only one thing—an important message from one of the Mossad agents he had personally recruited and planted around the world. Placing messages in the drafts folder on a shared account was a simple way to communicate without sending an email that could be intercepted in cyberspace. This account indicated the sender was Tyler Kensington in the U.S. The cryptic message said, "I may have stumbled on a terrorist plot. We need to talk."

8

MARCH 26

Alpharetta, Georgia
8:12am

Regan held out her hand and willed her mouth to form the words, "I'm Regan Hart, it's nice to meet you, Tyler."

"Most people call me Ty. I was named after the city where I was born in Texas. It got its name from one of the most unpopular Presidents in history, John Tyler."

Ty noticed Regan looked as if she were about to cry. "Sorry, I don't know why I'm telling you all this. You're upset. What's wrong?"

Regan's lip started quivering again but she steeled herself against the tears. "It's been a really bad night. I got in last night from Paris only to realize I had forgotten to pay my electricity bill, so I have no power."

"Okay, but that shouldn't be too difficult a problem to fix. We can call Georgia Power and they can turn it back on." Ty wondered if she got this upset with every problem.

"That's not the worst part," Regan said, sniffling. "Somebody broke into my apartment last night and stole my purse, which had my cell phone in it. I was coming outside to ask one of my neighbors to use their phone to call 911."

"Maybe I can help you. I'm a private investigator and I know some of the officers in the Alpharetta Police Department. You can use my phone. It's in my house, come on over."

As they walked up the sidewalk, Ty wished he had taken time to get properly dressed before retrieving his paper. But he didn't expect to meet a lady in distress—and certainly not someone as pretty as Regan. To shift her attention away from his appearance, he asked, "Did you notice anything else missing?"

"No," Regan said. "I searched the house pretty thoroughly in case the intruder was still there. I didn't notice anything else missing—except for a gift that I was bringing from a coworker to her sister here in Atlanta."

Regan paused. "Now that's weird. Why would they take that gift when there were other valuable things they could have made off with?"

"I dunno. Criminals are pretty dumb sometimes," Ty said, opening his front door and leading Regan into the kitchen.

He handed her his iPhone5 and said, "Here, use this."

"This is just like my phone. Thanks."

"So you have an iPhone5? Did you install the Find my iPhone app?"

Regan's eyes got larger as she understood what he was saying. "Of course I did! I can look on my laptop and find out where my phone is! Why didn't I think of that?"

"Do you want to call 911 first?" Ty asked.

"What do you think I should do?"

"I'd say let's look for your phone first because if we can locate it, we can send the police directly there and save some time."

Regan started out the door toward her house and suddenly stopped. "Uh. This won't work. With no power, my Wi-Fi is down."

"No problem," Ty said. "You can use my laptop."

Regan sat down in front of Ty's 15-inch MacBook pro, which looked massive compared to her slim MacBook Air.

As Regan logged into her iCloud account she was already feeling better. Using this ingenious app, she could not only locate her phone, but she could also remotely lock her phone and even erase all her data. She could also activate her phone to play a loud alarm for two minutes. But since the phone had been stolen, she wasn't going to give the thieves a heads-up by activating the alarm feature.

When she entered her password, a map appeared on the screen and in the middle of the map was a small green circle representing her phone.

At first she didn't recognize the map. Ty was leaning over her shoulder and she caught a light scent of soap. Ty said, "Hey, that's our neighborhood. According to this map, your phone is just down the street!"

Regan zoomed in on the location. Ty was right. Her phone was only four houses down the street.

"Those creeps!" she said. "I can't believe that my own neighbors would rip off my purse!"

Ty said, "Not so fast. Let's go look."

Saving the screen image, Ty took the laptop and walked out his front door with Regan right behind him.

If a neighbor had looked out their window, they would have

wondered about this strange couple. Ty was still dressed in his robe and slippers, carrying a laptop down the middle of the street, with Regan trailing behind in her sweatshirt and jeans.

"It should be right about here," Ty said. "Here, hold this please." He handed her the laptop and started searching in the azalea bushes in front of one of the townhomes.

"Bingo!" he said, as he retrieved a large, black Coach bag. "Is this your purse?"

"Yes! It is!" Regan grabbed her purse and started digging through it. Her wallet was there and she opened it, breathing a sigh of relief that her cash was somehow untouched. But she was more interested in her only credit card—a Centurion American Express with no spending limit. She removed the titanium card from its protective sleeve and said, "Thank goodness! They didn't take any of my money or my credit card."

"That is strange," Ty said. "So this wasn't a typical smash and grab. What did they take?"

"Well, I guess that leaves the only thing missing is that gift I brought from Paris." She didn't notice then that the card containing Bridget's sister's address was also gone.

Ty wrinkled his brow but tried not to alarm Regan. "Come on back to my place. Let me brew you a cup of coffee. You can tell me everything you know about this gift."

9

28 YEARS EARLIER

NOVEMBER 18, 1985
Salman Pak (south of Baghdad), Iraq
5:35am

The fluorescent lights cast an artificial pallor over the tables and scientific instruments in the lab. Dr. Saad enjoyed coming to the lab early so that he could concentrate on his work before the other scientists arrived. This facility was the main research center for Saddam Hussein's initiative to develop biological weapons. To the global scientific community, and especially the BWC (Biological Weapons Convention), this facility was part of Iraq's State Establishment for Pesticide Production. But Dr. Saad and the other scientists knew that the lethal fruit of their labor would never be used against insects. Saddam believed that he was the reincarnation of the great Babylonian King, Nebuchadnezzar. His lofty plan was to be the ruler of the ancient Babylonian empire, which would include all of the

Middle East. In so doing, he would eliminate the worst pest of all—Israel.

Dr. Saad privately thought he was a little crazy, but all great rulers were considered eccentric. He was just grateful to have such a good job. As a child, he had been fascinated with science. He had proven to be a prodigy in the field and after graduating from the University of Baghdad, his government had paid the full cost for him to obtain a Ph.D. in Microbiology and Biochemistry from the prestigious Georg-August-Universitat in Göttingen, Germany.

When he graduated, he was immediately hired as head of research at this facility. The job came with a three-bedroom flat, an automobile, and a large enough salary to easily support his growing family of a young son, Akmed, and a daughter, his little princess, Ameera.

For a genius, his job was relatively simple. He and his staff provided the chemical ingredients to purify several biological toxins including botulinum toxin, ricin, and aflatoxin. They obtained biological samples of these toxins from the U.S. Centers for Disease Control. The World Health Organization guidelines encouraged the free exchange of biological samples to be used for "medical research."

His work had been an unqualified success. In the past six years, his department had grown over a half-million liters of biological agents at the Al Hakum production facility.

Dr. Saad was particularly proud of his pet project with botulinum toxin, though he remained somewhat ambivalent about its true purpose. He approached his work purely as a scientist, trying to perfect the development of the most efficient toxin. Compartmentalizing his work kept him from focusing on the grisly potential consequences of a madman having access to a stockpile of 19,000 liters of concentrated botulinum toxin. Of course, Dr. Saad kept these thoughts to himself so he could keep his job and take care of his family.

To a chemist, this toxin was a work of art. Botulinum is a protein and toxin produced by the bacterium Clostridium botulinum. It is the most acutely toxic substance known. A tiny amount, two parts per trillion, administered intravenously or intramuscularly would be fatal. But Dr. Saad's perfect weapon was designed to be dispersed as an aerosol—and as little as 13 parts per trillion, when inhaled, would be deadly. Botulinum toxin paralyzes human muscles—arms, legs, face. But when it is inhaled, it first paralyzes the lungs—specifically the muscles that draw air into the lungs. This is what makes botulinum toxin the perfect weapon to inflict maximum pain. Death is slow and agonizing because the infected person is aware of their inability to breathe, and they soon suffocate from lack of oxygen.

Dr. Saad had read in the medical journals that its chemical cousin, botox, was just starting to be employed by ophthalmologists in the West to correct *strabismus* (the condition causing someone to be cross-eyed). It was also being used to treat *achalasia*, a spasm of the lower esophagus.

He smiled as he considered the potential if Western dermatologists figured out a way to use botox for the cosmetic treatment of wrinkles. One study he had read suggested that tiny amounts injected into the face and forehead of subjects removed wrinkles. That might be a goldmine, but he suspected that Saddam had other plans for the botulinum.

Dr. Saad had heard the rumor that Saddam planned on testing the botulinum toxin on Kurdish prisoners. *What a waste of good poison,* Saad thought. *The science doesn't lie.* He shuddered to imagine the horrendous way they would die—within minutes. The research showed a 100% lethal rate—much more accurate and deadly than a bullet or a bomb. As he booted up his computer for the day's work, he once again quietly hoped this deadly virus would never be used against an enemy. But those decisions were beyond his pay grade.

10

DECEMBER 26, 1986
Abu Ghraib Prison (West of Baghdad, Iraq)
12:20pm

Jawid Hosni shuffled into the sterile room with fourteen other Kurdish prisoners. He rubbed the raw skin on his wrists, thankful to have the shackles removed. He immediately noticed that the room had the clinical appearance of a medical lab. Before Saddam Hussein arrested him with a trumped-up charge of sedition, Jawid had practiced medicine in the Kurdish city of Erbil.

The walls were covered with shiny white tile and the floor was polished concrete. There was an ominous drain in the center of the floor.

The single overhead light cast a harsh shadow over the stainless steel table in the center of the room. Fifteen metal chairs were placed around the table. In front of each chair were a notepad, a sharpened pencil and a cheap pen.

Jawid thought it was the most sterile conference room he'd ever seen. A rectangular window that Jawid suspected was a one-way mirror dominated one wall. In each corner of the room near the ceiling were small cameras trained on the table.

What's going on? Jawid wondered.

An hour earlier, a high ranking Republican Guard officer had assembled these "high profile" prisoners to announce a breakthrough in their cases. Saddam, in his beneficent mercy, was willing to offer them a free pardon. To gain their freedom, each of them only had to document their previous involvement in organizations and activities aligned against Saddam's Ba'ath party. By including the names of other dissidents, they would not only be released but also handsomely rewarded.

This news led to elation among the group. Some of the prisoners sat down to write out their confessions. Jawid picked up a pencil to write as well. He would gladly concoct a faux-confession if it would get him out of this place. After five months in Abu Ghraib he would have sold out his own mother. But Jawid was suspicious of the offer at the same time. His suspicion turned to fear when he heard the whooshing sound of the metal door being sealed. His eardrums felt the pressure as the room was hermetically sealed to be airtight.

Sweat trickled down the faces of the prisoners as they shared Jawid's growing anxiety. The musky smell of fear filled the room. Jawid glanced up to the vents as he heard a soft hissing sound. Small clouds of vapor appeared as some kind of gas was released into the room.

Jawid was numb with the stark realization that he would never leave this room alive. The bitter truth came crashing into his mind like an avalanche of terror.

Jawid knew that Saddam had been developing biological weapons for several years. There was no way to know what gas had been released in the room, but Jawid knew it would be fatal. He silently prayed that it would be cyanide because death would come violently—but quickly. But his prayer for quick death went unanswered.

The other prisoners started to panic when they heard the hissing. They began to detect a slightly sweet odor. Wakil, an overweight lawyer from Mosul, ran to the door and started screaming. He clawed at the seal of the door and then pounded on it with both of his fists. After a couple of hysterical minutes, he was exhausted. He turned around and slid down the wall to a sitting position on the floor. He desperately sucked in deep breaths, wheezing from the exertion.

Jawid said, "Calm down, Wakil. They want us to panic. Save your energy."

Several moments passed. Then ten minutes. Then thirty minutes. For a brief moment, Jawid hoped that the gas wasn't harmful after all. He didn't have a watch, but he suspected that almost an hour had passed since they had entered the room. The other prisoners were growing restless. He looked for unusual symptoms in their behavior, but everyone seemed to be acting normally.

After another thirty minutes had passed, Jawid noticed that he had a hard time focusing his eyes. He squeezed his eyelids shut and opened them, willing his eyes to focus. But he was seeing double and it was taking a conscious effort to even keep his eyelids open.

The other prisoners were beginning to display symptoms of distress as well. Wakil panicked again and ran to the mirror. He slammed his fists on the glass and yelled, "Let us out of here!

We've signed our confessions!"

He continued to pound his fists and yell until he began to hyperventilate. Then he turned and looked at the other prisoners with horror in his eyes. He struggled to inhale, but it was as if his lungs were already full and there was no more room for oxygen. He grabbed his throat with both hands in a desperate reflex to try to force air into his starving lungs. His eyes were bulging out of their sockets. His face turned purple and then red as his cells demanded the oxygen-rich blood. He lost consciousness and collapsed into a heap on the concrete floor.

Jawid rushed over and felt for a pulse in his throat. He could feel a steady but weak heartbeat. "Wakil! Wake up! Can you hear me, Wakil?" But there was no reply.

The other prisoners began to experience the same symptoms. They rubbed their eyes to try to focus, and some grabbed their throats as it became more and more difficult to swallow—much less breathe.

Some of them fell on their knees begging for mercy from Allah. But their words became slurred and Jawid could hardly understand them. They fell to their faces and lay on the floor motionless as if in a coma. One by one, they began to die.

Jawid's medical knowledge served to intensify his fear. He suspected that the gas was some kind of inhalation toxin that caused muscular paralysis. He could feel his throat closing and he realized that he would soon lose all control of his muscles—including the ability to breathe.

Desperate to delay his death, Jawid's anger grew. His fear was replaced with a fierce determination to stay alive.

When he felt his throat constrict, he grabbed the sharpened

pencil on the table and felt for the soft area in his throat where the trachea was closest to the skin. Without hesitation he plunged the tip of the pencil into his trachea. Blood spurted from the hole, but he didn't care.

He needed a way to keep his self-administered tracheotomy open, so he desperately looked around. He quickly grabbed one of the cheap ink pens and unscrewed the two sections. He removed the ink cartridge and spring and jammed the bottom half of the plastic pen into his throat.

As he fell onto his back, he felt a slight flow of air seeping in through his trachea—but he knew that he didn't have much time. His brain willed his larynx to scream, and in his mind he could hear himself shrieking at the top of his lungs. But there was no sound heard in the room. Only silence.

As his mind became foggy, his last thoughts were of his family in Erbil. He saw his wife, beautiful Hiba, his precious gift from Allah, smiling at him. Then he saw the faces of his four children.

Mercifully, Jawid's brain shut down from lack of oxygen. He lost consciousness several minutes before his other vital organs died. He lay on the concrete floor with the other prisoners, looking grotesque with the bloody pen still protruding from his neck.

Then there was only stillness in the room. The floor was littered with the remains of fifteen prisoners who had died the most horrible death imaginable.

A disembodied voice of a technician came over a hidden speaker. "The time is 15:32. The experiment was a complete success. None of the subjects survived after inhaling the agent.

Now reverse the airflow to remove the toxin back into the secure containers."

A colonel in the Republican Guard, who had supervised the test said, "Send word to Dr. Saad that his botulinum toxin works better than we could have imagined. And have some prisoners clean this room and burn the bodies. I can still smell Kurds."

11

PRESENT DAY

MARCH 26
24 Rue de la Bûcherie
Paris, France
3:02pm

Ameera cradled a hot cup of tea in her hands and gazed out the window of her luxury, seventh-floor Paris apartment. Although she cared nothing for wealth, she had to admit that it was nice to live on the exclusive Rue de la Bûcherie in the coveted 6th arrondissement of Paris. She stared out across the Seine to the Ile de la Cité. Hundreds of tourists were streaming across the Pont Neuf to visit the majestic Notre Dame Church.

Since she and her father had launched their campaign, money had been no problem. Enormous sums of euros were deposited every week into her personal bank account at ABC (Arab Banking Company). Every Friday morning, after prayers at the ornate Grande Mosque, Ameera would casually walk into the ABC Office on the Avenue des Champs-Élysées. She never wrote a check or used her credit card—those left electronic trails.

Instead, using a different teller each time, she typically withdrew €20,000. Folding the 40 colorful €500 notes, she placed them in the side pocket of her Hermes Birkin handbag. Then she walked down the wide sidewalk to the café she frequented every Friday. Sitting at her favorite table, she faced the street and enjoyed a cup of tea while watching the crowd to ensure that no one was trailing her.

She suspected that the anonymous source of these unlimited funds came from the Muslim practice of the *zakat*. One of the five pillars of Islam, the *zakat* requires Muslims to donate 2.5% of their accumulated wealth to ease the financial hardship of other Muslims. In addition, wealthy Muslims often give more than 2.5% of their wealth—a level of generosity called *sadaqah*—to achieve additional divine reward.

The annual *zakat* from the Muslims in the oil-rich countries of Saudi Arabia, Kuwait, and the U.A.E. amounted to billions of discretionary dollars. In Saudi Arabia and Pakistan, government-run revenue offices collected the *zakat* much like the I.R.S. does in the United States.

Much of this money is sent to poorer Muslim countries like Afghanistan and Bangladesh where it provides food for millions of hungry Muslims. In addition, the *zakat* is used to fund thousands of *madrasas*—schools for young Muslim boys. Most of the boys, a million or more, are being indoctrinated in the radical *Wahhabi* branch of Islam that originated in Saudi Arabia.

But Ameera knew a dirty little secret about which the majority of Muslims were clueless. As a financial wizard, she surmised that her personal bank account was being fattened by the *zakat* as well to further the vindictive plans of a Muslim extremist group. In 1996, Osama bin Laden had issued his inspiring *fatwa* declaring jihad against Israel and the United States. Since that time, a substantial amount of the *zakat* had been channeled to fund the work of the mujahidin around the world.

Ameera never imagined that she would be on jihad, but the loss of her family had reversed the course of her life. Before the Americans had murdered her mother and brother in a drone attack, her main desire had been to build a successful career as a currency trader. As a bonus, she'd hoped to find a husband and raise her children in the way of Islam.

But since that fiery morning, her life had been swept up in her father's all-consuming passion—punishing the infidels. Unlike her father and the other Muslim extremists on her team, she was hardly a courageous warrior. Anxiety was her constant companion. Growing up in Yemen, she had developed an innate dislike of Americans. She felt the loss of her family with the same intensity of her father, but sometimes she wondered what avenging their death with more death would accomplish.

Now, as she stared across the Seine, she was filled with uncertainty and doubt. Nervous energy had consumed her mind since she had taken the first step in the plan by delivering the package to Regan.

She had carefully followed the instructions given to her by her team leader, Yamani. He was a highly trained former Iranian soldier who was a longtime Al-Qaeda operative. Yamani's fellow mujahidin had been secretly studying her co-worker, Regan, for many weeks. They had used every cyber resource available to develop a profile of her personality. Of the five possible American females who worked at GWA with Ameera, Regan had been chosen for her compliant personality. If it were possible, she even seemed too kind. She was the kind of person who, if you stepped on her foot, *she* would apologize.

Ultimately, however, Regan was chosen to be the mule to unwittingly carry the package from Paris to Atlanta because she had also proven honest and trustworthy. The research team had discovered that she had never stolen so much as a paper clip from her employer. Ameera knew that Regan's vitae (provided on her employment application) indicated that she listed herself as a Christian, but she and Regan had never discussed religion. Ameera assumed Regan was like millions of other misguided Christian infidels. Islam revered Isa (Arabic for "Jesus") as a great prophet. However, Ameera believed that claiming Isa was equal to Allah was the worst kind of blasphemy.

***

Once she had been given the go-ahead, Ameera introduced herself at work to Regan (going by her French cover "Bridget") and attempted to befriend her. She feigned an interest in visiting America and asked Regan to tell her about her life back in the States.

Regan was reticent to divulge much about her life, but Ameera was trained to observe and hone in on details and small, incidental facts that most people did not realize they shared in the course of casual conversation. She would assemble these details to form a working profile of Regan, however incomplete. In their brief visits, Ameera discovered that Regan was from

Atlanta, Georgia, where she worked for another office of GWA. She was consumed by her work and had no close friends or family members.

On one occasion, their conversation touched on romance. Regan had confessed that while she had gone through several boyfriends in college, there were no men in her life. They commiserated that they both felt married to their jobs.

Regan piled up thousands of frequent flier miles shuttling back and forth from her two offices and homes. Ameera had learned that Regan hated bothering with carry-on luggage and only took her purse on the plane. She always checked her suitcase. This detail was information that was critical in making the final decision to use Regan.

Even though Regan seemed to be the perfect choice, Ameera was worried. Would the package be discovered during the checked baggage X-ray? Would Regan be stopped and searched by U.S. Customs agents? There were so many variables.

Her tea had cooled by now, so Ameera poured it in the sink. For the tenth time in the past few minutes, she glanced at her iPhone5 again, hoping to hear from her contact in Georgia that the package was safely in their hands. Once Ameera received word, she would be on her way to Atlanta as well. Their strategic part in the holy jihad would move into the next phase.

12

MARCH 26

East Point, Georgia
6:00am

Yamani carefully maneuvered the dilapidated Ford mini-van through the neighborhood of tenement houses and government-subsidized apartments. In the early morning hours, traffic was light. He made sure to keep his speed below the posted limit. He brought the van to a full stop at every stop sign. The last thing he needed now was to be pulled over for a traffic violation.

He and his team had chosen this area of southwest Atlanta because of its diversity. Although there were frequent police patrols, the officers devoted most of their time to drug traffic and the frequent domestic violence calls.

Yamani stared again at the package sitting in the passenger seat. He had been told it was harmless in this state, but he still was anxious to deliver it to Dr. Saad.

He drove around the block twice to make sure he didn't have a tail before parking on the curb two blocks away from his apartment. He texted a number he had programmed into his iPhone to let his team know he had arrived with the package.

After parking, he carefully placed it in his backpack and pulled his hoodie down over his head. With one final glance down the street, he climbed the stairs to the third floor apartment. He knocked three times and then paused and knocked once again. He stepped away from the door and watched as the peephole darkened and one of his fellow soldiers looked out.

Yamani spoke the pre-arranged code phrase that indicated he was alone and not followed. "Is Martel in there? It's, me, Slick. Let me in."

After a moment, he heard the three deadbolts disengage and the door opened.

Yamani walked into the room and looked at his three fellow jihadists. "Salaam alaikum," he greeted them. Breathing a sigh of relief, he carefully removed the backpack and handed it to Dr. Saad.

"How did it go?" Dr. Saad asked.

"No problem. We found the courier's house from the address Ameera hacked from her employment record. We cut the power to her house and disabled the alarm before she arrived. I planted the explosive device behind her water heater. Then we left and waited at a nearby convenience store."

Dr. Saad nodded for him to continue. "Ali was stationed at the arrivals area at the airport and identified her as she left. He followed her home from the airport to make sure she was in her house. After she went inside, we waited for two more hours before our infrared sensor indicated she was in bed asleep. I thought we might have to search for the package, and we had our night-vision goggles, but the stupid girl left it right by the front door for us! Her purse was there as well. It was child's play. After I retrieved the fake Atlanta address Ameera had given her, I tossed the purse."

Dr. Saad interrupted, "And the device...?"

Yamani looked at his watch. "It should explode in about four hours."

Dr. Saad seemed pleased. He took the package over to the dining room table and began to carefully unwrap the gold foil paper. The paper was actually a high-tech invention that was just starting to be used by the wealthiest drug smugglers in the world. It was treated with a finish that employed stealth technology. Even though checked bags passed through the X-Ray at airports, the image on the screen appeared as pages of paper, mirroring the appearance of an actual book. You could fool machines, but it was more difficult to fool trained dogs that could sniff out drugs and explosives. The stealth foil, however, was also coated with a new technology that created a soap-like material to simulate the smell of ink on paper.

Dr. Saad was relieved to have the package. He hadn't trusted the technology enough to allow one of his own team members to transport the book in case they got caught.

He set the foil aside in case it needed to be re-used. Inside the wrapping was a textbook entitled, "Organic Chemistry." He chuckled at the title and gently opened the book to reveal the cutout area inside the pages. Using tweezers, he removed the small shavings that smelled strongly of fresh ink and gently placed them in a plastic bag.

Next, he removed a white plastic rectangular case. It was

cool to the touch, confirming that the dry ice had kept the chemical agent at the proper temperature. Inside the dry ice packages were four metal cylinders, each six inches long. Double sealed within the metal cylinders were vials containing a highly concentrated solution of botulinum toxin.

Dr. Saad smiled as he moved the vials to the refrigerator. He said, "Phase one of our plan is accomplished. It was the most difficult. Now we are ready to launch phase two. And inshallah, we will bring the Great Satan to its knees by unleashing more death on the infidels than the blessed 9/11 attacks!"

The team members shouted, "Allah Akbar! Allah Akbar!"

13

MARCH 26
Alpharetta, Georgia
9:50am

Regan's coffee had long since cooled, but she sipped it anyway, too disturbed to notice how dreadful it tasted. It still seemed like a bad dream. Someone had broken into her house and only stolen a mysterious gift and an address where she was supposed to deliver it. The only good part of the dream was that she was sitting across from a guy who looked like he walked in from a cover shoot for *GQ Magazine*.

Since they had retrieved her purse with her cell phone from the bushes, Ty had taken the time to change out of his pajamas and robe.

His new attire consisted of a pullover sweater, jeans, and casual shoes. Regan tried not to stare, but she could tell that there was a muscular chest and a flat waist under the sweater. She pushed that thought out of her mind as she tucked her hair behind her ear for the hundredth time. For the hundredth time, she also wished she had taken time to put on her makeup and fix her hair. She had to look like the winner of the Miss Frumpy

USA contest. But Ty didn't seem to notice.

"So, you basically don't know much about this girl, Bridget, who gave you this gift to bring back to Atlanta?" Ty asked.

"She's a currency trader at the firm in Paris. For the past few weeks, she's been talking to me. She is a conservative Muslim who always wore a head covering at the office, but she always wanted to talk to me about America. Her English is barely passable and she told me she wanted to practice with me."

"Describe the gift to me."

"I don't know much about it…it was wrapped up and about the size of a school textbook. It weighed about three or four pounds, I guess. I could barely squeeze it in my checked bag."

"Did you unwrap it?" Ty asked as he took her coffee cup to refill it.

"Thanks. No. It was wrapped in some kind of thick gold foil, and I never opened it."

"Wait. Weren't you asked by the security officers in Paris if anyone gave you a gift to bring to the U.S.?"

"Well, yes. But I was in such a hurry that I didn't want to be delayed any more than I was." Regan rubbed her forehead. "I can be so dumb sometimes!"

"Well, there's nothing we can do about it now," Ty said gently. "But my gut tells me that we should try to find out what that gift was. Apparently, it was something important enough for someone to steal it from you."

"What should we do?" Regan asked.

Before Ty could answer, they heard a loud "Whump!"

Regan jumped and said, "What was that?"

"Sounded like someone fired a shotgun down the street.

But discharging firearms is illegal in this part of the city."

Regan got up to walk to the door. But Ty reached out and said, "Why don't you wait right here, I'll check it out." He opened his hall closet and removed a leather holster that held his 9mm Beretta Cougar 8000. He slung the holster over his shoulder and grabbed a jacket to cover it.

"I'm not staying anywhere. I'm coming with you," Regan insisted.

"Fine. But stay behind me. It could be nothing. Ready?"

Ty opened the door and detected the first wisp of smoke. "Something's burning." Regan ran past him and looked both ways before yelling, "It's my house!" Then she tore off running across the yard toward her front door.

Ty saw that the house was already full of smoke and flames were licking the curtains. Thick, white smoke was curling from under the eves. He sprinted after Regan and tackled her before she reached her driveway. "You can't go in there!"

"Let...me...go!" Regan bit off every word in a voice full of rage.

As she fought to escape, Ty wrapped one muscled arm around her, pulled out his iPhone and dialed 911.

"Fulton County Emergency Center. What is your emergency?"

"There's a house on fire. The address is 3320 Foxtrot Circle in the Highlands Townhome Development."

The calm voice of the 911 operator responded, "I'm sending help immediately. Are there any occupants still in the house?"

"No," Ty replied.

"Are there any pets in the house?"

Ty turned toward Regan who was squirming like a snake to escape his arm. "Do you own any pets?"

Still struggling, she muttered, "No. I've been thinking about getting a dog—a big one. But I'm never here enough to care for one."

"I don't need a story. I just need an answer."

Ty put his phone back to his head and replied, "There are no pets in the house."

The operator said, "Stand by. The fire department is rolling toward your location now. Does anyone need emergency medical care?"

Ty was tempted to request a couple of valiums for his new neighbor. "We're okay. And I can already hear the sirens. Thanks for your help." He hung up.

By now, Regan was too exhausted to struggle. She looked up and said, "I'm okay, really. Will you go back into your house and bring me my purse?"

Ty didn't trust her. "You don't need your purse."

She had regained her composure enough to use her all-men-are-stupid-voice, "Well, if you want to roll around here on the grass a little longer while we watch the fire spread to my car, we can certainly do that."

Ty looked over his shoulder at her Mercedes parked a few feet from her front door.

Regan continued with increased volume, "Or...you can get your fat rear off me, get my keys from my purse and move my car!"

Ty shot like a flash back inside his house sweeping up her purse. Within seconds, he delivered it to Regan who was now sitting up brushing grass and leaves from her hair.

She quickly searched through her purse and found the key fob. She pressed the remote start, and the engine purred to life. As the smoke boiling out from her townhome grew thicker, she ran and unlocked the car, slipped behind the wheel and carefully backed out into the street.

She parked several houses down because she suspected the area in front of her house was about to get crowded.

Before she got out of her car, she took several deep breaths. Her safe and private world was shattering right before her eyes. For someone who preferred to fly under the radar, she was attracting a heck of a lot of attention all of a sudden.

She glanced at her house in flames and tried to think of anything in there that she couldn't live without. She had her wallet, keys, phone, and her iPad with her. Inside was mostly just stuff she had accumulated. There were no photo albums to save because all of her images were stored digitally. She thought about her expensive clothes and make up, but all of that could be replaced.

If there was a silver lining to this massive cloud of smoke, it was that this townhome was simply a place where she slept when she was working in Georgia. She had intentionally refrained from giving it any personal touches that might make it a home.

She glanced in her rearview mirror in time to see the fire truck wheeling down her street. The firemen sprang into action before the truck stopped in front of her house. They started attaching hoses to the truck, and in less than 30 seconds there were two powerful streams of water shattering her front windows and hissing into the flames. The white smoke became even thicker. By this time, curious neighbors had gathered in the street to watch the action. Regan realized again that she didn't know the names of a single neighbor.

She knew she should emerge from the safe cocoon of her car, but she was too mentally exhausted to even move. Fortunately Ty ran over to the first fireman. They were talking and gesturing and then Ty pointed at her car. As the fireman started toward her, she looked at her reflection in her mirror and shuddered. "Who is *that* crazy woman?" Her hair was disheveled and still had grass and leaves nesting there. She laughed as she realized that she looked exactly like one of those horrible celebrity mug shots.

She calculated that she had about thirty seconds before she had to confront the approaching fireman. She quickly opened the console beside her and snatched her spare brush and pulled it several times through her long, blonde hair. With practiced speed, she pulled out her make up kit and applied some powder. But there was no time to fix her eyes. Just as the fireman knocked on her window, she grabbed her Ray Bans and slid them onto her face.

At least she looked acceptable as she exited her car.

"Ma'am, is that your home?"

"Yes, officer." Regan wondered if a fireman was an officer, or if you only had to say that to policemen.

"Just to verify, can you give me your name and address?"

"Regan Hart. 3320 Foxtrot Circle, Alpharetta."

"Do you know how the fire started?"

"No, officer...I mean, sir. I was inside the home of my neighbor and we both heard a noise."

"What kind of noise?"

"It's hard to describe. At first, Ty thought it was a shotgun, but it sounded more like a loud thump to me."

"Okay, please stay here until we're ready to leave."

Regan retreated back to her car as the surreal scene played out over the next hour.

***

"That's all for now, ma'am. Looks like the fire should be under control in a few minutes. I'm sorry about your loss. The fire marshal will be by this afternoon or tomorrow to investigate the fire. There won't be much inside that will survive the fire, smoke, or water damage. But make sure you don't try to recover anything until after he makes his report. Do you have a friend or family member that you can stay with for a while?"

Regan tried to manage a half-smile and said, "Oh, I'll be okay."

But inside her head there was a voice screaming, "You'll be okay? You don't have any family or friends to help you. You're a loner, remember?"

Regan got back into her car. She felt like it was her only remaining possession. Less than twelve hours had passed since she returned last night, but her world had tilted so fast that it left her dizzy.

She reclined the driver's seat and closed her eyes to consider her options. Within seconds, she was asleep.

After Ty looked through her car window to make sure she was okay and saw she was sleeping, he returned to his townhome. His cover job was working as a private investigator, but he was actually a recruited Mossad agent assigned to the U.S. to combat global terrorism. As an American citizen, he could travel to countries where Israelis were forbidden. He had just returned from his latest assignment in Dubai. He had been waiting for his next mission, but there was something about Regan's story that set off warning bells in his mind. He needed to contact his Israeli handler, Solly.

He sat down in front of his MacBook and logged into a proxy server that couldn't be traced. He accessed his special email account and looked in the drafts folder. There were no new messages from Solly. So he began a new email and typed: "I may have stumbled on a terrorist plot. We need to talk." He didn't click on send. Instead he left it in the drafts folder. Ty knew that Solly never went more than a few hours without checking in with his agents, so he expected to hear back soon.

14

MARCH 26

Negev Desert
8:50am

After reading Ty's email, Solly unpacked his satellite phone and dialed the sixteen-digit Mossad number to access a secure line. When prompted, he punched in his twelve-digit PIN and heard what sounded like a normal dial tone. But this wasn't just any phone line. This line employed cutting-edge scrambling technology that was more advanced than anything the CIA possessed. The scrambled line changed frequencies every two seconds based upon a random algorithm developed by Israeli scientists. Solly punched in Ty's direct cell phone line.

Ty recognized the unique ringtone at once. The incoming call displayed "Uncle Bill" on his screen. Utilizing their personal recognition code, Ty answered and said, "Uncle Bill. It's good to hear from you. How is Aunt Pat?"

Solly replied, "Aunt Pat is still in the hospital. Thanks for asking."

After confirming that they were on a secure line, they both relaxed.

"How are you, my friend?" Solly asked.

"I'm good. I wrote because I've stumbled on a possible threat and I need your help."

"Tell me about it."

Ty recounted the story of meeting Regan and finding her purse. He described their conversation about the mysterious gift. But the clincher was the house fire. There were too many things happening to be a simple coincidence.

"What do you know about this Regan Hart?" Solly asked.

"Not much. I just met her today. I've seen her pull into her driveway a couple of times in the past few months, but she's hardly ever here. She seems to be on the level. She was scared and seemed pretty upset."

"What can I do?"

"Let's start with the Muslim girl Bridget who gave Regan the present. She works at Global Wealth Advisors in Paris. Of course, that may not be her real name, but if you can track her down and get a picture, I'm sure Regan can identify her."

"No problem," Solly said. "I've got several operatives in Paris and we can get on that today."

"Thanks. Do you think this is something worth pursuing?" Ty asked.

Solly paused. "Without a doubt. We have access to the U.S. Homeland Security airport cameras for all arriving international flights. Two weeks ago, their advanced facial software program in Atlanta International Airport scored a hit on a former biological weapons expert, Dr. Hakeem Saad. He was Saddam Hussein's chief chemist overseeing biological weapons development. After the first Gulf War, he fled Iraq and moved to Yemen where he assumed the identity of a university teacher living a normal life. But a couple of years ago, he disappeared from the radar. Then U.S. Customs got this hit on him when he entered the U.S."

Ty said, "I'm surprised that Homeland Security gives you access to their system."

Solly said, "Well, they haven't exactly given us access. We hacked into their system. Anyway, U.S. Customs pulled Saad aside for questioning and thoroughly checked his belongings. Nothing was found and he convinced them that he was just visiting his sister."

"Hmm. But you think Regan's package has something to do with him?" Ty asked.

"I don't know, but with Saad being in the Atlanta area, combined with your story about this package, and the explosion, my threat sensor is going off. In this business, I've learned that there is no such thing as a random coincidence."

Ty said, "Okay, I'll see what I can learn from Regan. Thanks, Solly. By the way, how's the archaeological tour guide business?"

"Busy as usual. Most of these wanna be archaeologists arrive with hopes of finding the Lost Ark or the Copper Scroll. But after two days of digging in the hot sun, they're ready to head back to an air-conditioned hotel."

Ty laughed and said, "Yeah. After a few days, I was ready to quit. But you convinced me to stick it out."

"Yep, sometimes I meet some interesting people. And some of them are even former U.S. Marines like you, Ty. I remember when I first met you there at the Qumran dig. That was a good day for both of us."

They agreed to speak again soon and disconnected their call.

15

12 YEARS EARLIER

JUNE 24, 2002
Qumran, Israel
5:30am

Ty awoke by instinct at 5:30am. Years of serving in the U.S. Marines had conditioned him to sleep soundly while having his ear and mind constantly attuned to any hint of danger. He was camped out near the Qumran excavations where he was part of an archeological team excavating a new area of the Yahad compound. He and the other amateur archaeologists were led by Solly. The sight of an Israeli with a full beard and a full Aussie accent to match amused Ty. He was ending his three-week dig and was already regretting having to leave this quiet, peaceful place.

It was still dark and the only sound was that of a gentle breeze caressing the side of his tent. As he inhaled, he detected a pleasant whiff of the salt from the Dead Sea less than one-quarter mile from the camp.

He had climbed to the tops of some of the tallest mountains

in North America including Mt. Rainier and Mt. McKinley. At those altitudes, the air was thin and the temperatures plunged. But at the Dead Sea, the lowest point on earth at 1,300 feet below sea level, Ty marveled at the contrast. Here, the temperature was always warm and the air was thicker with oxygen and calming bromine than at any other place on the planet.

Ty lay in his sleeping bag and took a brief inventory of his life. After high school he attended Baylor University on a baseball scholarship. He had a mean fastball and a sinker that dropped a couple of feet. He had visions of making it to the big leagues. That dream disappeared one afternoon when he was playing a pick-up basketball game with some of his friends.

He had been on a fast break, soaring above the rim for a YouTube-worthy reverse slam-dunk. After the dunk, the ring finger of his throwing hand got tangled in the net somehow. As he fell, he could feel the tendons on the inside of his arm strain and then tear. The medical trainer of the baseball team, who was an orthopedic surgeon, ordered an MRI and later diagnosed Ty with medial epicondylitis. After one dumb-jock stunt, his baseball career was over. He never threw again with any speed. He graduated with a degree in sports kinesiology. He wasn't ready to enter the work-a-day world, so he and his best friend spontaneously enlisted in the Marines. He immediately qualified for Officers Candidate School and graduated at the top of his class.

By this time, he knew he wanted to fly—and fly fast, so he applied to the Marine Air Corps School. He soon found himself flying T-34s out of Whiting Field in Milton, Florida. He excelled in all of his qualifying stages, and it wasn't long until he strapped himself into what would become his favorite set of wings: an F/A-18 Hornet.

The Hornet fulfilled his need for speed. With a top speed of Mach 1.8, it was its vertical climb performance that literally took Ty's breath away. The Hornet could climb at a heart-stopping rate of 45,000 feet per minute. The only other aircraft in the world rumored to climb faster was the Russian Mig-29.

Once Ty gained the hours and the rank to fly the way he wanted, he had a favorite tactic to break in new Weapons Systems Officers sitting in the cockpit behind him. He would start his takeoff roll down the runway. After reaching rotation speed, he would lift off the runway a few feet, retract the gear and engage the afterburners. Screaming just above the runway, when he reached the end, he would pull back on the yoke and put the Hornet in a near vertical climb, barrel rolling the aircraft several times before quickly leveling off at 32,000 feet. Any WSO who survived that initiation without depositing their lunch in their helmet won the respect of the entire squadron.

When Ty was deployed in the air campaign of the Gulf War in 1991, flying wasn't fun. It was dangerous work. Ty was a squad leader of the first waves of what would grow to over 100,000 sorties over Iraq. After 88,000 tons of bombs had been dropped, there wasn't much left of the Iraqi military and civilian infrastructure. Even though his aircraft deployed smart bombs, Ty knew with certainty that he had killed dozens, maybe even hundreds, of Iraqi soldiers and citizens. This combat experience was why Ty felt an immediate connection with an older soldier like Solly. They had both been in combat and killed the enemy.

After leaving the Marines, Ty had bounced around to several

jobs but he didn't like wearing a suit and keeping office hours. Once your work involves strapping on a super-sonic fighter jet, it's impossible to match that kind of excitement.

Many ex-military pilots became airline or charter pilots, but Ty didn't think he could stand the boring hours of sitting in the cockpit monitoring systems. He needed some adventure.

He was thumbing through a *National Geographic* one day and came across an article about eco-archaeological tours in Israel. That captured his interest, so he applied with the Israeli Antiquities Authority. Three weeks later in the summer of 2002, he found himself at the Qumran excavations.

A week after arriving at the Qumran dig, Solly had invited Ty to travel to Masada with the group, the site of Herod the Great's most ambitious palace. Masada is a raised 1,200-foot plateau with sheer cliffs on each side—virtually impenetrable. In 72 A.D., a group of Jewish rebels fended off the Romans for nearly a year from this fortress. When the Roman general Silva arrived, he was astounded to discover that the Jews had preferred death to slavery.

The members in Ty's group prepared to board the cable car to ride to the summit of Masada, now one of the most popular tourist sites in Israel. He noticed a thin trail winding up the side of the mountain fortress.

"Hey, Solly, I'm going to run up that trail. See you at the top, okay?"

Solly, always ready with a bit of Jewish history, replied, "That's the snake trail. Josephus wrote that it made the legs of even the strongest men tremble."

"I can handle it. I've competed in triathlons in Georgia," Ty said confidently.

"Okay. I'll join you," Solly said.

Ty didn't know just how old Solly was, but his full beard was grey.

"Let's go, old-timer," Ty challenged. "But I'm not going to slow down for you to take rest stops."

Before Ty knew it, Solly had started off jogging toward the base of the trail. Ty followed. He lagged behind in case he needed to give Solly CPR.

They ran back and forth on the switchbacks climbing the 1,200-foot tall mountain. Solly was widening his lead in front of Ty. He turned around once and yelled, "Let's go, kid! You don't want to let an old-timer beat you, do you?"

Ty increased his pace and narrowed the gap. Even though it was only a 45-minute run, the severity of the switchbacks and the steepness of the trail made it seem like hours. With only a couple of hundred feet left to go, they were side by side. Neither man was speaking as they exerted maximum energy to beat the other. Ty called upon his entire physical reserve and tried sprinting the last few yards, but to his surprise, he couldn't pull away from Solly. They both arrived at the wooden loading platform for the cable car at the same time.

A group of tourists waiting to board the cable car for the return to the visitor center stared at the two men as if they were crazy.

Exhausted, Ty and Solly were bent over with their hands on their knees, gasping for air. Neither could speak.

Then when they could finally take a full breath, they both started laughing. They couldn't stop. Finally, Solly threw his arm around Ty's shoulder and said, "Mate, you wouldn't think that either of us are very competitive now, would you?"

Ty smiled and said, "I've got to hand it to you, Solly. I thought the only way you were going to make it to the top of this mountain was on my shoulders!"

Still chuckling, they walked through the entrance gate together where the other members of their group were waiting and wondering what joke they had missed.

That race had launched a strong friendship that had changed Ty's life. In the evenings he would often talk to Solly about flying sorties over Iraq.

One evening Solly and Ty sat awhile after dinner and Solly told Ty about his near-death experience in the Yom Kippur War of 1973.

16

40 YEARS EARLIER

OCTOBER 6, 1973
The Valley of Tears
Northern Israel

As a fresh eighteen-year-old recruit of the Israeli Defense Force, Solly had heard all the stories about the War for Independence and the Six Day War in 1967. Since the ceasefire with Egypt was holding, there was a chance he wouldn't even see combat.

But all of that changed on Yom Kippur, the Day of Atonement, when Egypt and Syria launched attacks on Israel. Israel had so few weapons and soldiers that the survival of the young nation was in doubt. It was later reported that Israeli Prime Minister Golda Meir considered suicide. Her cabinet met in emergency session and developed plans for operating a government in exile. Complete annihilation seemed certain.

The two-pronged attack on Yom Kippur was intended as both a strategic advantage and a national insult. Yom Kippur is the one day of the year that all Jews, secular and religious, refrained from work. Israel's enemies assumed that their soldiers wouldn't fight on this holy day. But the plan backfired because their enemies did not understand Israel's defense strategy.

The Israeli Army is a citizen army made up of all former members of the IDF who are under age 45. All Israeli youth, male and female, are required to serve in the Israeli Defense Force for three years when they turn 18. For the next three years, the young members of the IDF are trained to fight. They also man the borders to protect Israel from invasion. If attacked, they are expected to hold the line until the citizen army can be mobilized.

In 1973, each member of the citizen army was a part of an intricate telephone tree structure. In the event of an attack, each member would receive a call and, in turn, they would call the five people on their list, who would call their list and so on.

In an ironic twist, if the Egyptian and Syrian forces had attacked on any other day than Yom Kippur, it would have been unlikely that Israel could have assembled their entire army in less than 36 hours. But on Yom Kippur, everyone in Israel is at home. With the streets and roads empty for the holiday, Israel was able to mobilize their entire citizen army in less than six hours.

In the north, Syria invaded Israel with a force of over 1,400 Soviet-built T-52 tanks. These massive war machines were equipped with state-of-the-art night-vision capability. Going out to face this Goliath was the David-sized Israeli armored division, less than 200 Centurion tanks strong. These dinosaurs from the British had been used in World War II. Slower and smaller, the Israeli Centurions rolled into the Golan, seemingly on a suicide mission against such a superior force.

The Syrians easily broke through the thin Israeli line of tanks in a fierce nighttime attack. They penetrated the Israeli forces so quickly and deeply that they were soon among the Israeli tanks without even realizing it. In the smoke and confusion, it became difficult to distinguish between the Israeli and the Syrian tanks.

Israeli Commander Avigdor Kahalani stared out of his tank at the red tail lights of what he thought were his own Israeli tanks. According to actual radio transcripts from that night, Kahalani barked at all the Israeli tanks to turn off their lights immediately. They all reported their lights off, but the tanks in front of Kahalani were still displaying small red lights. He commanded his force to start firing at any tank with lights still on.

Kahalani yelled, "Fire!" His gunner said, "Range, sir?" Kahalani shouted, "No damn range, just fire!"

The fighting became so fierce that Kahalani's gunner shot one tank at point-blank range, then turned to shoot another. Just as Kahalani looked up, he saw the bore of a Syrian tank barrel pointed directly at him less than ten meters away. There was no time to reload and fire. But in another unbelievable turn of events, the Syrian tank gun jammed and Kahalani's tank destroyed it before it could reload.

This heated battle continued day and night for over 36 hours. At one point, only seven Israeli tanks remained operational. Kahalani knew that this would be their final stand. Defeat meant that the Syrian force would soon overtake Tiberius then on to Haifa and Tel Aviv. The nation born again in 1948 would be pushed into the sea less than 30 years later.

He commanded his tanks to spread out along a ridge called

the Little Hermon. Perhaps by spreading out they would give the appearance of being a larger force. The Israeli tanks reached the summit of the ridge and began firing down on the Syrian tanks in the valley. Several Israeli tanks were completely out of shells, but they joined the line to add to the show of force.

Exactly what happened next is often debated. Many people call it a miracle. At the West Point Military Academy, instructors teaching about the Valley of Tears officially call it "The Impossible."

Perhaps the Syrian commander did what the Israelis wanted and mistook these few tanks as a first wave of reinforcements. We will never know for certain why, but with certain victory only moments away, the entire Syrian force suddenly turned around and retreated back into Syria. Many of the Syrian soldiers even deserted their tanks with the engines still running. Israel was saved. Goliath had fallen to David again.

The Syrian army left behind 260 wrecked tanks, 500 armored personnel carriers and numerous other vehicles. The burning hulks littered the battlefield that would become known as Emek Ha Bacha, the Valley of Tears.

The Syrian commander was interviewed later about issuing the command to retreat. A journalist asked why he hadn't advanced against the Israeli tanks on the ridge and won the war. He replied, "I'd like to see you cross that mountain if you saw an entire row of white angels standing on the ridge—and a white hand from heaven motioning you to stop." Some attributed his statement to Post Traumatic Stress Syndrome. But there are those of Solly's generation who believe it was nothing less than divine intervention.

17

JUNE 30, 2002

Qumran, Israel
9:40pm

When Solly finished telling Ty about the Valley of Tears battle, he bowed his head solemnly as if he were praying.

"How do you know so much about the details of that battle?" Ty asked.

Solly was silent for more than a minute. When he looked up, his eyes were filled with tears.

"I was only eighteen, and it was my first combat. I was the loader in Kahalani's tank," he said softly.

"In one hour that night, we destroyed 18 Syrian tanks. I thought I would die many times. We fired until we had no more shells. We were an easy target every time that we retreated to refuel and reload, but we were never hit. I can't say that about many of my friends—my neighbors and comrades. Over a thousand of our men died in that battle."

Ty knew when to speak and when to be silent, so he held his tongue.

Solly continued, "So, my friend, I understand how you feel.

It's hard to forget when you take another man's life—even in war."

Solly rose from his chair and said, "Goodnight, Ty. Sleep well. I want to show you something really special tomorrow." With that, Solly left.

18

The Israel Museum
Jerusalem 6:20am

Ty and Solly had left the digging site in Qumran when the sun was still hiding behind the Jordanian Mountains across the Dead Sea. They grabbed a mug of coffee from the camp kitchen and jumped into Solly's Mitsubishi Montero SUV.

Within minutes, they turned west passing Jericho where Solly pointed out that it is the oldest continually inhabited city in the world. Then they started the steep climb up to Jerusalem, ascending 1,200 meters in only thirty minutes.

Next, they drove through the biblical city of Bethany where from the top of Mt. Scopus Ty gazed at the layout of Jerusalem ahead of him. He would never tire of looking at this city.

As they pulled into the empty parking lot of the Israel Museum, Solly pulled on his beard and asked playfully, "So, Ty, do you believe in miracles?"

Ty possessed an uncanny memory for pop music from all generations and usually had a song running in his head. He said, "Sure, all I need is a miracle..." He started tapping on the dash like a drum, crooning the chorus of the 80s hit. Solly, who also loved music, said, "Mike and the Mechanics, 1985" and joined in the chorus as well. They couldn't remember the verses, so they just repeated the chorus several times.

Ty laughed at their off-pitch tune and said, "No, seriously. I don't believe in miracles. I'm not even sure I believe in God. If you ask me, there is a rational explanation for most things that people call miracles."

Solly and Ty started walking together toward the museum. "I used to believe the same thing, Ty," he began. "But when I look at the existence of modern Israel, I am forced to admit that *we* are a miracle."

As he was prone to do, Solly then launched into a brief but fascinating account of Jewish history as they walked. Ty appreciated these off-the-cuff opportunities to learn from Solly's wealth of experience and research.

Solly continued, "For over eighteen centuries, Jews were spread around the globe, and Israel did not exist, but these Jews never lost a sense of their history and culture. Born out of the ashes of the Nazi Holocaust, Israel was chartered as a nation in 1948. It was just a small sliver of land on the Mediterranean coast. A few days later, twelve different Arab countries attacked us, although Israel didn't even have an organized army to speak of. Somehow, we won this War of Independence in 1948, but Jerusalem remained completely controlled by the Jordanians. We were attacked again by overwhelming odds in 1967. When you compare the size of the armies that attacked us that second time, there is no way we should have won again. But in six days, we had pushed the enemies back and we gained control of

Jerusalem for the first time in over 2,000 years."

"That's amazing," Ty agreed.

Solly continued, "I already told you about the miracles of the Yom Kippur War, right? And in the first Gulf War when you flew missions, Saddam Hussein fired scores of Scud missiles into Israel, but not a single person was killed." Solly drew a breath. "Not only have we experienced many miraculous military victories, our language is a miracle in itself. How else can you explain the fact that the Hebrew language was a dead language for centuries? It is the only ancient dead language that has been revived and is spoken by schoolchildren today. No one in Egypt speaks ancient Egyptian, and when was the last time you heard an Iranian speaking ancient Babylonian? But my grandkids speak and read the same language of Abraham and Moses."

By now, Solly and Ty were standing outside the entrance to the museum. Waving his arm back behind him, Solly grew more animated as he spoke. "This entire land had become a desert wasteland. How have we been able to turn an area that is 80% desert into one of the most fertile areas on the planet? Today, Israel exports flowers and fruit to every continent. The prophet Isaiah predicted the time would come when we would fill the earth with fruit."

Ty said, "Well, all those events could still be coincidences..."

Solly grinned. "The word 'coincidence' isn't in God's vocabulary. Wake up, Ty, these things can only be explained as miracles. But maybe you need to see for yourself."

Solly walked up to the armed guard and showed him a card. They were allowed inside. There was a metal detector and X-ray for visitors to the museum, but Solly ignored it.

Ty smiled and whispered in the vacant hallway, "Did your family donate money to this place or something? How are you able to walk right in?"

"I'm a member of the Israeli Antiquities Authority," Solly replied. "Plus, they all know me around here because I've spent months working on a special project."

"What project?"

"You'll see."

Solly led them toward a solid black wall with a fountain at its base. The fountain was turned off. Past the black wall, there was a strange looking building that looked like a giant, white Hershey's kiss. Suddenly Ty recognized it from photographs. It was the Shrine of the Book built to preserve and display most of the Dead Sea Scrolls.

They walked down a set of steps that said, "Authorized Personnel Only." At the bottom of the steps, they came to a thick steel door with a security camera pointed down at them. Solly punched a code into the keypad and smiled up at the camera. After a loud "click," he pushed the door open.

"How much do you know about the Bible?" Solly asked as they walked down a long corridor.

"Not much. I used to tell my fellow jar-heads that my mom had a drug problem."

Solly cast a wary eye toward him.

"She drug me to church and Sunday school when I was a kid! I remember learning a few verses and attending something called Vacation Bible School. But it wasn't much of a vacation!"

"Have you read *any* parts of the Bible?" Solly pressed.

Ty thought for a moment. "No. When I was a teenager, I

lost interest in church and the Bible. Baseball became my god and I guess you might say I worshipped on the holy hill called the pitcher's mound. I was required to take some Bible classes in college, but I don't remember much about them."

Ty added, "And we didn't do much Bible reading in the Marines, trust me."

As they entered what appeared to be a sterile lab, the overhead lights automatically switched on. In the middle of the room were four long tables where different scrolls could be easily unrolled and studied. Polished wooden lockers lined the four walls. Each locker had a keypad and a sign in Hebrew that Ty couldn't decipher.

"Pretty cool," Ty said looking around. "I've heard about the Dead Sea Scrolls, but I never thought I'd actually get to see them."

Solly added water and grounds to a coffee maker in a kitchen area and turned it on. Over his shoulder he said, "Many of these are facsimiles of the original scrolls. The real scrolls were preserved for almost 2,000 years in the low humidity of the caves near Qumran. But in the 60 years since they've been discovered, they've suffered more deterioration than the previous nineteen centuries."

Solly got two coffee mugs out of the cabinet. "For instance, the massive Isaiah scroll you see under the display glass upstairs is an exact copy of the original. It's called the Great Isaiah Scroll because it's the largest and the best preserved of all the scrolls. It's 734 centimeters long and contains 45 columns that include all 66 chapters of the prophecy. And the words in it are exactly the same as you would read in a Gideon Bible in a hotel room, which really needles the guys who want to say the Bible is inaccurate." Solly grunted a laugh under his breath.

Ty glanced at one of the scrolls on the table. The Hebrew characters made it appear as if a chicken had walked through ink and then made its way in straight lines up and down the paper.

"Can you actually read this?" Ty asked incredulously.

Solly shook his head and said, "Ty, remember, my kids and grandkids can read these scrolls. The 23 letters of the Hebrew alphabet haven't changed in thousands of years."

Going back into professor mode, Solly continued, "The syntax and grammar are different, and so it would be like you trying to read Chaucer's Canterbury Tales in old English. You'd know the letters and most of the words, but you might not recognize all the meanings."

He pointed to the scrolls. "These contain portions of every book of the Old Testament except one, Esther. And some suggest that the Essenes in the Yahad Community who copied them refused to accept Esther because it doesn't contain God's name. These scrolls provided copies of the Scriptures that are 1,000 years older than any copies in existence prior to their discovery in 1946. That's an eternity of provenance in the literary world."

"So, they just tell a bunch of historical stories, right?" Ty inquired.

Solly smiled and placed his hand on Ty's shoulder. "You've got a lot to learn, my friend. This is going to be fun."

19

The Israel Museum
Jerusalem 8:30am

Solly handed him a mug of hot coffee and the two of them settled onto short stools at one of the long tables. Solly replied, "Much of what people call the Bible contains historical accounts of the Jewish people. But a large part of the Bible contains prophecy— predictions about the future. Prophecy is like history in reverse."

"Are you gonna go all Nostradamus on me, Solly?" Ty teased, sipping his coffee and noting its strong flavor.

Solly replied, "Bear with me, buddy. If you keep that tiny brain of yours open for a while, you're going to learn something today. When you read an ancient prophecy in the Bible, and then study history and discover that the prophecy was exactly fulfilled at a later date, you can't ignore that kind of evidence."

Ty looked confused, rather than convinced.

Solly decided to switch tactics at that point and said, "Just sit there and let me give you the short version of my story."

"Ten years ago, I was an all-out skeptic about anything to do with the Bible or religion in general. I was raised in a Jewish family, but we didn't really practice Judaism. We seldom attended synagogue, and I never even studied enough to pass my bar mitzvah. When I came to Israel, I was too busy learning Hebrew, working on a kibbutz, and getting ready to serve in the IDF. I got married and had a family, but I became more and more bitter about religion. I came to believe that the ultra-orthodox Jews were actually enemies of the State of Israel."

Solly took a sip of coffee and continued. "Later, when I came to work for the Israeli Antiquities Authority, there was a wise old Professor named Dr. Silverman who took me as his apprentice. Like you, I thought all these scriptures were just interesting old manuscripts like the writings of Plato or Josephus. Dr. Silverman knew better. He had been a history professor at Hebrew University when he was hired to be the curator for the scrolls. He devoted the last 30 years of his life to the preservation and interpretation of these scrolls."

Ty silently thought about how boring that job sounded.

Solly said, "I'll cut to the chase, as you Americans say. Dr. Silverman's study of the prophecies of the Old Testament scrolls led him to study the writings called the New Testament. Through this extensive study, he became convinced that Jesus of Nazareth was the Jewish Messiah."

"Come on," Ty said, "You're not going to tell me the Jewish curator of the Dead Sea Scrolls became a Christian!"

"That's not what I said. The term 'Christian' was originally a term of derision that was used against the early followers of Jesus. Dr. Silverman would say that he had become a 'complete Jew.'"

"What's a 'complete Jew'?" Ty asked as he drained his coffee.

"The earliest followers of Jesus were all Jews. They were able to maintain their Jewish culture along with their belief that Jesus was their Messiah. Dr. Silverman did the same thing."

"I agree that Jesus was a great teacher and all that. But you don't swallow that Messiah stuff, do you, Solly?" Ty inquired.

A huge smile emerged from Solly's thick beard. His eyes sparkled as he said, "I do more than *that*! I'm also convinced that Jesus was the Messiah. And I believe he died on a cross not far from here. He was buried nearby, and after three days the tomb was empty. I believe he's alive today in heaven. And one day he will return to claim his rightful place as King over Israel."

Ty shook his head in disbelief. "Is this one of those revival-type services? Is a choir going to start singing? Is this where I fall on my knees and you slap me on the head or something?"

Solly wasn't offended in the least by Ty's deflection. "I love your sense of humor, Ty."

"I guess you're also a 'completed Jew,' as you say, right?"

"Guilty as charged, my friend. I believe Yashua ha Mashia!"

"Okay, I'm curious now. What happened to change your mind?"

Solly said, "I thought you'd never ask. Remember, I'm a digger. I dig in the ground and find treasures from history. When I hold the Bible in one hand and my tools in the other, I see that the Bible *is* accurate. No single archaeological find in Israel has ever contradicted the Bible. It's not just a bunch of fairy tales or myths. And that just motivates me to dig into the Bible for other treasures."

"Give me an example," Ty said.

"I could give you hundreds, but here's one that your simple brain can understand."

Ty smiled and rolled his eyes.

"The New Testament states that there was a Roman procurator by the name of Pontius Pilate. He interviewed Jesus during his trial. Most scholars scoffed at the idea that Pontius Pilate ever even existed because there is no historical record of him in the Roman annals. This caused many scholars to assume the disciples of Jesus concocted the entire story after he died."

Ty nodded.

"Anyway, Dr. Silverman was a young archeologist and part of the dig at Caesarea by the Sea in 1961 when he heard excited shouts coming from one of the covered pits. He dropped his tools and ran to see what had been unearthed. And there he saw the words carved into an ancient limestone relief in Latin: 'Pontius Pilatus governor of Judea.'"

"So, that proved he was real?" Ty asked.

"Well, Dr. Silverman was convinced and this was before he had studied the New Testament. I'll never forget the day that he patiently sat down with me and showed me Hebrew passages from the scrolls predicting the coming of the Messiah. Then he opened a New Testament to read the descriptions about how Jesus accurately fulfilled these prophecies."

"Like what prophecies?" Ty was getting interested now.

"Well, 750 years before it happened, Micah predicted that the Messiah would be born in a little town named Bethlehem," Solly said. "That's a no-brainer because I'm sure you celebrate Christmas. The Jews had expected their Messiah to be a military king, but the prophecies predicted just the opposite. I can show you on the Isaiah scroll where he predicted that the Messiah would be despised and rejected, a man of sorrows. That he would suffer for our sins. That God would lay on him all of our iniquities. Those predictions are senseless unless you read them in light of how Jesus was treated by the Jewish leaders during his trial and crucifixion."

"Okay, so..." Ty said hesitantly. He was stumped because he had never heard any of this before.

"Ty, the precision of these prophecies is amazing. About 500 years before it happened, Zechariah also predicted that the Messiah would ride into Jerusalem on the foal of a colt. Check. That's what Jesus did. The Psalmist predicted that his hands and feet would be pierced. Check. The Psalmist also predicted that the soldiers would gamble for his possessions. Check."

"So how many of these Old Testament prophecies about the Messiah were fulfilled by Jesus?" Ty asked.

"About sixty. Some biblical scholars dispute a few of them, but there are 33 prophecies that can't be disputed. That is evidence that I couldn't ignore. And neither could Dr. Silverman."

Solly paused and placed his hand on Ty's shoulder. "And unless you suffered brain damage from all that high-altitude flying, you can't ignore it either."

"Well, it sounds interesting, but it will take more than some old scrolls to convince me. I'm afraid I've become a hard-core skeptic," Ty admitted.

Solly laughed. "You're a tough nut to crack—you remind me of myself ten years ago." He paused and said, "I've been debating with myself whether or not to show you something even more remarkable from the scrolls."

Solly paused again and asked, "How much can I trust you?"

"From one warrior to another," Ty said, "you can trust me. Remember, our Marine Corps motto is *semper fidelis*—always faithful. After telling me what you went through in that tank battle, I feel like there's a bond between us. So what else do you have to show me?"

Solly looked around and said quietly, "This *really* is one of those things that if I show you I may have to kill you."

"I'd like to see you try, old man," said Ty.

20

The Israel Museum
Jerusalem 8:50am

Solly led Ty to a thick door with a separate set of entry protocols. He leaned over and placed his right eye against a scope for a retinal scan. Then he spoke clearly, "Solomon Rubin, 6578985."

There was a sound of electronic locks opening as Solly pushed the heavy door open. The fluorescent lights came on automatically. Ty could sense that the temperature and humidity of this room was carefully controlled.

Solly snapped on surgical gloves from a sterile dispenser. He tenderly removed a large scroll from a glass container.

He explained, "Literary experts know that one of the most important Dead Sea Scrolls was the War Scroll. But there was another scroll found with the War Scroll. The text of this scroll has never been released to the global academic community. Dr. Silverman named it the 'Messiah Scroll.' That's what I'm about to show you."

Solly began carefully unrolling it. "Through the years, some have protested that Israel hasn't released all the scrolls. Of course, we have officially denied that. But now you know."

"What's so special about this guy?" Ty asked.

"To those of us who truly understand its meaning, it makes predictions that clearly reveal Jesus as the Messiah."

"I thought you already talked about all that from the Old Testament," Ty said.

"No, these aren't prophecies like the ones written by Isaiah and Micah. These prophecies are not part of the Bible, but the leader of the Essene Community, a mysterious man who was only known as the Teacher of Righteousness, wrote them. They date to only a few years before Jesus was born. For instance, the Teacher predicted that the forerunner of the Messiah would be a man who would announce the true Kingdom of God and use water to symbolize repentance and forgiveness."

"Are you talking about John the Baptist?" Ty asked.

"Very good," Solly said. "It's hard to read it any other way. And there is evidence from another scroll called the Community Scroll that a man named John was a part of the Essenes before he left to preach and baptize."

"I'm getting confused," Ty said. "Was John a member of the Essene Community or the forerunner of the Messiah?"

"Yes," Solly deadpanned. He stood to his feet and paced around the room while he spoke. "I believe both of those statements are right. There is evidence that the Teacher of Righteousness recognized John and commissioned him to leave the Community to announce the coming of the Kingdom of Heaven."

"Well, I'll be a monkey's uncle," Ty said.

"No, that was Charles Darwin's line," Solly replied without skipping a beat. He continued, "You can see why the Israeli government chooses not to release this information identifying the true Messiah as Jesus. It would create an earthquake of protest from Orthodox Jews. But we haven't gotten to the most amazing part yet."

Solly smiled like a little boy at Christmas.

"What can top that?" Ty asked.

Solly returned to his seat and carefully leaned over the Messiah Scroll until he found a place to start reading: *A generation after the Messiah is cut off, the mighty enemy will come from the West and destroy the Holy Temple.*

"When did that happen?" Ty asked.

"Well, this is nothing new. Five hundred years earlier, the prophet Daniel predicted the same destruction of the Temple," Solly said and pulled a well-worn New Testament from a nearby shelf and thumbed through the pages. "A few days before Jesus was crucified, he approached Jerusalem from the Mount of Olives and made a similar prediction. As he looked at the city, he began to weep because he knew its destruction was coming."

Solly drilled his finger down the page and said, "Here it is in Luke 19:41-44. Listen to what Jesus said, 'If you, even you, had only known on this day what would bring you peace—but now it is hidden from your eyes. The days will come upon you when your enemies will build an embankment against you and encircle you and hem you in on every side. They will dash you to the ground, you and the children within your walls. They will not leave one stone on another, because you did not recognize the time of God's coming to you.' To answer your question, one generation after Jesus was crucified, this very thing happened. In 70 A.D., the Romans sacked Jerusalem and destroyed the

Temple. They even pried the rocks apart to get at the gold that had melted between the blocks. We understand that prophecy because we can look back and see how it was fulfilled. But it's this next section that had Dr. Silverman scratching his head until he died."

Ty leaned forward, anxious as Solly unrolled another section of the scroll and began to read.

The people of the King will no longer need a Temple of stone and gold because Yahweh will build His true temple in the hearts of His people.

Solly paused, "The next two sections predict how the people of the King will take his good news to the west and conquer the enemies who destroyed Jerusalem. This wasn't a military conquest; it was a spiritual victory. Of course, we know that in 313 A.D. the Roman Emperor Constantine declared Christianity to be the faith of the Empire. But here's the part I want to read to you."

Moving his finger down half a page, Solly continued reading from right to left, *After forty generations, the people of the King will cross the Great Sea to the West and then cross the Greater Sea beyond. They will establish a nation to be a beacon of light for the world.*

"I don't get that one," Ty said.

Solly explained, "We know that the Great Sea is the Mediterranean. The only thing that would be a greater sea would be the Atlantic Ocean, right? A generation is roughly 40 years, so that would mean approximately 1,600 years after the Messiah was killed that this nation would be established. Does that ring a bell?"

"I think I know where you're going with this, but how could this be about America?" Ty asked.

"Remember, prophecy is a miracle. It is history in reverse. Your President Ronald Reagan continually called America a 'shining city upon a hill.' This was a direct reference to the words of Jesus in Matthew 5:14. For much of its history, America has been a moral and spiritual beacon for the world. But prepare to be blown away; this next part will amaze you."

Solly continued, "I'll translate this as literally as I can."

After seven generations, the light of righteousness in this land will fade and the Adversary will attack the people of the King. Four silver vultures will fly against the nation of light. These giant vultures roar and bellow smoke in their wake. One vulture will attack the great fort. One vulture will fall to the earth. Two vultures will destroy the strong towers. The smoke of the torment of the attack will rise into the heavens and the wail of the dead will ascend into the sky. The people of the Enemy will rejoice and dance in the streets over the carnage.

Ty felt the hair on the back of his neck vibrate. Fear like he hadn't felt since he first flew into combat gripped his mind. He tried to process what he had just heard.

"No way," Ty said, "You're pulling my leg, Solly. Tell me this is a joke. There's no way that could be talking about the 9/11 attacks."

"My friend, I wouldn't joke about the worst terrorist attack in history. Dr. Silverman died before he ever knew the meaning, but as I watched CNN last fall my jaw dropped as I saw the jets hitting the World Trade Center and the Pentagon. When I saw smoke from the towers rising over Manhattan and the news about the fourth jet crashing in the Pennsylvania countryside, I knew that this prophecy was accurate."

"Why haven't I heard about this before? Who knows about

this?" Ty demanded.

"Only a few leaders in our country have access to this scroll," Solly said. "And what good would it have been to release this prophecy after the fact? Nobody would believe it anyway."

"Well, thank you for shaking up my world," Ty said.

"I'm not finished," Solly replied.

"What do you mean?"

"There's more."

Solly continued to read from the scroll.

...The people of the land of light neither humbled themselves nor repented of their sins. They rebuilt their fort and their towers, but their hearts were hardened. The Adversary gave them rest for a season to lull them to sleep. Yet they ignored Yahweh's warnings and played in their green pastures. Then the Destroyer interrupted their games and came upon the land to strike them down with a cloud of death. Thousands of the wealthy leaders perished as their breaths were ripped from their throats.

"Huh? I don't get it," Ty said. "When did that happen?"

"It hasn't happened...yet."

21

The Israel Museum
Jerusalem 9:10am

"What does this mean?" Ty asked.

"If the first prophecy of 9/11 was accurate, that would lead me to believe that there is going to be another massive terrorist attack on the U.S. This description sounds exactly like a bioterrorism attack."

Ty was silent for a moment. "So, why are you showing me this?"

"Ty, it's time for you to know the truth about what I do. I'm more than just an archaeology guide and a member of the Antiquities Authority. Those are just cover jobs. I'm a member of Israel's clandestine service."

Ty smiled and shook his head, as if he couldn't accept this final bit of information. "So you're telling me that you're a member of Mossad?"

"Now, I seriously have to kill you," Solly said. "Actually, I'm a one-man branch of Mossad. After the 9/11 attacks, I brought the words of the scroll to the attention of the Prime Minister and the head of Mossad. After the implications were fully realized, they authorized me to use any means possible to uncover and attempt to disrupt this next prophetic attack. We've given it the code name Cloud Strike."

"Again, I don't have a clue why you're telling me all this," Ty said.

"Simple. I want to hire you to work for me in America," Solly said. "I've recruited several dozen agents in strategic countries around the world to help me sniff out the Cloud Strike threat."

"But you don't know anything about me," Ty protested.

"I knew Marines were dumb, but are you so thick-headed that you don't think that Mossad has resources to vet you?" Solly laughed. "Tyler James Kensington, born in Tyler, Texas, on September 24, 1971. I can even quote your E.R.A. for the years you pitched at Baylor before you messed up your elbow. In fact, I could tell you how much money—or should I say how little money –you have in your bank account back in Atlanta. No current romantic relationships..."

Ty held up his hands and interrupted, "Okay, okay. I get it. Are you serious?"

"I'm a good judge of men. I've never picked a bad apple, and you have what I'm looking for. I know you're scheduled to leave Israel next week. Why don't you stay here in Jerusalem for a few more weeks and let us train you? We'll put you up at the King David Hotel, on our dime—that's an improvement over your sleeping bag, don't you think?"

He continued, "After spending some time with me, we'll send you back to Atlanta. You can continue your work as a private investigator. Of course, we know that you are starving for a lack of good-paying clients. We can even send you some legitimate clients."

"But if I work for Mossad, won't I have to tell the U.S. government about it? Would I be breaking any law?" Ty asked.

"You could tell them, but I wouldn't suggest it. We have ample evidence that there are moles placed in every American intelligence service, from the C.I.A., to the F.B.I., to the N.S.A. Of course, Israel and the United States are allies and we share intelligence to a point. We won't be asking you to break any laws. You'll actually be doing a great service for your country."

Solly said, "I know this is a lot for you to take in, but I felt that I had to show you this clear and present evidence of danger to your country before I recruited you."

Ty's head was spinning slightly as he realized that his life was about to take a new trajectory. He stared Solly in the eyes and held out his hand to shake. "Where do I sign up?"

"Good choice, mate! That's the jarhead I know!" Solly said and shook his hand.

22

PRESENT TIME

MARCH 26
Alpharetta, Georgia
5:30pm

Regan was dreaming. It wasn't a sweet dream but a nightmare. She was running from a faceless pursuer. In her dream, she whipped out her iPhone, but she couldn't get it to go to the correct screen to make a call. She didn't recognize any of the symbols and apps that appeared on her screen. As she ran for her life, she was consumed with frustration. She started pushing the icons on her screen, and when nothing happened, she started tapping the screen with her fingernail.

"Tap, tap, tap." She could hear the sound getting louder in her dream. "Tap, tap, tap tap tap."

Her eyes flew open and she realized she was still in her car with her seat reclined. She'd been asleep and someone really was tapping on her driver's side window.

As she swam her way to the surface of her confused thoughts, reality hit—and it hit hard. She was parked in front of the burned-out shell of her house.

The tapping on the window continued. She turned to see Ty standing there with a hot cup of coffee. "Wake up, sleepy head. We have guests."

Regan opened the door and thankfully accepted the cup of java. Several men in firefighting outfits were sifting through the ashes of what had been her home just hours earlier.

"The guy with the ball cap is the Fire Marshall. They've been here for over an hour and he told me he wanted to talk to the owner of the house," Ty said. "You were sleeping so soundly I hated to wake you."

"Thanks. I'm okay," Regan managed. She had just spoken a big, fat, white lie. She was far from okay. *What was happening?* she thought.

A tall African-American with kind eyes walked over. He took off his thick gloves and offered her his hand. "Ma'am, I'm Tom Woodard, the Fire Marshall, and I want to say how sorry I am for your loss."

"Thank you. I'm Regan Hart," she said as she stepped out of the car and numbly took his hand.

"Miss Hart, we've called in the ATF, the Alcohol Tobacco and Firearms, because we discovered that this fire was caused by an IED."

At first Regan thought she heard him say IUD and she almost burst out laughing. How could that cause a fire?

"A what?" she asked.

"An IED, ma'am, an Improvised Explosive Device. Insurgents in Iraq and other Middle Eastern countries are experts at making them. If you have some accelerant like gasoline or gunpowder, it's a simple device that can be made from a few items purchased at your local home improvement store. We don't see many of these things around here. I need to ask you a personal question. Do you have any enemies who might want you dead?"

If Regan had been playing a game entitled, "Ten Questions that you think you'll never be asked in your life," that question would have made the top three. She ran a quick mental inventory of people who might not like her. Ex-boyfriends. Disgruntled clients. One of her former bosses, who was a jerk.

"No. I honestly can't think of anyone who would want me dead," Regan finally replied.

"Well, you're lucky you weren't in the house when the device exploded," Tom said. "Where were you, by the way?"

"I was at Ty's house having coffee," she answered. *Did they think I had something to do with this?* she wondered.

Tom glanced at her fresh cup and then at Ty, assuming they were a couple.

"Oh, I hardly know the guy," Regan was quick to say. "I just met him a few hours ago. It's a long story. Do you want to hear it?"

"Save it for the ADF report. They'll interview you before they leave. Be sure to hang around for the next few hours, okay?"

Regan wanted to scream. *I don't have anywhere to go, can't you see?* But instead she composed herself and said, "Thank you, Tom. I'll be nearby."

As Tom walked away, Ty stepped up and gently guided her arm as they walked. He said, "Back to my house, I've got some updates for you."

Once they were seated in his den, Regan sipped her coffee,

shell-shocked.

Ty said, "At first I was a little suspicious about the story of the missing gift, but the fire and the IED sealed the deal. We're dealing with something sinister here. Apparently your friend Bridget in Paris gave you something to bring into our country. Whatever it was, it was important enough to remove the evidence—you."

"This is starting to sound like an episode of 24 or something," Regan said, tucking her knees under her. "I say it's time to call in the cavalry. The ATF is already here. Let's call in the FBI, the CIA, and any other agencies with initials we can find."

Ty said, "Not so fast. We need some help, but these agencies often start fighting and posturing for control and it can become a Keystone Cops routine."

"Who are the Keystone Cops?" Regan asked innocently.

"Never mind. While you were napping in your car, I called a friend of mine who is a global expert in these kinds of situations. I mentioned to him that our first step is to find Bridget, if that's even her real name. I told him she worked at GWA with you in Paris and gave him the general description that you gave me."

Ty paused to let this information sink in.

He continued, "My friend has some friends in Paris who have been looking for her. It seems that the girl named Bridget LeMeux no longer works for GWA. She left a short resignation note the day she delivered the gift to you. In fact, we only found two records of a Bridget LeMeux in Paris. One is nine years old and the other is sixty-nine. They pulled her employment application, but it was a dead end. Her information was bogus. In her employment picture, her hijab covered her face so much that she could be one of thousands of Muslim women in Paris."

"I've seen her many times without her hijab in the break room with just women colleagues around. She's pretty. Even elegant. But what I don't understand is how your 'friends' could gather all that information in a few hours," Regan said. "What is it you said you do for a living?"

"Well, these friends are, er, pretty well connected," Ty said, ignoring her question. "But start connecting the dots here, Regan. It seems that she worked at GWA just to befriend you to give you a package to bring to Atlanta. Do you have a better explanation?"

Regan wasn't ready to think she was caught up in some espionage scandal. "How about she got tired of working there and wanted to return home to wherever she was from? And what if she really has a sister in Atlanta and wanted me to bring her a gift? Does everything have to be a conspiracy with you?" Regan hadn't noticed that her voice had gotten louder.

Ty held out his hands palms downward and said, "Settle down, there, girl. Then how do you explain that only the gift and your purse were taken? And that they tossed your expensive purse? And how do you explain the explosive device? Come on, Regan, wake up and smell the burning hulk next door."

"Okay, you could be right," Regan admitted. "But what do we do now? I need to return to Paris to my job and my other apartment."

"Why don't I go with you and let's find Bridget? She's the key to solving this mystery," Ty said.

"Excuse me? Let's see, I've known you for less than..." Regan glanced at her Ice sports watch, "...twelve hours, and you want me to take you to Paris with me?"

Ty flashed his smile, which Regan noticed was slightly crooked. "Hey, don't let it go to your head. I'm a private investigator, remember? This is what I do. I don't have any pending cases now and I promise I'll be a perfect gentleman."

A big part of Regan really wanted this mysterious man to travel with her. He seemed to be smart—and kind. And he definitely wasn't hard on the eyes. These past twenty-four hours had unsettled her, however. Her gut instinct told her to say, "No thanks," and walk away and never see him again.

Ty could see that Regan was debating with herself trying to decide about accepting his offer.

Ty pushed his luck. "I'll make a deal with you. This will be purely professional. I'll stay in a hotel instead of your apartment. If you get tired of me at any time, just give me the word and I'll be gone in a flash. But I want to solve this mystery, and I think you could use a little back-up right now."

Regan was leaning toward saying yes. She paused, "Okay, Ty. I appreciate your offer to help. When do you want to leave?"

"Is any time better than the present? It doesn't look like you need to get anything from your house since it's in ruins. Why don't you stop by Target and pick up a few things you need, and I'll make the travel arrangements?"

Regan replied, "Oh, I can handle the travel. Our company has its own travel agent, and I'm Diamond Status on Delta. I can even use some of my miles for your ticket if you can't afford one."

Ty just smiled and said, "You head on to Target. I'll call my friend who has an interest in this case. I might be able to do one better than your Delta offer."

"But the Fire Marshall said I had to talk to the ADF agent," Regan said.

"Give me your cell number and I'll give it to him. He can call you with questions. I'll give him my word that I won't allow you to escape from my custody," Ty said with a smile.

Regan and Ty exchanged contact information. "I'll call you with our travel plans when I nail them down," Ty said and walked her to the front door.

As Regan got in her car to drive to Target, she still hadn't figured out this guy who had suddenly appeared in her life. But she wasn't going to complain—yet.

23

Gwinnett County Airport (LZU)
9:45pm

Following the directions on her iPhone Google Maps app, Regan pulled into the small parking lot in front of a single building of the Gwinnett County Airport. *This has to be a mistake,* she thought. *I thought we were going to Paris, and this is a tiny airport.*

After Regan had grabbed a few essential items at Target, including a basic Samsonite suitcase, her phone signaled an incoming text. Ty's text read, "I've arranged transportation. Meet me at Gwinnett County Airport." He included a link to the location.

She always flew out of Atlanta-Hartsfield Airport. But these directions had taken her north toward Lawrenceville, Georgia. She was about to call Ty to see if there was a mistake when she saw him walking across the lot toward her. She watched him through her tinted driver's window. At six-foot-two with a lean frame, he walked with the smooth grace of a man who looked like he competed in marathons. It was hard to judge his age because his salt and pepper hair made him look a little older. Regan guessed that he was somewhere north of forty.

"Hey, you found it!" Ty smiled as he opened her door. "Let's grab your stuff and head out to the ramp."

"Are we taking a small plane to Hartsfield to connect with a larger one?" Regan asked hopefully.

"Nope." He looked at all the plastic bags containing her purchases. "Why don't you pack all these bags of stuff you bought into this suitcase?"

"Well, I don't want to put everything in my checked luggage. I need some of it on the flight," Regan said.

"No problem. Just put it all in the suitcase for now and we'll take it on the plane," Ty offered. He loaded the smaller bags, grabbed the handle of her suitcase and led her across the parking lot to the small terminal building.

Regan followed after him saying, "But this suitcase is too large to fit in overhead compartments..."

"No worries, mate, as one of my friends likes to say. This plane doesn't have any overhead compartments," Ty said.

Regan was completely confused. After they passed through the lobby, they walked out onto the ramp. It was dark, but the ramp was well lit. Regan saw over a dozen small airplanes lined up and tied down with ropes attached to their wings and tail. None of them looked like they could fly to Florida, much less Transatlantic.

"Hey, seriously. I don't like little airplanes. I'm not getting in one of those."

"No worries, mate," Ty said again, ignoring her growing petulance. "Our ride is over inside this next hangar."

They walked left of the small aircraft to approach a large hangar where the door was open. Light was spilling out from the interior.

Regan turned the corner and she stopped and stared with surprise. A large, gleaming white business jet was sitting on the polished floor of the hangar. It was a little larger than some of the regional Delta jets that Regan had flown, but it stood higher off the ground.

The sleek jet had three large letters on the tail—IAI. Workmen were fussing around the underside of the wings and wheel wells performing some last minute checks.

"What airline is IAI? And where are the other passengers? When did this airport start offering airline service?" Regan asked, trying to fill in the blanks.

Ty smiled, "Slow down. First it isn't an airline. The letters stand for Israeli Aircraft Industries—the company that built this little bird. We are the only two passengers. And no, Gwinnett County doesn't offer airline service. This is a private charter."

Regan was still overwhelmed. "You've got some explaining to do. What bank did you rob to charter this flight? You told me you were a private investigator, and I know you guys don't make much money. Who's paying for this?"

Ty led Regan to the air stair hanging down behind the left wing. "Come on in and we'll talk. I'll answer at least some of your questions."

He easily carried her heavy suitcase up the air stairs and disappeared into the cabin to the right. Regan reluctantly followed him and stuck her head in to check out the interior. To the left, she saw a small galley with a young man dressed in a black suit and tie preparing some delicious-looking food. Inside the cockpit, she saw a confusing array of instruments, lights, and what appeared to be two, large video screens. Two pilots were talking to each other and pointing to a list on one of the screens.

The pilot on the left was a young, attractive woman with short black hair. She glanced back at Regan and smiled. "Welcome aboard, Ms. Hart. Make yourself comfortable, we'll be ready to depart in about ten minutes."

Regan noticed that she spoke English with a strange accent that she couldn't quite place.

Regan glanced to the right and saw eight luxurious leather seats. Four of the chairs were facing a large table, and the other four were facing forward. Each seat had a large LED video screen that swung out from the cabin wall.

At the aft of the aircraft, Ty was placing her suitcase in a large closet. Beyond him, she saw a door that said "Lavatory."

He looked up and said, "Well, is this better than Delta?"

Regan entered the cabin and sat in one of the plush leather seats facing the back. "Okay, Ty," she demanded, "unless I get some answers I'm walking off this gorgeous plane right now. What's up with this jet?"

Ty sighed and said, "Well, it's a Gulfstream 280 manufactured in Tel Aviv by the Israel Aerospace Industries. It can cruise at Mach .8 at 42,000 feet. We can fly non-stop from here to Paris in less than ten hours."

"That's not what I meant, buster. I want a straight answer. Who owns this jet?"

Having had his fun, Ty relented. "Okay, I apologize. To be honest, I'm not sure whose jet this is either."

Regan started to gather her stuff to leave.

Ty spoke quickly, "But my friend in Israel is pretty well

connected. He is very interested in helping us track down the woman who gave you the package. Let's just say it's a matter of national security. He told me this jet was already in D.C. on some kind of diplomatic mission. He had them fly it here and offered to let us use it to get to Paris. That's all I know."

"How do I know that you're not kidnapping me and holding me for ransom or something?"

Ty flashed his crooked smile. But Regan wasn't laughing. "Oh, you're serious. Okay, well, how could you not trust a face like mine?"

Despite her reservations, a deeper part of Regan was telling her that she could trust this handsome man. She had an independent streak that always prevented her from asking anyone for help. But her life had turned upside down overnight. The thought of having someone to help her solve this riddle had some merit as well. Her analytical mind weighed the pros and cons, but she was undecided.

Ty continued, "Okay, here's what else I know. Remember, you asked for this." He took a deep breath.

"My friend works for the Israeli government. He has reason to believe that there may be a plot to launch another terrorist attack on the U.S. There's already a suspicious foreign bioweapons scientist who arrived in Atlanta a couple of weeks ago. The fact that your package disappeared and your house was bombed raised the threat level in his mind. He wants me to try to unravel any connection between your package and a terrorism threat. The only place we know to start is to find your friend, Bridget."

Regan tried her best to remain calm, not wanting Ty to see

that her heart was racing. "It sounds like a movie plot instead of real life, Ty," Regan said finally, holding onto one last hope that this really was all some cruel joke. "I still don't know..."

"I know. I'll tell you what. You wanted to return to Paris to your job and apartment. Just let me take you there. If you decide to ditch me when we arrive, I'll say goodbye and you'll be rid of me. I'll do this on my own. But I could sure use your help. I've never even been to Paris."

"Well, okay. At least I can help you learn your way around the city of lights," Regan said. She was too tired to argue anymore. "Let's go."

"Great!" Ty said. He jumped up and leaned into the cockpit. "We're ready to go when you get your clearance."

The attractive Israeli pilot said, "I've already filed our flight plan. Since the tower is closed here, I'm talking to Atlanta Center Clearance Delivery on my cell phone."

Ty nodded.

She continued, "We'll take off VFR and copy our clearance once we're airborne. Flight computer is showing nine hours and forty minutes to Paris-Le Bourget. Please have Ms. Hart fasten her seat belt and we'll be ready for startup and taxi in less than a minute."

24

Gwinnett County Airport
10:12pm

Ty settled in across from Regan and launched into his best flight attendant imitation. "The captain has illuminated the fasten seat belt sign indicating that you should fasten your seat belts and turn off and stow away all electrical devices. To fasten your seat belt, insert the metal portion..."

Regan smiled.

"Sorry, I've always wanted to do that," Ty said, pleased that he'd made some progress with amusing his travel companion. "Who in the civilized world is too dumb to know how a seat belt works?"

Regan pointed at his seat and said, "Apparently, you're that person because you haven't fastened yours yet."

He quickly snapped the belt in place. The jet began its take off roll and was soon airborne. After a few minutes, Ty said, "We have nine hours to get to know each other. Why don't you start your story by telling me when you were born?"

He looked at his watch and pushed a button on the side like he was starting a timer. "Ready? Go."

Regan looked at him blankly. *Is he kidding me?* she thought.

"Gotcha," he joked. Regan breathed a sigh of relief.

"No, seriously, you're right. You don't know anything about me, except that I like to joke around. And I don't know much about you either. Do you have a better idea for spending the next few hours? Play Boggle?"

Regan caught herself smiling again.

"Okay, well, what do you want to know?" she asked.

"Anything you want to tell me. Start wherever you like."

Feeling like she was caught between a job interview, a first date and a hidden camera reality show, Regan began hesitantly.

"Well, I work in Paris, as you know…"

"Tough job," Ty said, nodding. "Do you speak French?"

"Are you going to interrupt me every five seconds? I speak just enough French to be dangerous," she replied coolly.

Ty said, "Whoa. I'm sorry. Go on. I won't interrupt you."

"I actually just transferred over there last year, so I have barely had time to settle in. I went to Georgetown and got my degree in public relations. Then I went on to Harvard and got my MBA. I was hired by Global five years ago to work in global commodities markets."

"The only thing I was interested in in school was sports," Ty said. "And girls."

"I can see that about you," Regan said with only a half-smile this time. Just then, the cabin steward came from the galley offering a tray of four glasses of water with lemon slices.

"Still or sparkling?" he asked, leaning the tray toward the two of them.

"Still, thank you," Regan said. Ty took the glass of sparkling.

"Cheers," he said. "Here's to Paris!" and raised his glass toward hers.

He genuinely seemed interested in whatever she was telling him, Regan noticed. They talked easily over the next hour, Regan sharing with him about how she grew up on the outer edges of Alpharetta with her large family of three brothers and a younger sister. She was raised by a single mom after her dad died in an accident. Her brothers had all been very protective of her and her sister since their dad died.

"Yep," she laughed. "I didn't go on a date until I was seventeen—and I don't think they thought I was old enough to go out then either."

"I bet!" Ty said. "So did you date much in high school or college?"

"I guess so. I had a serious relationship or two, but I guess I was more into the career thing than settling down." This was getting awkward, Regan decided, so she steered the conversation to a safer topic.

"Tell me about where you went to school," she offered.

"I am a Texas boy, born and raised."

I thought I heard an accent, Regan mused.

"Played baseball on a scholarship until I tore my tendons up in my right elbow. I got out of school with a sports kinesiology degree. But I was restless so I joined the Marines and became a pilot. Fought in the first Gulf War. When I came back I didn't know what to do. I had a buddy in Atlanta who owned an insurance adjustment firm, so I went to work with him just to pay the bills. It was pretty boring. After a few years, I walked away and started pursing my passion, archaeology. I traveled around participating in some digs, taking odd jobs where I could to make enough money to survive. I can live on very little."

"How did you get into private investigating?" Regan asked.

"Well, my friend's father owned the company and he suspected one of his executives was embezzling money. I started looking into the case for him and it turns out I was pretty good at solving mysteries."

Ty downed the rest of his water. "If you are looking for a way to make big money, there are probably a lot better ways than becoming a private investigator, of course. But it has its perks, too. I love being independent and being curious about the unknown."

Regan asked, "So, should I picture you slumped down in your car with a Styrofoam cup of coffee in one hand and a camera in the other waiting to get a picture of someone's husband coming out of a strip joint?"

"You'd be surprised what all we PI's get into," he said, smoothing back his hair from his forehead.

Ty and Regan continued to dig into each other's past over a delicious meal served by the cabin steward. After the fruit compote dessert, they were both yawning.

Ty pointed at the moving map display on the forward cabin wall that traced the flight path over the Northern Atlantic. "It looks like we've got about six hours until we land. I'll bet you're exhausted. Why don't we try to sleep?"

"Sure." Regan said. She thought she would just recline in her seat and try to rest. But when she turned around, she saw that the cabin steward had changed the configuration of one of the aft seats into a flat bed—complete with pillows and a thick duvet. There was a curtain that could be closed for privacy.

"That's your bunk. Sorry you'll have to rough it," Ty teased. "Just let me use the restroom in the back and then I'll settle into my forward bunk."

Ty emerged from the bathroom with his toothbrush. As they passed each other in the narrow aisle, he looked down into her eyes for a moment and said, "Good night, Regan. Thanks for trusting me."

Ty held his gaze a little longer than required—as if he were trying to look into her soul, Regan thought. She was surprised to feel her heart beat a little faster. She wanted to blush for some reason. It had been a long time since she had felt anything like that—if ever. And she didn't really like it. She was trying her best not to like this stranger, but her resistance was weakening.

"Good night, Ty. Sleep well."

25

MARCH 27

37,000 feet above the Atlantic Ocean
1:35pm

The cabin steward gently shook Regan's shoulder and said, "Ms. Hart. We're an hour out from Paris-Le Bourget Airport. Would you care for some breakfast?"

Regan came out of a deep sleep and wondered for a moment where she was. And who was this stranger speaking to her? Then she remembered.

"Sure," Regan said with a voice still thick with sleep. "Just give me a few minutes to freshen up."

After emerging from the lavatory, Regan felt like a new woman. She had slept for almost five hours. The two beds had been reconfigured as seats again and a healthy breakfast was set on a table in front of Ty. He looked better than any man should after just awakening.

"Good morning, sleepy head," he said cheerfully.

"Good morning. How long have you been up?"

"I only slept an hour or so. Since then I've been online communicating with my friend in Israel. Hungry?"

Regan realized she was famished. Even after dinner last night, all the tension had made her crave nourishment. She dug into the cheese omelet and the fresh croissant. The chilled orange juice tasted freshly squeezed and the coffee was delicious. Between sips and mouthfuls of food she managed, "So, have you learned more about our search for Bridget?"

"Slow down, there. We have plenty of food for seconds," Ty teased.

Regan grinned and reached for another croissant. "I've never flown on a private jet before. I've got to admit that I could get used to this."

"Me too. The good news is that my friend's contacts in Paris have now verified Bridget's existence. They interviewed some of your fellow GWA employees and one of them had some digital pictures she took at a work party. In one of the pictures, Bridget's hijab was off. While you were sleeping, these guys have accessed some very sophisticated facial recognition software and discovered that Bridget's real name is Ameera Saad."

"But why would Bridget use a fake name?" Regan asked.

"I'm not sure, but that's not all. Do you remember I told you that my Israeli friend had determined that a bioweapons expert arrived in Atlanta a couple of weeks ago?" Ty asked.

"Sure. But what's that got to do with Bridget, I mean, Ameera?"

"Do you care to guess what this bioweapons expert's name is?" Ty asked.

"I have no clue. And I don't like playing Sherlock. Just tell me."

"Dr. Hakeem Saad."

"So, is that Ameera's husband?" Regan asked.

"No, her father," Ty said and filled Regan in on Dr. Saad's past.

"So where does that leave us? What are we supposed to do?" Regan asked.

"We know who Ameera is, but we don't have a clue where she is. We don't even know if she's still in Paris. My friend still wants us to try to find her," Ty explained.

"Ha. Fat chance!" Regan said. "There's got to be at least 50,000 Muslim women in Paris, and most of them wear a burka or a hijab. Besides, I've got to get back to work. You're on your own. I'm done with this little mystery. Thanks for the ride home."

"Well, it seems that one of GWA's largest clients has a special interest in this little mystery. They called the President of GWA in Atlanta and guess what? You're on a paid leave of absence to help me run down this lead."

"Well, what if I don't want to?" Regan argued. "I really like my calm, boring life. I enjoy looking at numbers all day. I'm not interested in the kind of spy adventure you're describing."

Even as Regan spoke those words, she heard a voice saying, *Really? Are you sure you want to continue your sad, boring, safe life? All alone? Every night?*

Regan relented, "Oh, okay. I'll try to keep you from getting totally lost for a couple of days."

"Thanks, Regan," Ty said. "I was hoping I could count on you."

Just then the cockpit door opened and the co-pilot said, "Buckle in, please. We've started our descent into Paris-Le Bourget. We should be on the ground in ten minutes."

***

The sleek Gulfstream 280 touched down lightly on the single runway of Paris' main business jet airport. As they taxied to the ramp, Ty turned to Regan and said, "Do you have a car in Paris?"

"No way," Regan said. "The traffic is crazy. I use the Metro most of the time. But if I'm in a hurry, I never have a problem getting a taxi. Parisian taxi drivers are the least friendly in the world, but they get you to where you're going. Would you like for me to recommend a hotel?"

"Uh, I already booked La Maison," Ty said.

"Wow, that's just around the corner from my...wait a minute! Don't tell me that you know where my apartment is located!" Regan's temper was rising again. "Have you been snooping into my personal life?"

"Take it easy," Ty chided. "Again, my friend has access to a lot of information, and before he asked me to help you, he had to learn your basic profile. If you had given me a chance, I would have told you that I know where you live and I'll be staying nearby."

"Who is this friend of yours, James Bond? I'd certainly like to meet him sometime."

Ty flashed his winning smile and said, "His name is Solly, and I'd love for you to meet him. You'd love him."

"I don't know about that," Regan said. "I don't like people prying into my private life."

"Regan, I'm really sorry that you're involved in this," Ty apologized once more. "But when Bridget, uh Ameera, picked you to deliver that package, you became part of this. I'd love for us to be able to find Ameera, and then you can go back to your normal life."

"I don't know if my life will ever be normal again," Regan lamented.

"Well, they say excitement is the spice of life..." Ty said, trying to perk her up.

"Yeah, and I hate spicy food, too!" Regan said and looked away to gaze out the window. But not before Ty saw a tiny smile curl at her lips.

26

**La Maison Hotel
Rue Jean Goujon
Paris, France
4:22pm**

"I guess I should stop being surprised," Regan said. "I expected us to grab a taxi, but it was nice to have that private car deliver us here."

"Solly only does things first class," Ty said. "Are you sure you'll be okay to walk to your apartment from here?"

"Sure, it's only half a block away. But, of course, you already know that," Regan said with sarcasm.

"I already apologized once for that, but I'm still sorry, ma'am," Ty said, using his best Southern drawl. "Why don't you let me make it up to you by treating you to dinner here at the hotel?"

Regan thought about how there wasn't anything in her apartment to eat. She wanted to decline on principle. Instead, she found herself saying, "Sure. Why not? I'll see you back here around 8:00pm." It felt good to turn the tables on Ty and be the one who made the plans now that they were on her turf.

"That's perfect. See you then."

***

After soaking in an indulgent hot bath for an indolent amount of time, Regan felt much better. She had eaten at the La Maison restaurant several times before. The La Table du 8 Restaurant was very elegant. Having never been to Paris, Ty probably thought it was like a sidewalk bistro, so she hatched a wicked plot to out-dress him. She had only seen him in jeans and boots and knew that he would be embarrassed to be the only guy in jeans in the restaurant.

She smiled as she carefully applied her makeup. She was a casual kind of girl, but she could dress up on demand. She dried her thick, long, blonde hair and then brushed it until it shone. She put on her favorite short blue dress to bring out the blue of her eyes. She hated heels, but she slipped into a pair of stilettos so the height difference between her and Ty would be less. To finish off the look, she hung a blue topaz necklace around her throat and added matching earrings. She looked at herself in the mirror and liked what she saw. She didn't consider herself to be runway model pretty, but all the guys she had dated had told her she was gorgeous. Still, she figured all guys told all girls the same thing.

As she stared at her reflection, she realized that she hadn't been this excited about meeting someone for dinner since... well, she couldn't remember when. But then she frowned and said aloud, "This is just business, that's all."

At 8:05, Regan walked through La Maison's small lobby into La Table du 8 Restaurant. Each small table was covered with a white tablecloth and set with the finest china, silver, and crystal.

As Regan walked in, every man looked at her with desire, and every woman looked at her with envy.

Where was Ty? For a moment she thought the lousy bum had stood her up. She was about to turn around when a figure toward the back of the room stood up. It was Ty. She hadn't recognized him because she'd never seen him dressed up. He was wearing a navy blue silk sport coat with a tangerine-colored handkerchief over a light blue, open-collared dress shirt. Silk khaki pants and light brown Gucci shoes completed his outfit. His hair had always been a little unkempt, but tonight it was swept back and she noticed the natural waves on top.

"Wow!" Ty said. "As we say in Texas, you sure do clean up well!"

"Thank you, sir," Regan said. "And I must say that I like this look on you." She wasn't disappointed at all that her plan to out-dress him had failed.

Ty held the chair back for Regan to be seated. During the course of the evening, they enjoyed a wonderful dinner and shared a bottle of expensive French wine. They kept the conversation centered on the same getting-to-know-you topics from the previous evening on the jet. When coffee was served, Ty got down to the business at hand.

"Let's start by you telling me again everything you know about Ameera. Tell me how many times you spoke with her. What she looked like. Describe every detail you can remember about her clothing and speech."

Regan closed her eyes and tried to recall what she remembered about Ameera. "She was about my height, five-foot-eight. She was very fit, so we probably weigh about the same and I weigh ... well, that's no business of yours," Regan said.

Ty held up his hands in mock surrender.

She continued, "Like I said, her English was very poor. The first time she approached me, she asked if she could practice her English. She spoke fluent French, and I heard her speak in another language to some of the employees. I didn't recognize it, but in hindsight, it was probably Arabic."

"If you were describing her appearance to an artist, how would you direct him to draw her?" Ty asked.

Again, Regan closed her eyes and tried to recall. "She was a beautiful woman. She had dark hair and eyes. She had an olive-skinned complexion and very pronounced cheeks, in a pretty way. She only removed her hijab when there were just females in the room. I heard the guys in the office talking about how she was stunning. But they called her the ice-queen. When any of them tried to flirt with her, she would look at them with a gaze that would freeze hot water. Sometimes she refused to even talk to them. I would recognize her if I saw her, for sure."

"Tell me about her clothes."

"Now, that's interesting. Her dress was usually plain and dark with a long hem. You could tell it was expensive material, but she didn't dress to attract attention. And yet she had a collection of purses and shoes that all of the other women talked about."

"What do you mean?" Ty asked. "She had a variety of expensive Prada, Louis Vuitton, Chanel, Max Mara, Bottega Veneta, and Gucci purses. And they looked real—not knock-offs. The same with her shoes. One of the girls in our office was a fashion hound. She said Bridget wore Dior, Proenza Schouler, Fendi, and Jimmy Choo. Those are all very expensive labels.

And she had dozens of them."

"Did she seem to be wealthy?" Ty asked.

"She made a lot of money as a global currency trader because she got a salary and worked on commission. But she didn't make enough money at GWA to afford those kinds of accessories."

"So, where do you buy that kind of stuff?" Ty asked.

Regan laughed, "I'm not a shopaholic, but I do enjoy stalking good bargains. You don't find many bargains with those brands. But there's only one place in Paris where all of those stores are found together."

"Where's that?" Ty asked.

Regan pointed over her shoulder. "Two blocks from here. The Avenue des Champs-Élysées."

"Well, let's start looking there tomorrow," Ty said.

"Good luck. It's probably the most famous shopping street in the world. Thousands of shoppers crowd the sidewalks every day. It will be like searching for a needle in a haystack."

"Great! That sounds like my job description," Ty said and signaled for the check.

27

March 31

**Avenue des Champs-Élysées
Paris, France
2:12pm**

Regan and Ty had spent the last four days strolling up and down the Champs-Élysées. They had decided their best cover was to pose as a couple on vacation. The first time Ty casually grabbed her hand to complete their ruse, Regan had instinctively swatted it away.

"Sorry," she mumbled and offered it back to Ty.

"It's just for appearances, Regan," Ty said between clenched teeth.

After four whole days of shopping and sitting at the various sidewalk cafés, Regan had become familiar with the touch of Ty's hand. She secretly enjoyed it when they strolled hand in hand. She cherished the meals they shared together. But she kept reminding herself that this was strictly business.

While they were walking and shopping, they were surreptitiously looking at the faces of the women they passed—especially those wearing a burka or hijab. But none of them were Ameera. They couldn't even be certain she was still in Paris. Their initial excitement about spotting her in one of the upscale stores had faded. They had frequented some of the stores so many times that the salespersons welcomed them with, "You're back, I see!" Regan had purchased a few of the purses and shoes to keep up the appearance. She was having fun now.

Ty was always patient and gracious to give his opinion when she asked in character, "What do you think of these, honey?" *At least he wasn't paying for them*, he thought.

It was Friday afternoon, and they were both discouraged. They decided they would try one more day of searching, then give up and talk about plan B. The only problem was that there was no plan B. If they lost Ameera, they were at a dead-end.

Suddenly Regan's grip on Ty's hand tightened. "I think that's her!" she whispered.

"Where?"

"Over there, at that sidewalk café. She's at a table facing the street."

"Are you certain?" Ty wanted to know.

"No, I'm not certain! We need to get closer."

They decided to get a table near her and order lunch. After being seated, Regan slowly turned her head to look full into the face of the girl she suspected was Ameera. Their eyes made brief contact and there was a moment of full recognition for both of them.

Without hesitation, Ameera sprang to her feet and started running down the crowded sidewalk, shoving shoppers aside from behind.

"Let's go!" Ty shouted as he took off in pursuit.

Ty and Regan were running as fast as they could, trying desperately to keep Ameera in sight. They almost tripped over her expensive heels that she kicked off to run faster.

Angry shoppers and tourists were shouting at them. Even in a city of rude people, this was a level of rudeness that was unacceptable.

Ty was fast. He ran with the graceful stride of an athlete. He left Regan behind as he steered around people toward his target fleeing less than half a block away.

***

Ameera was fit as well. She worked out four days a week at a fashionable gym near her apartment. She was caught off guard staring into the sea-blue eyes of Regan Hart, but at that same moment her training kicked in. As she ran, she fished a throwaway cell phone from a side pocket in her purse. She punched the speed dial for the only number programmed into the phone.

After two rings, a voice said, "Yes?"

"My identity has been blown. I need extraction from Paris immediately," Ameera shouted into the phone as her bare feet pounded the sidewalk.

"What's the code and your ID number?" the voice on the phone asked.

"You know who this is, you idiot!" she shouted in Arabic. "I don't have time to play silly spy games. I'm tossing this phone. Have someone meet me in the alley behind my apartment in one hour. Call Yamani and tell him."

Ameera smashed the phone on the side of the building

where she was running and tossed the remains into a trash barrel. She could hear the objections of the people behind her being shoved aside. She glanced around and saw a tall man dodging people. He was gaining on her.

Ameera darted right and ran blindly into the stream of traffic. Cars and buses honked their horns and drivers leaned out their windows, cursing at her in profane French. She dodged cars, sliding across the hood of a taxi and reaching the other side of the street. The man wasn't far behind. He was holding up his hand maneuvering between the hectic traffic.

In desperation, Ameera looked ahead. A plan formed in her mind. She quickly veered off the wide sidewalk toward a large Nike store. It was crowded with shoppers. She knew most of these stores had a security person stationed at the front door to keep beggars from walking in and to prevent shoplifters from just walking out.

She ran up to the burly guard inside the door and grabbed his shirt. Sobbing, she cried out in French, "Please help, there is a bad man chasing me! He tried to assault me. Please help me!"

She released the guard and ran into the store. She grabbed a shirt, shorts, and some running shoes off the rack that appeared to be her size. At the last minute, she pulled down a black Nike cap from a shelf, along with a backpack, and charged into a changing room.

Ty saw Ameera run into the Nike store and he increased his speed thinking she would be trapped. He ran through the front door, right into the arms of the security guard. Before Ty could react, the guard grabbed him and tripped his legs out from under him. He pushed Ty down on his stomach and twisted his right arm behind his back.

"What are you doing?" Ty yelled.

"Not so fast, monsieur! You can't get away with assaulting a woman," the guard said in heavily accented English as he placed his knee in the small of Ty's back.

"You don't understand! The woman I'm chasing is a terrorist. Let me up!" Ty growled with his face pressed against the cool concrete floor."

"Tell it to the police," the guard said. He turned to another employee, "Pierre, call the police!"

Ty was at a disadvantage because the guard outweighed him by sixty pounds and was half his age. But Ty was desperate. He relaxed his arms as if he were surrendering to the guard. Then he rolled his shoulders and body to the right and felt the guard leaning left to regain his balance. Ty quickly reversed his roll to the left. Using his left hand, he pushed off the floor and spun his body under the grip of the guard. He swung his right elbow around and felt it connect with the cheekbone of the guard.

In less than two seconds, Ty had the guard on his face with his knee in his back.

"How does that feel, Junior?" Ty asked. "I don't want to hurt you. I'm going to let you go because I've got to find the woman who ran into this store."

The guard was too dazed to answer.

Just then Regan ran into the Nike store.

"Ty! Where's Ameera? Who is this guy?" Regan yelled breathlessly.

In the distance, they could hear the rising and falling tones of a Paris police car getting louder.

"She ran in here and I lost her. This guy tried to stop me. Fan out through the store and see if you can find her!" Ty said.

***

Inside the dressing room, Ameera removed her hijab and her black dress and quickly changed into the sporty shorts and t-shirt. She ripped the price tags off all the items, but she couldn't remove the theft prevention locks. Cursing in frustration, she shoved her feet in the shoes. They were a little small, but they would have to do. She piled her thick black hair up on her head and stuffed it under the cap as she pulled it down over her forehead.

Then she dumped the contents of her Prada purse on the seat. She grabbed the cash and her remaining cell phone and anything else that might tip off her identity and piled it into the backpack. She stuffed her dress and hijab in her purse and threw it under the seat.

As she calmly walked out of the changing room, she could hear a commotion in the front of the store. She could also hear a police siren. She wanted to flee, but she decided that she should be patient and wait for the right time to exit the store. She glanced at her reflection in the mirror and hardly recognized herself. Still, her eyes were a giveaway. She removed her Chanel sunglasses from the backpack and put them on. Then she re-checked her image. Perfect.

Meanwhile, Ty and Regan frantically searched the store. There were at least 50 shoppers and several of them were wearing hijabs. Glancing carefully, they eliminated them one by one. Regan spotted a female shopper across the store with a cap and glasses. Something about the way she was shopping, or wasn't shopping, caught Regan's attention. It seemed that she was watching Regan in a mirror. As Regan moved toward her, the woman eased toward the exit of the store.

"Ty, this way!" Regan shouted.

Regan had an angle and arrived at the end of the aisle before Ameera did. She grabbed her by the shirt and said, "Bridget! Ameera! Whoever you are, why did you use me?" Regan wanted to hold onto Ameera just long enough for Ty to reach them.

Ameera pivoted and grabbed a handful of Regan's hair and pulled her head down violently onto a glass and steel display case. Regan screamed and released her grip. Blood poured out of the wound in her forehead and Regan felt faint.

Ty sprinted toward the exit to catch Ameera. As she ran, Ameera pulled down two displays of athletic shorts to slow down her pursuer. She ran past the security guard who was still sitting on the floor holding his head from the blow to his jaw.

Alarms sounded as Ameera passed between the theft prevention detectors. But there was no security guard to stop her. Ty was only a few seconds behind her. At that moment, three officers with the French police arrived and the security guard pointed at Ty. He shouted, "He is the man. Stop him!"

The policemen grabbed Ty. As he struggled to get away, he said, "I'm after a possible terrorist. Let me go!" But two of the officers pulled his arms behind his back. A third officer snapped cuffs on his wrists. He looked up to see Ameera walking swiftly down the street away from them. She glanced over her shoulder and after delivering a wicked smile, she disappeared into the crowd.

28

24 Rue de la Bûcherie
Paris, France
1:30pm

Ameera was out of breath when she unlocked her apartment. She had walked out of the Champs-Élysées area and caught a taxi. She had the taxi drop her off two blocks from her apartment and she was winded from climbing the stairs. She had almost been captured, and she was angry with herself. Her hatred for Regan and that man was intense. Why were they looking for her? Had their plan been uncovered?

Ameera had been planning for the possibility of an emergency evacuation. First, she needed to change her appearance. She went into her bathroom and took scissors to her hair. In a matter of minutes, her sink was full of the long, black hair that had been a source of pride for her. Using a kit purchased from a hair salon for such an occasion, she began the messy, smelly job of dying her new hairstyle.

Afterwards, she stared into the mirror. Her hair was now short and blonde. After thoroughly cleaning up, she completed her transformation with contact lenses that changed the color of her eyes to hazel.

She tossed several stacks of euros into the backpack along with a few clothes and toiletries. Fifty minutes after arriving, she left her apartment for the final time. Walking down the stairs, she arrived at the alley. A black Citroën was idling across the block. She walked over and got in without saying a word. The car drove off. Ameera wondered with regret if she would ever see Paris again. It didn't matter. This was war and she was a foot soldier.

"What is the evacuation plan?" she asked the driver.

"We will drive to the port and take a ferry to England. In England, we'll drive to London. From there, you'll fly to Toronto and we'll smuggle you across the U.S. border and drive you to Atlanta."

The driver turned and asked, "Do you have the money?"

"Yes, it's all here in my backpack. How will I smuggle it into Canada?" Ameera asked.

"In London, we'll use the euros to buy diamonds. They're easier to transport. You'll have a normal looking carry-on with wheels with a secret compartment. But first you need a new passport."

After driving for 90 minutes, the driver arrived in Calais. He pulled into an underground garage of a tall apartment building. The driver handed Ameera a hijab and said, "Wear this until we get upstairs."

Once inside the apartment, Ameera stood in front of a screen while a digital camera snapped her photograph. The technician said, "Take thirty minutes to get a bite to eat or something to drink. Your new passport will be ready then."

Ameera visited the restroom and surprised herself when she looked in the mirror. She still wasn't used to her new appearance.

She was sitting in the kitchen drinking a cup of strong, bitter coffee when the technician tossed a French passport on the table. "Check it out."

Ameera opened the passport and saw a blonde girl staring back. Her new name was Lucille DuMond. Although she knew the passport was created minutes earlier, it had the appearance of having been used. As she thumbed through the pages, she noticed stamps from Russia, Canada, the U.S., and Brazil.

"This won't pass muster at a U.S. Immigration station, but it will work for you in Canada," the technician said.

Ameera put the passport in her bag and stood up. "Let's go. I've got a war to join and I don't want to be late."

29

Commissariat de Police
5 rue Clément Marot
Paris, France
5:30pm

Ty had been placed inside an interview room and left alone for over an hour. His wrists were raw from the handcuffs that still cut into his skin. He had protested to the policemen that he was an American citizen and demanded a call to the U.S. Embassy. The officers spoke very little English and beyond the word "croissant," Ty's French was non-existent. They had confiscated Ty's passport, wallet, and phone. He had no clue where Regan was or how she was doing after being attacked by Ameera. And to add to his frustration, he didn't have any way to contact her. He had made a mess of things just when he was hoping to impress her.

Finally, the door opened and a man in a suit said with a thick accent, "Good afternoon, Mr. Kensington. I am Inspector Canne. Please come with me."

"Where are we going?" Ty asked.

But the inspector had already turned and left the room. Ty

followed. "When do I get my passport and wallet back?" he demanded.

"Soon," the inspector replied, without a hint of concern.

Ty was led down a set of stairs to an underground garage where dozens of French police vehicles were parked. Inspector Canne led him to a black Peugeot and opened the back door. His hands still cuffed, Ty got in and Inspector Canne got into the front passenger seat.

As the car drove away Ty said, "Where are we going? I want some answers."

"You shall have them. Soon," the inspector replied.

Ty hadn't realized how tired he was. All the tension of the last several days and the delayed effect of jet lag combined to edge him toward sleep. He tried to keep his eyes opened but failed.

"We have arrived, Mr. Kensington," the inspector said, jolting Ty out of his slumber. His accent reminded Ty of Inspector Jacques Clouseau from the Pink Panther movies Ty watched growing up.

Ty sat up and stared out of the windshield. He recognized that he was back at the Paris-Le Bourget airport. They were driving up to the same Gulfstream 280 that had delivered him and Regan three days earlier.

The car stopped and Inspector Cannes got out, walked around to Ty's door and opened it. With a key he removed from his pocket, he unlocked Ty's handcuffs. Then he handed him a plastic bag containing his passport, wallet, and phone. He said, "Your ride awaits, Mr. Kensington. Just be glad you have some influential friends. I released you on the condition that you will never return to my city."

"No problem," Ty snarled. "I don't plan to come back here unless the French improve their manners."

Ty climbed out of the car and walked across the ramp. The sun had set and the area was dark except for the light peeking out from the cabin of the jet through the open door. Ty climbed the air stairs and heard voices and laughter coming from the cabin. Once inside, he turned right and couldn't believe his eyes. Solly was sitting across from Regan, obviously charming her with his wit and stories. Regan had a bruise and an ugly cut on her forehead, but it had been closed with butterfly stitches.

Solly's face broke into a grin. "Well, it's about time you made it, Ty. Ms. Hart and I have been having a delightful time getting to know each other. But your criminal escapades have put us behind schedule. Strap in and let's go."

Regan smiled and said, "You were right, Ty. Solly is a blast. He's much more fun than you described."

Ty moved to Regan and pulled her to her feet. He embraced her and said, "Regan, I'm so happy you're okay. I saw the blood...I thought you might be seriously injured."

"No worries, mate. Remember?" Regan said, pushing Ty away awkwardly and retaking her seat. "Ameera just outsmarted us and outfought us. But I'm not going to let that happen again."

Ty turned to Solly and said, "Solly, what are you doing here? How did I get out of jail? And where are we going?"

"You sound like me," Regan joked. "So many questions, Mr. Private Investigator."

Solly replied, "I had a hunch that you might need some help. I was already on the way here when I received a call from one of my agents that you had been arrested. Mossad has a limited number of 'get out of jail free' cards with the French government. I burned one for your sorry behind today. You owe me, big time. Plus, you owe me for your stay because I checked you out of the hotel and collected your luggage."

"Just put it on my expense account," Ty shot back.

Regan added proudly, "Solly is taking us back to Atlanta."

Ty took a seat. Now he was really confused.

"We're certain that Ameera has left Paris," Solly explained. "I have another hunch that she is going to be joining her father in the U.S. If we can find him, we will find her. They're up to something, and it can't be good. We've gathered more Intel on Dr. Saad and he's a very dangerous man. I believe their activity may be a fulfillment of the Cloud Strike prophecy I read to you. We've got to see if we can stop them."

Ty said, "I'm all in. But why is Israel, and Mossad specifically, so interested in stopping an attack on American soil?"

"America is Israel's strongest and most loyal ally. In a world where we have few friends, we must help the one friend we have. Did you know that Mossad provided the U.S. with credible threat warnings before the 9/11 attacks?" Solly asked.

"I'd heard that, but I never knew if it was true or not."

"It's true. I was part of the team that gathered and provided the Intel to the C.I.A." Solly shook his head and said, "But the C.I.A. basically ignored it. And they were in such a competition with the F.B.I. and the N.S.C. that they didn't share it."

Solly looked over at Regan and quipped, "America has too many acronyms."

He turned to Ty and said, "This time, we aren't bringing

them into the loop unless it's absolutely necessary."

30

APRIL 1

**42,000 feet above the North Atlantic Ocean
3:22am**

The Mossad-owned Gulfstream 280 clipped along at a rate of nine miles a minute. It followed the great circle route and was currently near the southern coast of Greenland. The outside air temperature was -60 degrees Celsius, but inside the richly appointed cabin it was warm and pleasant. Solly used a Bluetooth connection from his iPad to display graphics and information on the 42-inch flat screen on the forward cabin wall.

Ever the tour guide, Solly began his lecture about the man whose face currently appeared on the screen. "Regan, Ty knows some of this, but I want to fill you in on the characters we're dealing with. The man you see is Dr. Hakeem Saad. He has a Ph.D. in microbiology and in biochemistry. By most accounts, he is brilliant. If he hadn't been working for a maniac, he might have won a Nobel Prize. But instead, he was the chief bioweapons developer for Saddam Hussein in the 1980s."

Solly pressed the remote and the picture changed to an aerial view. "This is a satellite picture of the bioweapons laboratory. It appears to be as large and well-equipped as any lab in the world."

The next slide was the production and storage facility. "As you can see, it's as large as a modern U.S. refinery. The Iraqis were able to destroy most of their bioweapons before Baghdad was invaded. But a few scientists who worked with Dr. Saad have reported that they produced tens of thousands of liters of ricin, aflatoxin, anthrax, and botulinum. That's enough to kill a third of the world's population. Saddam utilized ricin against the Kurdish insurgents, and there are reports that several thousand Kurds died and were buried in a mass grave."

"Saad and his family escaped Iraq during the first Gulf War—when you were dropping bombs on their heads, Ty."

"Hey, those were smart bombs, remember," Ty objected.

"Yeah, but some of them were flown by dumb pilots," Solly countered. "May I continue?" Ty nodded.

"Our agents lost track of him for several years, then he reappeared on the radar as a chemistry professor at a university in Sanaa, Yemen. There was no indication that he was involved in bioweapons development for a couple of decades."

Regan interrupted, "What made him change?"

Solly answered, "Our undercover agents in Yemen believe they've discovered a turning point. A couple of years ago, there was a U.S. drone strike on a Yemeni Al-Qaeda leader. Everyone in his vehicle was killed, but the burning vehicle rammed into Dr. Saad's house. His wife and son were killed and Ameera was injured. We suspect that's why he's in Georgia, seeking revenge. And that's why we're on our way to Atlanta."

Regan said, "How could they launch an attack using something that I carried in that gift? It didn't weigh more than three or four pounds."

Solly said, "That's the missing piece of the puzzle. We have no clue about what bioweapon he might have smuggled in. However, some of them are so highly toxic that just a small amount can kill hundreds or even thousands of people. Over the past ten years, the FBI has uncovered and thwarted three attempts by terrorists to poison city water supplies in the U.S."

"I never saw anything on the news about that," Regan said, turning toward Ty.

Solly replied, "It wasn't on the news, Ms. Hart. Most Americans would live in abject fear if they realized how many plots have been stopped before they could be launched. Remember, the goal of the terrorists is to create terror—fear. U.S. officials know that running those kinds of news reports would accomplish much of what the terrorists desire."

"So do you think these guys will attack a water supply again?" Ty asked.

Solly ran his hand through his beard and said, "Something tells me they've learned their lesson. Water supply facilities have heightened security controls."

"Then what will they try?" Regan asked.

"If they're smart—and I think they are—they'll disperse the bioweapon as an aerosol," Solly said.

"How would they do that?" Ty asked.

"Have you ever seen a truck driving through your neighborhoods during the summer spraying for mosquitos?" Solly asked.

"Sure." Ty and Regan answered simultaneously.

"A terrorist could hijack one of those trucks and fill the tank with a bioweapon. They could create a lot of havoc in a short period of time," Solly said.

"Maybe we should contact the cities around Atlanta that spray for mosquitos?" Ty offered

"Maybe," Solly said. "But if I were a terrorist and I wanted to kill the most people, I wouldn't use a truck. I'd use a plane."

31

APRIL 4

East Point, Georgia
9:25pm

After traveling for three straight days, Ameera was exhausted. She had arrived in Toronto and had no trouble clearing Customs. From there, she was taken to a remote area near Sarnia on the Canadian-U.S. border where she was met by a team that smuggled her across. She had then slept for much of the 12-hour drive to Georgia. She pulled a floppy hat over her head and face and slipped into the Atlanta apartment under the cover of darkness. She hadn't seen her father in over a year and she was excited about being reunited.

"Papa!" Ameera ran into his arms when she saw him.

"My princess!" Dr. Saad said. After their embrace, he held her at arm's length and said, "Who is this blonde girl? I don't recognize you!"

"I had to change my appearance after the American devils recognized me in Paris," Ameera said.

"I'm glad you've joined me. After all our planning, the time has come. We are here in the enemy's land to punish them for their violence and bloodshed toward our family," Dr. Saad said.

"How is the work going, Papa?"

"Come see for yourself."

They walked out the door of the apartment and down the stairs. A block away, they entered what appeared to be an abandoned warehouse. Dr. Saad pushed a speed dial number on his cell phone and a large door opened. Inside the small lobby, two other team members, Ali and Nasser, looked in bewilderment at the girl with the short, blonde hair.

Ali spoke up and said, "Who is this stranger with you?"

"This is my daughter, Ameera," Dr. Saad said.

The two men instantly recognized their teammate then and greeted her, "Salaam alaikum, Ameera." Ali and Nasser were his lab assistants and drivers. They were scientists like him, but they had pledged to die for the cause if necessary.

Dr. Saad punched a code into the keypad beside a door and it opened for them. They walked into a modern lab with over a dozen large metal boxes that looked like oversized stainless steel refrigerators. But there were no doors or handles.

"These are the molecular multipliers. You can think of them as chambers where the toxin is multiplying and expanding like yeast placed in a refrigerator. With the concentrated samples you sent by your friend, we've been able to make almost 500 gallons of botulinum toxin."

"Come." Dr. Saad then led Ameera through another door into a room that felt like an industrial refrigerator because it was so cold. She saw dozens of yellow plastic jerry cans, each having a capacity of over seven gallons.

"The toxin is very stable at this temperature. It isn't until it is warmed up that it becomes lethal. In a few more days, we'll have our target of 500 gallons," Dr. Saad said proudly.

"So when do we attack? And what is our target?" Ameera asked.

Dr. Saad paused. "I could tell you, but there is still a chance this operation could be compromised. If you were captured, it would be better if you didn't know these details yet. Just be assured that we are going to deal a crippling blow to the arrogant Americans."

32

APRIL 5

Greene County Regional Airport (37J)
Greensboro, Georgia
75 miles Southeast of Atlanta
9:10am

Out of habit borne from almost 50 years of flying, Hap Potter glanced at the sky as he walked from his office to the hangar. He had already called the FAA weather service for the aviation forecast, but he still trusted his eyes and instincts.

After removing the padlock and chain, he put his shoulder against the heavy hangar door and groaned as he pushed it along the rail on the ground. There was a grating noise as the metal wheels gained momentum and then the door rolled open easily. Hap thought how easy it used to be to open the door when he was a young man. Now, he dreaded the first few feet of stubborn inertia.

Inside was his Air Tractor 602. The AT-602 was a turboprop-powered crop duster capable of flying almost 200 mph. This plane was a great improvement over the piston-driven engines on his earlier planes. The jet-prop enabled him to pull back on the yoke and climb at over 1,000 feet per minute. This was critical when he reached the end of a spray-run and there were tall trees bordering the field—which seemed to be the case in every field in Georgia.

Twenty years earlier, his crop dusting business had been booming. But times were tough. The EPA had cracked down on the pesticides and fungicides that farmers could use to control insects on their crops. And many of the younger farmers were going green. *Lousy tree-huggers,* Hap thought. This "going green" movement only meant less green in his wallet.

In the good old days, he would have four to five jobs a day during the peak growing season. Now, he was lucky to have three or four jobs a week. With the price of Jet-A fuel at $5.25 a gallon, he could hardly afford to fly. But it was what he loved. He couldn't do anything else. Since Doris had died last spring, his wife of 47 years, he didn't need as much money to live. At seventy-one, he was drawing some Social Security, but he needed a job to keep him alive.

Hap climbed on the small John Deere tractor in the back of the hangar. He earned some extra money from the Fixed Base Operator (FBO) by mowing the grass around the ramp and the single runway. He positioned the tractor in front of the tail wheel and connected the metal tow bar to the front of the tractor. He slowly backed the plane out of the hangar and pulled it across the flat, paved ramp where all the other airplanes were parked. He carefully positioned it in front of the gas pumps so he could refuel it. One pump provided 100-octane aviation gasoline for piston-driven aircraft. The price of 100-octane had soared to $6.25 a gallon. The other pump provided Jet-A fuel.

These days, few customers other than Hap used this fuel. There was a time when three Beech King Airs were hangared here, but two of them were long gone—sold because of the recession and the soaring costs of general aviation.

Hap connected the wire from the pump to the front landing gear to provide a ground that would prevent accidental ignition from static electricity. Then he positioned the metal stepladder in front of the left wing. Pulling the long fuel hose over his shoulder, he climbed the ladder and opened the fuel tank cap. He topped off the left wing tank and then repeated the process for the right wing.

When completed, he wrote down the amount of fuel on a ticket to be paid later when he got some cash. He towed the plane over to the Ag center where chemicals were stored to be used for crop dusting. Five huge white plastic tanks were set on a platform ten feet off the ground. He consulted his log to ensure the correct pesticide had been delivered to one of the five 500-gallon plastic tanks.

He walked around the fuselage behind the single cockpit and opened the hopper tank cap. The AT-602 had two hoppers, one behind the engine and one under the fuselage. Hap seldom used the one behind the engine—even after thousands of years of safe flying, the idea of a hopper leaking in front of the cockpit was a problem he didn't need to worry over. After donning a paper mask and rubber gloves, he placed the small hose from the chemical tank into the opening and attached it with a plastic clip. He returned to the chemical tank and pumped the plunger until enough pressure built up to force the chemical into the hopper tank on his plane. Satisfied that there was enough pressure, Hap climbed down from the elevated chemical tank and opened the spigot of the hose. The chemical started flowing into the hopper tank and gravity kept the flow constant. Hap watched the gauge on the side of the tank as the hopper filled. His capacity was over 500 gallons, but today's job only required 300 gallons.

When the tank was more than half full, he closed the spigot and stowed the hose back in the holder of the chemical tank. He was going to wait an hour or so before he took off. He wanted the ambient temperature to be high enough to prevent clogging of the spray vents, which sometimes happened in cool conditions.

As he walked back toward his office, he watched an old faded blue mini-van pull up into the lot of the FBO. He'd never seen it before, but there were always visitors here. Some people just liked to sit at a private airport and watch the planes take off and land.

Hap thought, *If that's why they came, it's going to be a boring day.* At one time, several Certified Flight Instructors used airplanes rented by the FBO to give private pilot training. But even that business had dried up. The FBO had sold their rental airplanes and barely hung on by selling fuel and providing an occasional charter in their old 1971 Beechcraft King Air C90.

Hap was the King Air charter pilot, but there weren't many customers. The King Air was a fine aircraft, but it was like driving a luxury car. It was just a matter of monitoring instruments. The autopilot took all the fun out of flying. He preferred the thrill of hand-flying his AT-602.

He was also the only Airframe and Powerplant (A&P)

mechanic on the field. The King Air and an assortment of two dozen aging single-engine aircraft on the field kept him fairly busy, but times were still tough.

Two men from the van walked through the FBO office and out onto the ramp. While public airports with airline service had strict access restrictions, the majority of local airports in the country had no security procedures.

One of the men was about thirty and had dark skin, but he did not look African-American. The other was an older man who was old enough to be the younger man's father. They walked toward Hap so he stopped and waited.

"Can I help you?" Hap asked.

"Yes, perhaps you can," the older man said. He had a very pronounced accent, like he was from Europe. "My name is Max Phillips. This is my son, Jake." He held out his hand toward Hap.

Hap shook hands with both men and said, "Pleased to meet you. I'm Hap Potter." The younger man's grip was strong, but he didn't speak. He just bowed his head acknowledging Hap's handshake.

"We wanted to speak to someone about a crop dusting job," the older man said.

"Well, I'm the only crop duster around here for sixty miles, so what can I do for you?" Hap was already thinking about a new client.

"We just bought a farm west of here and were told that we needed to spray for insects," the older man said.

"Sure. Whose property did you buy? I know all the farms in these parts."

The older man seemed to be taken by surprise. He said, "I'm

not sure of the former owner's name. I bought the farm through an agent and he served as the buyer for me. I just had some questions I wanted to ask about your service."

33

Hap adjusted the brim of his cap and stuck his hands in the front pockets of his coveralls. "Sure. Ask away," he replied, always happy to help a potential new customer.

"How much do you charge?" the man wanted to know.

"I charge by the hour. I have a Hobbs meter in the plane that records the time when the engine is running. I charge $400 an hour for the time on the meter. You pay for the chemicals."

"How long does a typical job take?"

Hap smiled. This fellow didn't seem to know much about farming, but there were all types inhabiting these parts lately. "Well, it depends on how large your field is and how dense you want the coverage to be. With normal coverage, I can spray 125 acres in one trip. I usually spray about 5 gallons per acre. Of course, you have to pay for the flying time from here and back."

"What is the capacity of your chemical tank?" the man asked.

"I can carry a little over 500 gallons in the hopper. At six pounds a gallon, that's almost 300 pounds of chemical. That can cover almost 150 acres."

The older man rubbed his chin as if he was calculating the cost. He walked over behind Hap's airplane and examined the eight spray nozzles below the trailing edge of the right wing. Hap followed him.

The man said, "I'm curious. What is the size of the droplets of spray that come out of the nozzles."

Hap almost laughed. In over thirty years of crop dusting, he had never been asked that question before. "Well, now, the nozzles only have two settings—fine and broad. For about 80% of my jobs, I use the fine setting. But I'll be danged if I know the size of the droplets."

"Sorry, I was doing some research on the internet before I came," the older man explained. "I read that on this model AT-602, the fine setting releases a droplet of about five microns."

"I'm impressed you can identify my crop duster," Hap said. "But I'll shoot straight with you, I don't have a clue how big a micron is. Are you some kind of a scientist?"

"I used to teach chemistry at Georgia Tech before I retired a couple of years ago," the man said.

"Well, if you need me to spray your fields, just let me know where and how much. I'll suggest how much chemical you should buy. But from the way you talk, you probably have that figured out," Hap said.

"It is good to meet you," the man said. "Do you have a card?"

"Sure." Hap hadn't given a business card away in several years. He pulled out his fat wallet and fished out a well-worn card. He handed it to the man.

"Potter's Crop Dusting," the man read aloud. "Do you have an email or a website for your business?"

Hap grunted and said, "Nope. I never got into that whole internet thing. I live just fine without it."

"Okay, thanks. We'll call you when we're ready to do business." The man who called himself Max shook hands with Hap. His son did the same. And then they walked back through the FBO and drove off in the van.

Now that's a strange pair, Hap thought. *I wonder if the son can't talk. He never said a single word.*

As he resumed his walk back to his office, Hap suddenly recalled a pair of FBI agents who had visited him after 9/11. They told him then to report any strange inquiries about crop dusting. There was even a flyer about it that had been tacked to the bulletin board inside the FBO. But that was years ago, and Hap saw no reason to report the two men, given this small community. *What in the heck would a terrorist be doin' out here anyway?* Hap chuckled to himself.

Inside the blue van, Dr. Saad turned to Yamani and said, "Are you sure you can fly that plane?"

"No problem," Yamani said. "It's the same model I trained in when I was in Syria. I can fly it in my sleep. But how are you going to add the pay-load?"

"You let me worry about that," answered Dr. Saad. "I've got a plan. And inshallah, we will deliver a mighty slash with the sword of Allah against the infidels. They took my family, and I shall extract Allah's revenge."

34

APRIL 6

Augusta National Golf Club
Augusta, Georgia
7:30am

It was Bill Townes' first year as Chairman of the Augusta National Golf Club. As Chairman, he would be the official face of the Masters Golf Tournament that would begin in a few days. Every spring, the Masters attracts the top professional golfers from around the world. It is the first of the "big four" major tournaments of the year. But unlike the U.S. Open, the PGA Championship, and the British Open, the Masters is played on the same course every year.

The golf course and the tournament were the brainchild of Bobby Jones, who won the "grand slam" of golf in 1930 as an amateur golfer. At that time, that included the British Amateur, the British Open, the U.S. Amateur, and the U.S. Open.

Jones launched the first Masters Tournament in 1933. It has grown to become the most coveted prize in the golfing world. Jones contracted syringomyelia in 1948, and the crippling nerve disease rendered him an invalid until he died in 1971. He is still considered the President in Perpetuity of Augusta National Golf Club.

Bill looked out and saw that the lawn behind the iconic clubhouse was filled with members and employees. The members, in their distinctive green blazers, huddled into groups drinking cocktails. They chatted loudly with each other. There was an occasional laugh and a good-natured slap on the back. Meanwhile the employees gathered, quietly whispering about the upcoming tournament.

Several hundred volunteers called marshals would soon arrive from all over the world to guard the tee-boxes, quiet the gallery, and make sure the fairway margins were protected. These were coveted jobs jealously performed year after year by businessmen and professionals. These volunteers travel at their own expense and receive no stipend for their week's work. Their only reward is to be invited back to play one round each year on the immaculate course.

At the Masters, the spectators are not called customers or fans. They are religiously referred to as "patrons." During the practice rounds on Monday through Wednesday, over 30,000 patrons crowd the course each day just for the chance of seeing professional golfers practice. Cameras are allowed during the practice rounds, but cell phones and cameras are strictly prohibited during the competition rounds Thursday through Sunday.

For the weekend, the real patrons arrive. Each day over 35,000 patrons flood the wide spaces between the fairways and set up their Masters lawn chairs on hills overlooking the course. They fill the grandstands surrounding several of the most picturesque holes. Their tournament badges (not tickets) are worn like medals of honor. Tournament badges are coveted and passed down from generation to generation. The face value on the badge for each round is only $75. The tournament rules prohibit re-selling Masters badges, but the practice is widespread. If someone wants to attend all four days of the tournament, they can do it by shelling out $10,000 - $15,000. A weekend badge to the Masters tournament is the hardest ticket in all of sports to obtain.

Membership at Augusta National Golf Club is by invitation only. There is no application. The club has around 300 members, and when a slot is open, a club member suggests a replacement. If there is no objection, that person is invited to join. The initiation fee is a closely guarded secret, but it is rumored to be less than $25,000. The club makes millions of dollars each year from CBS who pays for the privilege of televising the Masters. So the annual dues for members are rumored to be less than $3,000.

But Augusta National Golf Club isn't about money; it's about prestige. Every member is a leader in sports, politics, or business. It was the ultimate boy's club until the club admitted two female members in 2012.

Bill realized that he had massive shoes to fill in his role as Chairman. All the invitations had gone out and the best golfers in the world, both professional and amateur, would be arriving in a few days.

He tapped the microphone on the portable podium and said, "Ladies, and gentlemen, let's call this meeting to order." The employees immediately turned and listened attentively. The Members continued to talk and laugh until Bill called their attention saying, "Gentlemen, please. You'll have plenty of time to socialize over the next couple of weeks, but we have work to do."

The murmuring soon died, and Bill continued. "I want to welcome the Members and employees of the Augusta National Golf Club. Most of you have been here longer than I have, but a few of you are new so let me introduce myself. My name is Bill Townes. I was invited to join the Augusta National in 1992 when I was Chairman of ExxonMobil. I've since retired, like a lot of my fellow Members here, and I'm excited about serving as Chairman of the Club.

"When our President, Bobby Jones, first started the Masters in 1933, he had no way of knowing that it would grow into the most prestigious event in the world of sports.

"I'm sure some sports fans would disagree. They would rank the World Series, the Super Bowl, or the World Cup above the Masters. But think about it. Our golfers are gentlemen, who even call penalties on themselves. They want to win, but they display grace and courtesy to their other competitors. Where else does that happen in sports? Our patrons are the most well behaved sporting audience in the world. They are quiet and respectful at all times. They applaud every good shot and never direct hateful comments toward the competitors. In addition, we will have 60 million people watching the telecast from around the world."

Bill continued, "You all have your assigned areas of responsibility. My executive committee and I are going to do everything possible to make this the most enjoyable Masters in its fabled history."

He concluded, "Here we are in a small city in Georgia, but

over the next few days, the eyes of all the world will be on this place. Let's make sure we do our best."

35

East Point, Georgia
7:45am

Dr. Saad gathered his team together in his production warehouse. He had been waiting on this moment for two years. He glanced at those sitting around the table—Ameera, Nasser, Ali and Yamani. They were his family now. Like most Al-Qaeda cells, they operated independently from the knowledge of other terrorist cells. This afforded each cell plausible deniability if anyone was arrested and interrogated.

Dr. Saad spread a map on the table and said, "Here's the plan that Allah has given me to bring the Americans to their knees in humiliation. Americans are a fat, pleasure-seeking culture. While millions of their citizens are starving, they spend billions of dollars on their toys and sporting events. The game of preference for the wealthiest Americans is golf. Instead of using this fertile land to grow food, they plant grass where players compete to hit a little ball into a hole using a curved stick. It's a pathetic example of how decadent and indulgent these infidels have become."

Ali and Nasser scoffed in agreement.

Dr. Saad continued, "In a few days, the most important golf event in the world begins a two-hour drive from here. It's called the Masters Golf Tournament. Over 30,000 of the wealthiest and most important American business and political leaders will gather in Augusta, Georgia, to watch this spectacle. Millions of television viewers will be tuned in to the telecast. And, inshallah, we are going to give them a surprise they'll never forget. We will bring the Great Satan to his knees."

When Dr. Saad paused, Ali asked, "But how are you going to introduce the bioweapon to the people at the golf tournament? It would be impossible for us to get access to the golf course."

Dr. Saad turned to Yamani and said, "Yamani, why don't you explain our plan?"

Yamani said, "From the beginning of his fatwa, our leader, Osama Bin Laden, may Allah grant him Paradise, envisioned the possibility of using a crop dusting airplane to deliver an attack on the Americans. After the glorious 9/11 victory, the American authorities visited all the crop dusting airports in the nation. They warned about foreign pilots wanting to receive flight training. For about three years, the authorities keep frequent contact with the crop dusting operations, but over the last few years, they have become lazy in their vigilance."

Yamani swelled with pride as he continued, "Our blessed leader, Osama bin Laden, may Allah grant him Paradise, realized that it would raise too much suspicion for any of our operatives to receive pilot training in the U.S. again. So I was enlisted to learn how to fly a crop duster in Syria."

Yamani was already a military pilot for the IRIAF (Islamic Republic of Iran Air Force), so it was easy for him to transition to a simple crop duster. Syria had purchased several American-made models for their agricultural operations. Yamani became proficient in flying several models of the Air Tractor, which is manufactured in Olney, Texas.

Yamani added, "I have over 400 hours of flying time in AT-602. I'll be flying the crop duster that delivers the payload to the American infidels."

Dr. Saad picked up the narrative. "We have found a suitable crop duster airplane. It's located at an airport east of here almost halfway between Atlanta and Augusta."

"Okay, but how will we deliver the agent?" Ali asked.

Dr. Saad replied, "With the money Ameera brought us, we've purchased a refrigerated truck. We'll take the botulinum that is already stored in the plastic jerry cans inside our refrigerated facility and pour them into a stainless steel holding tank inside the refrigerated truck. We'll drive to the airport at 2:00 on Saturday afternoon. When we arrive, we'll transfer the agent to the chemical tank to fill the hopper of the aircraft."

"Why are we waiting until later in the day?" Nasser asked. "Wouldn't the toxin be more stable and easier to transfer in the cool morning hours?"

"Good thinking, Nasser," Dr. Saad said. "But I have studied this golf tournament. In the morning hours, the spectators are scattered throughout the entire course. However, toward the end of the day when the best golfers are finishing, the infidels are bunched together around the final four or five holes. It's a much smaller target to saturate at about 4:00."

Ameera remained silent, but nodded her approval.

"But when we arrive at the airport, won't there be someone

there to ask what we're doing?" Ali asked.

Yamani interjected, "There's an old man who owns the crop duster. But he won't be a problem. We've already scheduled to meet him that day. He thinks he's flying a job to lay pesticide down on a farm that we told him we own. I'll get rid of him and anyone else who might have the poor luck of being around. Nothing will stop us from our mission!"

Dr. Saad continued, "I estimate that the toxin will be effective as an aerosol agent within about 30 minutes after Yamani takes off. He will be over Augusta in about that exact time. Crop dusters are common in this part of Georgia. They generally fly so low that they don't ever contact any radar facility. So Yamani will circle northwest of the city until we give him the 'go' signal by radio."

Dr. Saad referenced the map containing an aerial view of the eighteen-hole layout of Augusta National Golf Club. Tracing the route with his finger, Dr. Saad said, "The prevailing wind is usually from the southwest. So, I suggest that Yamani approach from the west. He can descend to treetop altitude and start releasing the toxin. By following my plan, he should effectively introduce the toxin to 90% of the spectators and golfers."

Dr. Saad then activated his iPad to display photographs of the course and the location where the patrons congregated at the end of the day. The pictures showed a beautiful green golf course surrounded by budding dogwoods and azalea blooms.

"But isn't the FAA or the U.S. government going to respond to a crop duster flying over a crowded golf course?" Nasser asked.

"Of course," Yamani replied. "But it will only take me about four minutes to spray the toxin on the infidels. By the time I've finished, there's nothing anyone can do to stop me."

"How will you escape after you spray the poison?" Ameera asked.

"I don't plan on escaping," Yamani replied. "By the time I'm flying away, I expect U.S. fighter jets to be assigned to shoot me down. But I won't give them that satisfaction. I have decided to die as a martyr to achieve the hope of Paradise. As soon as I drop the payload of poison, I'll crash the aircraft into their beloved clubhouse, spreading even more toxin. Like my brave jihadists before me, I'll be shouting, 'Allahu Akbar' in my last moments." Yamani's face was shining as he thought with elation about the honor of killing and dying for Allah.

The room was silent as the team members contemplated the sacrifice Yamani was making.

"But what about the spectators and the golfers?" Ali asked. "What will happen to them when they breathe the botulinum?"

Dr. Saad leaned back in his chair and said, "I can't be sure because this agent has never been deployed outdoors. But it is the most acutely toxic substance known. That's why I chose it. If a person inhales as little as 10 nanograms per kilogram, it can be fatal."

Yamani said, "I don't understand that terminology. How much are we talking about?"

Dr. Saad explained. "A nanogram is one billionth of a gram. So basically, all a person has to do is to ingest a miniscule whiff of the toxin and the paralysis of their lungs will be irreversible."

Ameera unconsciously shuddered.

"Is there any cure, or antidote?" she asked.

Ali interjected, "There is neither. A person whose lungs were paralyzed could theoretically survive if they were immediately placed on a respirator. The respirator would breathe for them until the effects of the toxin wore off—which would be about 24 hours. But my guess is that there are not more than 20 respirators in the entire Augusta area, and there won't be adequate time to transport affected victims to a respirator."

"So what do you predict will be the end effect?" Ameera asked.

Dr. Saad paused and bowed his head before he answered. When he looked up, his eyes were full of emotion and tears. "Inshallah, we shall punish the Great Satan and achieve revenge for the murders of your mother and brother. I predict that almost all of the spectators and golfers will die a horrible death from this attack, just as my own family suffered. I have seen people die from this toxin. It is a torturous death of having full mental alertness but being unable to inhale. They die with the agony of knowing they are dying slowly. The tournament will be cancelled. It may never be played again. The chiefs of the industry and politics for the Great Satan will be gone. The richest golfers will be dead. With Allah's favor, we will strike a blow that will be greater than 9/11!"

36

APRIL 9

East Point, Georgia
3:13am

Ameera woke in a cold sweat. She was shivering as she fought her way to the surface of consciousness from her nightmare. It was the third night in a row that she'd had the same dream. She was exhausted but afraid to go back to sleep again, fearful that the dream would reappear.

During her waking hours, she forced her mind to refrain from thinking about the dream. But here in the silence of her bed, she couldn't escape her questions. What were the odds of having the same dream three nights in a row? It had never happened to her before. Was it a coincidence? Was it just an unexpressed fear that crawled to the surface of her mind?

In the dream, she was standing on a beautiful, green lawn surrounded by brilliant flowers. She realized that the setting matched the photographs of the golf course her father had displayed.

As she stood there, a man in a white robe approached her. Instead of being afraid of this stranger, she was flooded with a sense of peace and tranquility. The man never took his eyes off Ameera's face. He walked up to her, gently grasped her shoulders and smiled. He said, "Ameera. I am Isa, the prophet you have heard about all your life. But I am more than a prophet. I am Jesus, the Son of God. I love you, Ameera, and I want you to know me and love me too. I am the way, the truth, and the life. No one comes to God except through me."

The first night, she had forgotten it as a weird dream. The second night, she was baffled to have the same dream. But here in her bed on this third morning, she became convinced that it was more than a dream.

She had heard stories of Muslims dreaming about Isa, but she had written them off as Christian propaganda. But what she had experienced for three straight nights was no hoax. Islam taught that a prophet had visited each generation in history. Isa was considered one of the greatest prophets, but Muslims rejected the claim that Isa was the Son of God. To say such a thing was considered to be blasphemy. There was only one God, Allah, and Mohammed was his final and most important prophet.

If that was true, why was Ameera having these dreams? She knew she couldn't talk to her father or any of the team about what she had seen, so where could she find answers?

She opened her MacBook Air and saw that it was logged onto their remote server. This remote server in Pakistan changed their IP address so no one could trace the activity to this apartment. This also gave Ameera the assurance that no one on her team would be able to see what sites she had visited.

She brought the Google screen up and wondered what to

ask. She typed, "Who is Jesus really?" Incredibly, she saw a link to a website named whoisjesus-really.com. She clicked on the link and to her surprise the website had a drop down menu that allowed her to choose her language. She didn't expect Arabic to be one of her choices. However, there were nine different Arabic dialects offered. She clicked on Egyptian Arabic, spoken by the majority of the Arabic-speaking world.

As she read the website, tears started flowing down her cheeks. These verses from the Christian Bible told her that God loved her. She knew that Allah was great and mighty, but she had never even considered that the Creator would *love* her. Islam was a religion of duty and obedience. Obeying the five pillars was performed out of fear of punishment from Allah. In all of her religious duties, Ameera had never felt good enough to please Allah. Her eyes fell on the scripture, "For God so loved the world that he gave his one and only Son, that whoever believes in him shall not perish, but have eternal life." She had never read such powerful and freeing words.

The website's claims almost seemed too good to be true. *Everyone is sinful and our sin separates us from God,* she read. *But God's solution for our sin problem was to send Jesus to die on the cross for our sins.*

Islam taught that Isa was a virgin-born prophet who performed miracles, but they denied that he was crucified. But now Ameera saw that God required a perfect sacrifice for sin. Jesus was that sacrifice, according to the website.

Ameera continued to read and click dozens of other related links. She glanced at the clock on her computer and saw that she had been reading about Jesus for three hours. It seemed like only a matter of minutes. Her soul was drinking in this truth like someone thirsty receiving life-giving water.

Ameera eventually arrived at a website called Global Media Outreach. As she scanned the site, she saw that she could chat with someone from her own country, Yemen.

"Impossible!" she said softly under her breath. Nobody from Yemen believed these things about Jesus—it was illegal to believe anything other than Islam.

Ameera looked around to make sure nobody else was up yet. She had the brief urge to close her computer and forget this delusional episode. But after hesitating, she clicked on the link to Yemen. Nothing happened. *See, I was right,* she thought. *Nobody in Yemen believes this.*

To her surprise, Ameera suddenly heard a tone and saw a screen appear in the bottom right of the website. Then words began to appear in Arabic.

Hello. Do you want to speak to someone in Yemen?

After hesitating for what seemed like an eternity, Ameera typed her reply in the chat field.

Yes. But how do I know you're in Yemen?

Do you know Yemen?

It is my home country.

Are you here now?

No.

Where are you?

I cannot say.

Ameera drew in her breath. She could not believe this was happening. But she was still not convinced, so she continued typing, "If you know Yemen, you must know the name of our main seaport."

Of course, Aden. That's too easy.

What's the population of Yemen's largest city?

It's Sana'a and it has over a million people.

Ameera considered the answer and it sounded as if this person really was in Yemen. She typed, *Sorry to ask so many questions, but it's dangerous for me to be on this site.*

I feel the same way. What can I do for you? Do you want to know more about Jesus?

Ameera hesitated. She typed the words slowly, *I've been having the same dream for three nights.*

Tell me about your dream.

I'm standing in a beautiful garden. A man who identifies himself as Jesus walks up to me and takes me by the shoulders. He tells me he loves me and he wants me to know him. I feel a sense of peace and tranquility in the dream. But then I wake up terrified. What's happening?

You're not alone. The same thing happened to me.

What?

Two years ago, I had a dream that I was a passenger in a car involved in a terrible accident. In my dream, I was knocked unconscious, but when I opened my eyes I saw that Jesus was the driver. He said to me, "Come to me. I am with you. I love you."

What did you do?

Nothing to begin with. But I was haunted by the dream. I eventually found a Bible in Arabic and started reading. I discovered that Jesus died for me and that he is the Savior of the world.

Ameera typed furiously and wished time would stand still.

Are we going crazy? How can this be happening?

It's happening to thousands of Muslims around the world. They are turning to Jesus. In the Bible, the prophet Joel predicted, "I will pour out my Spirit on all people. Your sons and daughters will prophesy, your old men will dream dreams, your young men will see visions. Even on my servants, both men and women, I will pour out my Spirit in those days."

What should I do next? I cannot renounce Islam. My father would disown me.

I know the cost. My family considers me dead now. But I have a growing family of brothers and sisters in Christ.

How did you...

Someone making coffee in the kitchen interrupted Ameera's typing. She quietly closed her laptop and lay back down in her bed.

What's happening? she wondered. *Please Allah. Or God... or Jesus... please help me! I don't know what to do,* she prayed.

From the kitchen her father shouted, "Ameera! We're out of coffee again. And we need eggs and bread. You're neglecting your duty. Hurry to the corner store and buy some supplies!"

Ameera got dressed and walked down the stairs and out onto the street. It was a beautiful spring morning. The birds seemed to be singing louder and the trees and flowers seemed to have suddenly bloomed.

Ameera had noticed over the last couple of weeks that since her hair was blonde and she wasn't wearing her hijab, people treated her differently. Instead of avoiding her, total strangers would smile and say, "Good morning."

Is this the Great Satan? Ameera was no longer sure.

Ameera picked up the coffee, eggs, and bread and made her way to the single cashier. There was an elderly black lady in the checkout line in front of her. The lady was smiling and quietly singing a melodious song to herself. Ameera didn't recognize the tune, but she could make out some of the words. She leaned closer to hear what she was singing. "Precious name; Oh how sweet. Hope of earth and joy of heaven. Precious name; Oh how sweet. Hope of earth and joy of heaven. Take the name of Jesus with you..."

The cashier rang up the lady's groceries and started sacking them. Then the lady turned to Ameera and said, "Darlin', I'm going to pay for your groceries, too."

Ameera was startled. "W-w-why you do this?" she asked in her heavily accented English. "I have the money myself to pay."

The lady looked her in the eyes and smiled. "My pastor told us last Sunday that this week we should perform an act of kindness to strangers. Jesus said that if I give a cup of cold water in his name, I won't lose my reward. So, your money's no good here. I'm gonna pay for your groceries in the name of Jesus."

"No, you cannot do this!" Ameera protested.

The lady just patted Ameera's arm. "Now, honey. I'm doin' this 'cause Jesus loves you and I love you, too."

Ameera was too amazed to resist. She hadn't asked for any kind of sign from God, but it seemed as if he gave her one.

37

APRIL 9

3310 Foxtrot
Alpharetta, Georgia
9:34am

Regan walked out of the bathroom and into the den, still wearing one of Ty's terrycloth bathrobes. She dried her thick hair with a towel. "I can't tell you how much better I feel after a long, hot bath. It seems that I've been wearing those same clothes for weeks."

"How's your head?" Ty asked.

"I think the wound is healing, but I still have a killer of a headache," Regan admitted.

An hour earlier, they had arrived at Ty's townhome after landing at Gwinnett County Airport. As a matter of routine for international arrivals, U.S. Customs and Immigration agents were waiting on the tarmac as the Gulfstream G280 taxied to a stop. The agents boarded the aircraft. After carefully inspecting their documents, they cleared the passengers. Regan noticed that Solly had an American passport, although she thought Ty told her he was an Israeli. She looked up at Solly with a questioning look. Solly winked back, silently letting her know that she shouldn't ask anything in the presence of the Customs agents.

Solly, Ty, and Regan grabbed their luggage and made their way down the air stair onto the tarmac. Regan always felt a sense of pride whenever she returned to her homeland. But today, she only felt anxiety and fear. They made the short trek across the ramp to exit through the offices of the FBO. Solly had arranged to have a rental car waiting for him.

In the parking lot, Solly insisted that Regan ride with Ty, since her head wound was still puffy. Regan had already learned not to argue with Solly. She was a strong-willed person, but Solly's resolve was like a steel girder—unbendable.

Solly drove behind Ty and they soon arrived at Ty's townhome. As they pulled into the parking place, Solly stared at the burned-out shell of what had been Regan's home a few days earlier. Yellow police tape still circled the remains of the house. He realized that they were dealing with a formidable enemy who would stop at nothing to destroy innocent Americans.

Regan sat on the leather ottoman by the TV and continued to fluff her hair with the towel. From the kitchen, Ty yelled, "I've got breakfast! Who's hungry?"

Regan realized that she was famished. Food had been served on the flight back from Paris, but with her head pounding, she didn't have an appetite.

"I'm starving. I hope you cooked enough for an army!" Regan shouted back as she headed toward the kitchen. Solly followed her.

Ty said, "Nope. I'm a Marine, not an Army wimp. I fixed

enough for the entire Corps."

Regan stared in wonder at the kitchen island. Ty had set three places. There were large, frosty glasses of orange juice and steaming cups of coffee at each place. A large platter of scrambled eggs was set in the middle. Crispy pieces of bacon lined the outside of the platter.

Ty was wearing a gourmet apron with the U.S. Marine Corps seal emblazoned on the front. "Have a seat, you two," Ty said. "Dig into the eggs and bacon now. I'm also cooking waffles, so save some room for that."

Solly looked at the spread on the table and said with mock exaggeration, "Ty, I am insulted to the core. How *dare* you serve pork to a Jew, for heaven's sake!"

Regan was horrified.

Ty said, "Don't let him fool you, Regan. I've seen Solly eat pork before. He isn't always kosher."

Solly picked up a piece of bacon and said, "Well, as much as it disturbs my religious sensitivities, I wouldn't want to insult my host. When in Georgia, do as the Georgians do." He devoured the piece of bacon in three bites. "Those poor Orthodox fellas don't know what they're missing!"

"Besides," Ty said, "Solly calls himself a completed Jew—he believes in Jesus as the Messiah."

"Really?" Regan asked as she reached for the bacon.

Solly got serious for a moment. "Now, I don't call myself a Christian—that word carries too many meanings, especially in the Middle East. I'm a Jew who is following the teachings of Jesus. I spent an entire day once trying to convince Ty that Jesus is the fulfillment of the Old Testament prophecies about the

Messiah. But he's a tough nut to crack."

"I'm a nut, for sure," Ty said. "I just need some more time to figure this out. I've seen so many damaging things done in the name of religion that I'm still pretty skeptical." Ty turned toward Regan and Solly, holding a plate piled high with waffles. "Who's ready for some waffles?"

After putting away the sumptuous breakfast, the three friends refilled their coffee cups and returned to the den. Regan excused herself to change in the guest bedroom.

After a few minutes, she emerged looking refreshed and ready. Ty couldn't help stealing a glance at her. She had so many looks. When he first saw her at the end of his sidewalk, she had looked like a vulnerable princess in need of rescue. When she walked into the French restaurant, she looked like a fashion model. But Ty liked this look best. She had on jeans, a black t-shirt, and running shoes. Dressed this way, she looked like the All-American girl from next door. *She really is from next door—or from what's left of next door*, Ty thought.

Solly said, "Okay, let's talk about our next step. We're not certain that Dr. Saad is still in the Atlanta area, but until we receive a confirmation that he is somewhere else, we have to start here."

Regan said, "Why don't we pursue your hunch that the terrorists will attempt to use an airplane to disperse the poison dust? How would they do that?"

Solly said, "If I were a terrorist, I'd use a crop duster. After 9/11, it was confirmed that the leader of the suicide bombers, Mohammed Atta, had visited several crop dusting schools in Florida to ask about training. In addition, the American authorities arrested Zacarias Moussaoui before he could participate as one of the 9/11 terrorists. He is currently serving a life-sentence in a super-max prison facility in Colorado. When he was arrested, officials found a computer disc about crop dusting in his possession."

"Okay, if we start with that assumption, why don't we start investigating all the crop dusting companies in Georgia? There can't be that many," Regan said.

"Actually, there are 76 in Georgia," Ty said as he looked up from the screen of his laptop. "And if you add the crop dusting services in the adjoining states that are within 100 miles of the Georgia border, that number soars to over 150."

Regan said, "No problem. That's just fifty for each of us. Let's divide them up and start calling all of them and ask if they've had anything unusual happen at their operation."

"I love your positive attitude, Regan," Solly said. He ran his hand down through his thick beard as he thought about their options.

He looked up and said, "Ty, do you have a private pilot's license?"

"Yes, I've had my license since I retired from the military. But I haven't flown in a few years. After strapping on an F-16, it's pretty boring to be droning along in a Cessna 172."

"Do you have an old VFR sectional chart for the Atlanta area?" Solly asked.

"I think so, let me go look in my flying case." Ty left the room.

"What's a sectional chart?" Regan asked.

Solly replied, "It's like a road map for pilots. But it's more of an air map. It shows where all the airports are located and has topographical features like lakes, rivers, and mountains. The location and height of tall obstructions are listed as well."

Ty returned unfolding the large and colorful map and placed it on the coffee table, its edges hung over and touched the floor.

"This one is out of date," Ty said, "but not much has changed since it was legal. What are you looking for?"

"Give me a pencil and some string," Solly said.

Ty went into the kitchen and returned a few seconds later with a pencil and a ball of nylon string. "I think I know what you're doing," Ty said.

Solly unrolled a piece of string and measured off a length of it using the scale on the map. "I want to see which airports are within 150 nautical miles of Atlanta."

"I don't want to sound dumb," Regan said, "But what's a nautical mile?"

Ty said, "Well, we use statute miles when we're driving. But ships and aircraft use nautical miles. They're pretty close, but not exact. For instance, 150 nautical miles equals about …"

"173 statute miles," Solly said without looking up. He tied the length of string equal to 150 nautical miles to the pencil. Then while placing the end of the string over the approximate center of Atlanta, he drew a circle on the chart. "We start looking with all of the airports and crop dusting services inside this circle."

"But that includes large cities like Birmingham, Chattanooga, Greenville, South Carolina, Athens, Augusta, Macon, and Columbus," Ty countered. "That's too large an area. Why don't you bring your circle in to 75 nautical miles?"

Solly said, "I think you're right. Let's see where this leaves us." He shortened the string to the appropriate length and drew another circle, this one smaller than the first.

"That's better. Now, we're only looking at larger towns like Macon, LaGrange, Rome, Gainesville, and Athens," Ty said. "Let me cross-check the names of the 76 crop dusting services to identify the ones that are located inside that circle."

"Can I help?" Regan said.

Ty said, "Sure, I'll print out the list. You can start with the beginning and I'll start at the end. We'll meet in the middle."

Solly said, "You kids go to work. I'm going to step outside to make a phone call."

38

APRIL 9

CIA Headquarters
Langley, Virginia
10:55am

Tony Parker, the newly appointed Director of the C.I.A., was studying his iPad2, reading briefings from three-dozen chief agents scattered across the globe. These agents reported the threat levels from the same sources they'd been watching for years. Tony's inner threat level sensor was calm. He didn't get excited because these daily reports were most often like the boy who cried "wolf" too many times.

He was startled when his private cell phone rang. Like many Washington insiders, Parker carried a Blackberry for texting and emails and an iPhone for personal use. Only three people had his private number. Arthur Flowers, President of the United States, his assistant Frank Taylor, and Parker's wife, Penny. He glanced at the screen and read, "blocked" on the caller-ID. He started to reject the call as a wrong number, but he had a hunch. He had learned through the years to listen to his hunches.

"Hello," he said.

"Tony, how are you?" the voice replied.

Parker tried to place the accent, which sounded either Australian or South African.

"Who are you? And how did you get this number?" he demanded.

"No worries, mate. It's your old friend, Solly."

"Solly? Where are you? How did you get my private number?" he asked.

"I'm actually here in the U.S. And you don't want to know how I have your private number. But you know you can trust me."

The whole time Parker was head of MENA (Middle East and Northern Africa Analysis), Solly had been a great source of information and help. But they had lost contact with each other since then.

"Where have you been the past few years?" Parker asked.

"I've been digging around in the dirt of Israel for antiquities. And I've been digging around for plots against Israel or the U.S.," Solly added.

"How's the digging going?" he asked cautiously.

"I might have uncovered a threat that you need to know about."

"What is it?"

"I'm not sure if I'm ready to tell you or not."

"Why not, for God's sake?" Parker used more volume than he expected.

"Well, remember what you did with the intelligence we fed you before 9/11?" Solly said.

"That was a different time and a different administration," he replied.

"Okay, I'll toss you a bone. Tony, do you recall a drone attack in Yemen on an Al-Qaeda member named Anwar al-Rimi a couple of years ago?" Solly asked.

"You know I can't comment on that," he said. "Besides, that was a long time ago and we've participated in hundreds of drone missions."

"Let me refresh your memory," offered Solly. "A missile from a drone destroyed the vehicle al-Rimi was in, and in the process it ignited a fire in a house on the edge of that town. Two civilians died in the fire."

Parker was silent for a moment. Stalling for time, he pushed a button under his desk. Within seconds, his administrative assistant was standing in front of his desk. Tony scribbled a note: "Trace this call immediately."

He returned to Solly, "Again, I can neither confirm nor deny that we were a part of that mission. But you know that there is always a danger of collateral damage."

"Well, the surviving family members in that house call it murder, not collateral damage. And that attack stirred up a dangerous wasp's nest. I have a lead on finding where the wasps are."

"Tell me everything you know, Solly," Parker demanded.

"I don't know," Solly said, "With your lack of action on the info we fed you before 9/11, Mossad is reluctant to bring you fellas into the loop on this one. We may be handling it ourselves. Besides, I'm not sure if you still have moles operating in your system. I don't want to risk tipping off the leaders of this operation."

"Solly, you know that it's a violation of U.S. Federal Law for foreign intelligence services to operate on U.S. soil. If I find you withholding information relating to the security of our nation, I'll personally arrest you and throw you in Gitmo!" Parker was shouting now.

"Tony, you know me better than that. I only want what's best for Israel's strongest ally. Here's another freebie for you, friend. You should be finding everything you can dig up on Dr. Hakeem Saad."

Solly paused. "And I suspect you're tracing this call, so I'm hanging up. If you hear back from me again, it will be to ask for your help. Good talkin' to you, mate. Good day." Solly disconnected the call.

Parker looked at the phone in his hand and yelled at Frank, "Tell me you were able to get a location on that call!"

Frank stuck his head in the doorway and shook his head. "He hung up too soon. Sorry, boss."

Parker's threat level sensor was now off the chart. Solly was a senior Mossad agent and he wouldn't be here unless he had gotten wind of a legitimate terrorist threat.

He removed his glasses, closed his eyes and pinched the bridge of his nose with his right hand. Should he inform the President about this so-called threat or not?

His mind went back to the C.I.A. agents who had dismissed credible intelligence from Mossad before 9/11. He was determined to not make the same mistake.

He barked, "Frank, get our researchers digging into anything we have on a Dr. Hakeem Saad."

"Yes sir. When do you want it?" Frank asked.

"Yesterday! Now, get on it." He slumped in his chair and stared at the special phone that had direct connection with the White House. The only time he had touched it was during his orientation to his new job six weeks earlier.

With a deep sigh, he picked up the phone and pressed the single button on the console. He didn't have to say anything because a voice replied, "Yes, Mr. Director. How may I help you?"

For the first time in his short tenure as C.I.A. chief, Parker spoke the words that he had hoped he would never have to utter. "I need to talk to Mr. Holman and the President about a credible terrorist threat against the United States of America."

39

APRIL 9

Augusta National Golf Club
Wednesday practice round
9:45am

Yamani had used a fake driver's license to rent a Nissan Altima for the two-and-a-half hour drive from Atlanta to Augusta. When they arrived in Augusta, Yamani had exited I-20 at Washington Road and found himself in a traffic jam. Eventually they had been directed to park, astonished to discover the number of people already parked in the huge lot beside Berckmans Road.

As they exited the car, Dr. Saad and Yamani tried their best to blend into the Augusta crowd. Weeks earlier, they had gone online to StubHub and paid $1,400 for two tickets to the Wednesday Masters Practice Round. The staggering amount of money made Dr. Saad seethe with anger. His only consolation was the realization that he would soon deliver a crushing blow to this American indulgence.

As they stood in line outside the main entrance, they felt out of place wearing their strange American clothes. Ameera had visited an Academy sports store and purchased golf attire that looked like some they had seen fans wearing. For her father, she bought khaki slacks, a solid white pullover golf shirt and a black hat that had "Titleist" written on it. She had no idea what a Titleist was, but it was in the golf section. For Yamani, she purchased blue slacks and a red golf shirt with a pattern, and a "TaylorMade" cap. She also picked out brown Timberline boat shoes for both men. Dark sunglasses completed their outfits.

After waiting for twenty minutes in a line that moved fairly quickly, they found themselves inside the gate beside a huge shop where people were buying Masters memorabilia in a shopping frenzy. People were grabbing handfuls of shirts, hats, and other items related to the Masters.

Ameera had researched the tournament and suggested that they each buy a short Masters folding chair so they would fit in with the crowd.

Dr. Saad found two of the green folding chairs. He expected the price to be expensive, but he was surprised to find that they were only $16 each. He got in one of the long checkout lines served by several cashiers. The shopper in front of him was loaded down with dozens of shirts, sweaters, and hats. Dr. Saad heard the cashier say, "Your total is $4,324."

Dr. Saad shook his head as he thought again about the way these luxury-loving Americans lived. With his scientific mind, he calculated that this store would sell well over $500,000 of inventory today alone. And these weren't items that the customers needed to survive or to stay warm. *They are frivolous luxury items—mementos of their visit to this silly tournament,* he thought. As he stepped up to the cashier, he focused on the fact that in a few days he would give them something to remember for years to come.

"How are you, sir? Did you find everything you need?" The young girl asked.

"I'm fine. Thank you. Yes, this is all." Dr. Saad tried to speak without a trace of his Arabic accent.

After paying in cash, Yamani and Dr. Saad walked onto the grounds of the golf course. Dr. Saad had to admit that it was one of the most beautiful gardens he had ever seen. What a tragedy that the Americans restricted it to only a few visitors a year.

The pair walked with the crowd beside the steep downhill fairway of #10. Then, following Ameera's earlier suggestion, they walked to the left of the #14 green and turned right. They walked a little ways downhill and set up their chairs along with several thousand other people who were watching the action at "Amen Corner."

Ameera had explained that Amen Corner had nothing to do with religion. Years ago, a sportswriter had given that name to holes eleven, twelve, and thirteen.

Dr. Saad or Yamani neither understood nor were they interested in golf. Unlike the other patrons, they were only there as enemy scouts to get the lay of the land. They were pleased to see thousands of people congregating in such small, compact areas. Yamani studied the trees to see how low he could fly and deliver the agent. Many fairways were wide enough to land a small airplane. He saw several open areas where he could easily fly below the tree line.

After watching from that vantage point for about an hour, they moved over to the grandstands beside the putting green for #15 and the tee box for the par three sixteenth hole. From this position, they watched as the crowd yelled for the players on the tee box to hit their balls into the small lake beside the #16 green.

Yamani watched with disbelief as the players laid down new golf balls and chipped them into the lake, trying to skip them across the water. What a waste! He didn't know how much golf balls or golf equipment cost, but he was sure it was expensive. There were no golf courses in Yemen or Iran, which was Yamani's birthplace.

This is a sport for the rich and lazy, he determined. There was no athleticism involved.

Dr. Saad and Yamani continued to walk around the course studying the layout and where the crowds seemed to congregate. They had read on a video screen in the gift shop that the par three tournament would begin today at 12:30. As that time approached, the crowds moved from the main golf course to an area located to the left of the 10th hole.

By 1:00pm, most of the main course was deserted. Ignoring the par three tournament, Dr. Saad and Yamani walked back to Amen Corner where they had spent the first part of the day. Dr. Saad pointed back toward the clubhouse. "You'll make your approach low from the west. At the clubhouse, activate the sprayer. Then bank right and descend as low as you can to fly over this area where thousands of the spectators will be sitting. When you see this small pond, bank right and fly down the 13th fairway. There are trees near the green, so you'll want to pull up over the parking lot. Then bank left and fly over the grandstand area where we were watching the fools hit balls into the water. Get as low as you can to spray this group of spectators. Then fly up the 15th fairway, avoiding those few trees in the middle. Your last pass will be when you bank left and fly up the 18th fairway. Fly as low as possible as the land begins to rise. The largest group of spectators will be gathered around the 18th green."

Dr. Saad and Yamani walked slowly uphill back toward the top of the course where the clubhouse was located. They could hear the shouts and cheers from the crowd watching the par three tournament. When they finally climbed to the area behind the 18th green, Dr. Saad turned around and pointed down the fairway.

"As you can see, the land begins to rise from the beginning of this hole until where we're standing. If you're flying low enough, you should be able to spray this area from an altitude of only 20 or 30 feet."

Yamani was taking mental notes. He said, "Sir, this is an excellent plan. But as soon as I make a pass over the golf course, I'm sure the authorities will be notified. What will be their response?"

"You are wise to anticipate that," Dr. Saad said. "But I don't think they'll have time to stop you. First, you'll be flying so low that Air Traffic Control won't pay any attention to you. If you are considered a threat when you first appear, the authorities will probably suspect a terror plot. They will call the U.S. Military. There is a U.S. Army Base here in Augusta named Fort Gordon. But it is mainly an electronics and communications training center. They have one transport helicopter on base. There is a detachment of Marines at Ft. Gordon, and they might be mobilized to respond to you. But they aren't going to try to shoot you down over the crowded golf course."

"You have really done your homework for this attack," Yamani said admiringly.

"It is our glorious opportunity to honor Allah and gain vengeance for the murder of my family. I have planned this day every day for the past two years."

"Is Fort Gordon our only threat?" Yamani asked.

"The local police department and sheriff's office will respond. But I don't think they're going to try to shoot you down either. The nearest Air Force base is Robins Air Force Base. It is 160 miles southwest of here. I expect them to scramble a couple of F-16s. But you'll be finished long before they can arrive."

He turned around and pointed up the hill at the famous clubhouse. "May Allah give you the courage and strength to finish your mission by destroying this symbol of American luxury and decadence."

Yamani bowed his head and said, "Sir, I am honored to give my life in obedience to our Prophet." He then quoted the words of the Prophet in Sura 2, "On unbelievers is the curse of Allah. Slay them wherever you find them. Fight against them until idolatry is no more and Allah's religion reigns supreme."

"You are a brave soldier, Yamani. You will be honored among the martyrs," Dr. Saad confirmed. "America's arrogance will be destroyed by your act of sacrifice."

As Dr. Saad and Yamani walked out the gate into the parking lot, they were all alone. The security guard scratched his head and wondered why two patrons were leaving so early. But he figured they were just trying to beat the crowd. In fact, they had no trouble leaving the parking area. Soon they were cruising along well below the posted speed limit heading back to East Point to make final preparations.

40

The White House
1600 Pennsylvania Avenue
Washington, D.C.
4:32pm

Tony Parker waited nervously outside the Oval Office. He had been here many times before. The last time was for an ordinary briefing. However, this meeting was hastily arranged in response to his call. POTUS—the President of the United States—had rescheduled an afternoon and evening of appointments to carve out time to talk about this threat.

President Flowers' secretary walked out. "Mr. Parker, the President will see you now."

Parker walked into the Oval Office and the President shook his hand. "Good afternoon, Tony. I think you know everyone here. This is Secretary Nathan Hughes with Homeland Security. And of course, your counterpart at the FBI, Director Bridgeman Cagle, and my National Security Chief, Jason Holman."

Parker shook hands around the circle and thanked them for

agreeing to meet with him. He sat on one of the two facing sofas and turned to the President.

President Flowers leaned back against the front edge of his massive desk named Resolute. It was a gift to the U.S. by Queen Victoria. The desk was made from the heavy timbers of a British Arctic exploration ship, the H.M.S. Resolute, which had been abandoned when it became trapped in ice in 1854.

"So what do you have for me?" President Flowers asked.

Secretary Hughes spoke up first. "Sir, after Director Parker called, we've put together some Intel on Dr. Hakeem Saad." He nodded to a presidential aide who pushed a button on a remote control. A screen lowered from a panel near the ceiling beside the door going into the President's private study. Dr. Saad's picture appeared on the screen, smiling and standing beside some other gentlemen.

President Flowers commented, "He looks like someone's grandfather."

"This picture was taken a few years ago when he was a professor at the University of Science and Technology in Sanaa, Yemen. But before relocating his family to Yemen, he was the chief chemist for Saddam Hussein's bioweapons department."

"Did the Coalition ever find any evidence of bioweapons in Iraq?" President Flowers asked.

Secretary Hughes consulted his notes. "Dr. Saad escaped in 1992 after the First Gulf War. When Coalition troops invaded Iraq in 2003, he had been gone for over a decade. But they did find evidence that many forms of biological warfare chemicals had been developed. It's easier to dispose of bioweapons than WMDs."

"Why all the interest in him now?" President Flowers asked.

Parker spoke up. "Mr. Hughes, if I may..." Secretary Hughes nodded.

"Mr. President. Dr. Saad has been totally off the map for the past 20 years. However, his face was in our C.I.A. database of persons of interest. This facial recognition software ages the image to coincide with the actual age of the suspect." He nodded at the aide. A computer-generated picture appeared on the screen. "We suspect that Dr. Saad looks something like this today. And a few weeks ago, our facial recognition software registered a hit on him as he was entering the U.S. in Atlanta." He nodded again, advancing the frame. "Here's the image taken by an airport surveillance camera as he approaches U.S. Immigration and Customs."

The airport picture and the computer-generated photo were displayed side-by-side on the screen. There was no mistaking that they were the same person.

Secretary Hughes said, "Sir, the system worked as designed. He was detained and questioned by U.S. Customs agents. One of our Homeland Security agents was part of the interrogation."

"What happened? Where is he now?" the President asked.

There was uncomfortable silence for a few seconds as nobody wanted to answer that question.

Finally Secretary Hughes spoke up. "We released him, sir. We thoroughly checked his luggage and did a full body check. He claimed to be here on a weeklong visit to relatives in Atlanta. He answered all the questions to our satisfaction. And since he was so far down on the priority list, we had no reason to hold him. He even supplied a U.S. address where he would be staying."

President Flowers pushed himself from his desk and crossed his arms. "I think I know where this is going. I'm sure you checked the address and it's bogus."

"No, it's a legitimate address," Secretary Hughes said. "But the people there have never heard of Hakeem Saad and they have no relatives in Yemen."

"Great. Why are we suddenly even suspicious of this guy?" the President wanted to know. "Has he committed a crime or an act of terror?"

"No, sir. Not yet," Parker said. "But I have a very reliable foreign intelligence source who gave me his name in connection with a possible terrorist threat. It seems that Dr. Saad has a motive for revenge."

"What kind of motive?" the President asked.

Parker hesitated. "A couple of years ago, one of our drones killed an Al-Qaeda leader in Yemen. There was some collateral damage. We believe Dr. Saad's wife and son were killed in the attack. We also suspect he isn't working alone. To pull off a biological attack, he would need a team."

"God help us all," the President said, shaking his head. "Who is your source?"

Parker replied, "I think you can guess when I tell you that he's with the same group that gave the U.S. credible information about the threat of attacks a few weeks before 9/11. We basically sat on that Intel."

The President was quiet for a moment. "We're not going to make that mistake again." He turned to the F.B.I. Director and said, "Mr. Cagle I want your agents scouring the Atlanta area showing this photograph. I want to find this maniac and stop him before he can unleash some God-awful biological attack on our people."

Director Cagle said, "I'm on it, sir. I'll call our AIC now and give him an update. I'll be traveling to Atlanta myself to supervise the search."

When nobody moved for a couple of seconds, the President shouted, "What are you waiting for? Get out there and find these bad guys before we have another 9/11 on our hands!"

"Yes sir!" the four men said in unison and they stood up to leave.

41

APRIL 10

East Point, Georgia
4:22am

Ameera was having the same dream again. She was walking through the beautiful garden, admiring the stunning flowers. She could even hear the birds singing. She felt no fear. Only peace. And anticipation. Would the wonderful man Jesus appear to her again?

Soon she saw Jesus walking toward her. This time she ran and knelt before him. Before he could say anything, she looked up into his eyes and blurted out, "What's happening? Why are you coming to me? What do you want me to do, Jesus?"

Jesus reached out his hand toward her head and for the first time she noticed the angry wound on his palms. He placed his hand gently on her head and said, "Ameera, you are indeed a princess. But you can only be the princess I created you to be if you will join me in my Kingdom. There's nothing for you to do. I've done all there is to do. I died so you can be forgiven. All you have to do is let me love you."

He waved to his right and Ameera saw that there were

thousands of people in the garden lined up along the edge of the woods. They were cheering about something. Jesus said, "And I love these people too. And I want you to love them the same way I love you."

She wanted to ask him more questions, but she woke up. Wide awake. She wasn't shaking or sweating. She was smiling as she recalled her vision of Jesus.

Knowing she could not go back to sleep, she got up and booted up her laptop. She had spent much of the last day reading about Jesus. She didn't own a Bible, but she had discovered BibleGateway.com. As she scrolled down the various translations, she was amazed to find that they offered an easy-to-read Arabic version online.

An introduction to the Arabic version of the Bible suggested that new readers begin with the New Testament. Over the next few hours, she devoured the books of Matthew, Mark, Luke, and John. She had never heard these stories about Jesus. Her religion taught that Isa was a prophet, but the New Testament presented him as the Son of God. Ameera loved the way John told the story of Jesus in a personal way.

This morning, she logged onto the BibleGateway site again. Since she was also fluent in French, she searched for a French translation since it is a much more expressive language, known as the language of the heart. She scrolled down to La Bible du Semeur and started reading the Gospel according to John in French.

She would read a verse or two and then stop and ponder what it meant. As she proceeded into the first two chapters, the words started making sense to her, as if her eyes were being opened to a new and wonderful truth.

In John 3, she read the story of a very religious man named Nicodemus. She had always been taught that salvation comes by keeping the commands of her religion. But Jesus told Nicodemus that observing his religion wasn't sufficient. He said that a person had to be born again.

Ameera wondered how that was possible. And then she read how Nicodemus had the same questions. Jesus explained, "Flesh gives birth to flesh, but the Spirit gives birth to spirit."

It made sense that just as she had been born physically, it would be possible for her to be born spiritually as well. *There could be a new spiritual life for me,* she thought and a sense of peace washed over her.

She thought about this rebirth for a few more minutes and found herself praying, *God, tell me how I can be born spiritually.*

Just then her eyes fell on the sixteenth verse in John 3: *"Oui, Dieu a tant aimé le monde qu'il a donné son Fils, son unique, poiur que tous ceux qui placent leur confiance en lui échappent a' la perdition et qu'ils aient la vie éternelle."*

Ameera bowed her head and her eyes filled with tears. She saw teardrops falling onto her keyboard, but she didn't care. Something was happening. She *did* believe in Jesus. It was as if her life was starting all over again. Everything sinful she had ever thought or done seemed like a bad dream now. She was convinced that this moment was the beginning of something new and exciting.

Ameera continued to read the story of Jesus. Everything was making perfect sense to her now. Time stood still as she continued reading in John. She was learning about Jesus washing the feet of disciples when she heard her father in the kitchen.

He came to her closed door and pounded. "Ameera! Where is breakfast? This is an important day. We must leave soon to transfer the botulinum into the containers so we can transport it to the airport soon. Come out and get to work!"

His words hit Ameera like a punch in the gut. The plot. The attack. The plan. Were those people she saw in the dream the ones they were going to kill?

But what could she do? She couldn't tell her father or the other men what had happened. They might kill her. She didn't know what to do.

So she prayed. But this wasn't the memorized words of the fajr she had recited from her youth. She said softly, *Dear God, I need your guidance. I need your help. Please tell me what to do for the sake of your Son, Jesus. Amen.*

She stood up and walked into the kitchen. As she brushed her hand through her short blonde hair she said, "I'm sorry, Father. I'll have breakfast ready in a few minutes."

42

APRIL 11

3310 Foxtrot
Alpharetta, Georgia
3:00pm

Regan was frustrated beyond words. She and Ty had taken the list of 76 crop dusting services in Georgia and located each one on a state map. That left 48 crop dusting businesses within 75 miles of Atlanta. With Solly's help, they started making calls to each one. They soon discovered that most of them were chemical companies that only sold the crop dusting chemicals. They could recommend several pilots who had crop dusting planes. But some of those pilots were in the neighboring states of South Carolina and Alabama.

They found the names and phone numbers of some of these flying services and tried calling them. Some were disconnected. Most were answered by a voicemail. They weren't even sure what to ask those they did reach.

One conversation went this way. "Hello, Turner Spraying. What can I do for you?"

Regan said, "Are you a pilot of a crop duster?"

"That's what I do. Have you got a need for some spraying?"

"No. I was just wondering if any strange characters had visited you asking questions recently."

There was a pause for a few seconds. "Lady, most of the people I deal with are a little strange. I'm a little strange myself. I'm a beer-drinking, tire-kicking redneck and proud of it. So, do you have a job for me or not?"

"Uh, no. But these men would be..."

Click.

They didn't have much luck with any of the others either.

After spending two hours making phone calls, they were no closer to finding out anything about Dr. Saad and Ameera.

"What are we going to do?" Regan asked.

"Beats me," Ty said. "I feel like we're at square one still."

Solly said, "When I get to a spot like this there's only one thing to do."

"What's that?" Ty said.

"Pray."

"What good is that going to do?" Ty said. "Is God going to drop a note from the sky giving us the address where the terrorists are hiding?"

"He could," Solly said quietly. "But I've learned that when I calm my mind and ask him for wisdom he gives me some new ideas."

Ty walked away and went into the kitchen. "You guys can have your prayer meeting. I'm going to head out to Chick-fil-A to rustle us up a little supper for later." He grabbed his keys and left.

Solly turned to Regan. "I'm not a religious fanatic like Ty

thinks. But I have found that prayer works. Would you like to join me?"

Regan said, "I haven't been doing much praying lately, to tell the truth. But I do believe in God, and I was baptized when I was a teenager. It can't hurt."

Solly smiled and said, "No it can't hurt. But prayer always works best if you believe you're going to get an answer. It's called praying by faith."

"How do I do that?" Regan asked.

"You ask God for something and then you believe he will answer. Be quiet in your spirit and listen to see if he speaks to you in a still, small voice."

Solly and Regan bowed their heads and Solly prayed. Then he said, "Now, Regan, why don't you pray?"

Regan felt inadequate, and she didn't know the right religious words, so she just mumbled, "Dear God, please help us. We can't do this without you."

They both remained quiet for a few minutes and Solly said, "Amen. Did you get any kind of impression from the Lord?"

Regan said, "It was the strangest thing. Bridget...I mean Ameera kept coming to my mind."

"Did God suggest to you where Ameera might be?"

"No. I just felt the need to pray for her. That's so crazy because up until now, I have been mad at her for getting me into this mess. But suddenly I felt sorry for her."

Several minutes later, Ty returned with a large, white sack full of food. "I've got grub. Who's hungry?" He went to the cabinet and started pulling out plates and glasses to set the table.

Solly said, "My brain is too busy trying to figure out what

we can do, but my stomach is reminding me that I need to eat."

"How about you, Regan? Hungry?" Ty asked.

"Sure, maybe after we've eaten, our brains will work better," she said.

As they dug into the sandwiches, chicken strips, and salad, the three of them were silent. They were each in their own world trying to figure out the next step.

Ty turned to Solly. "Something's been bothering me about this whole Cloud Strike business for several days."

"What is it, buddy?" Solly asked.

As Ty cleaned off the table, he explained, "When you showed me the War Scroll in Jerusalem that seemed to predict the 9/11 attacks, I was fascinated. But the fact remains that even though you had access to that prediction, there was nothing you or the U.S. government could do to stop it. It seemed destined to happen."

Solly said, "I think I know where you're going with this. But regarding the first prediction, before it happened, we couldn't be certain that the four silver vultures were airliners. We had no way of knowing that the fortress was the Pentagon and the tall towers referred to the World Trade Center. It wasn't until after the fact that the prediction made sense. Our warning to the C.I.A. before 9/11 wasn't based on that prophecy. Mossad had intercepted online traffic between Al-Qaeda operatives that hinted at the plan to hijack scheduled airlines."

Ty said, "Okay, well, how do we know for sure that second Dead Sea Scroll prophecy is predicting some kind of biological attack?"

Regan looked at both of them, confused.

Solly said, "We can't be certain, but it sounds like that's what was predicted." He opened his iPhone and scrolled down to a certain app. He said, "Let me read it to you again. Regan, you haven't heard this yet. The prediction says, *The people of the land of light neither humbled themselves nor repented of their sins. They rebuilt their fort and their towers, but their hearts were hardened. The Adversary gave them rest for a season to lull them to sleep. Yet they ignored Yahweh's warnings and played in their green pastures. Then the Destroyer interrupted their games and came upon the land to strike them down with a cloud of death. Thousands of the wealthy leaders perished as their breaths were ripped from their throats.*"

Regan was astonished. She said, "Are you sure that's not a hoax? There are plenty of crazy people out there who try to fake ancient prophecies to scare people or to make money."

Solly said, "I wish that was the case. But the carbon dating on the scroll that contained this prediction verifies that it was written 2,000 years ago."

43

3310 FOXTROT
Alpharetta, Georgia
3:45pm

Ty sat down beside Solly and said, "Here's my point. Let's just assume for a minute that it's a genuine prediction. What makes us think we can do anything to stop it? We couldn't prevent 9/11. Maybe this attack is going to happen, and there's nothing we can do. If that's true, we're wasting our time and energy. Solly, this God that you believe in never changes his mind, does he?"

Solly stroked his beard out of habit. "It's interesting you should bring this up, Ty. As I've already told you, you should read your Bible more. It's true that God says in Malachi 3:6, 'I, the Lord do not change.' However, there are many incidents in the Bible where God was threatening to punish a nation for their sins, but there was someone who prayed for them and God delayed his judgment."

"Huh?" Ty said. "I don't remember hearing anything about that in my college Bible classes."

Solly answered, "We Jews can be a rather, um, stiff-necked people. Do you recall when Moses was leading the children of

Israel from Egypt to the Promised Land?"

"I saw the movie starring Charlton Heston," Regan interjected.

Solly looked at Regan and said, "The book is better."

Everyone laughed and the tense atmosphere broke a little.

Solly launched back into his Bible history lesson. "There were multiple times when the rebellious people rejected God's leader and God's commands. In response, God announced his plan to destroy them. But Moses prayed for the people—and God withheld his judgment."

"I don't remember that in the movie," Ty said.

"Here, let me read this to you," Solly said. He scrolled down his Bible app until he found Exodus 32. "While Moses was on Mount Sinai receiving the Ten Commandments, the people were worshipping a golden calf they had made, remember that?"

Ty said, "Yes, I think that *was* in the movie."

"Well, God told Moses that he was going to destroy all the people for their idolatry. But Moses prayed for the people and God listened. Here's what Moses prayed in Exodus 32:31-32: *Oh what a great sin these people have committed! They have made for themselves gods of gold. But now, please forgive their sin—but if not, then blot me out of the book you have written.* God was planning to wipe out the Israelites, but Moses interceded for them and God delayed his punishment."

"Okay, so I understand that. But Moses is dead," Ty said. "Who's going to pray the same prayer for America?"

Solly sighed and said, "Well, I know that many Christians in America are praying for their nation. They are asking God to withhold his judgment. We don't want America to suffer another 9/11. So for the past seven years, thousands of Jewish believers in Israel have paused every evening at 8:00pm to pray for your nation. We're praying that America will repent and that God will not punish you. So, I'm believing that even though this attack was prophesied in the scrolls, it still may be averted."

"Well, good luck with that one, Solly," Ty said. "We're no closer today to finding Dr. Saad than we were a week ago."

Solly said, "I'm not depending on luck..."

Regan shifted nervously in her seat.

Ty held up his hand and interrupted, "I know, I know, you're depending on God ...but where was he in 9/11 when all those people were killed?"

Solly was stunned by Ty's angry response. But he knew they were all under a lot of pressure. He said gently, "God was in the same place he was when his only Son suffered and died."

44

APRIL 12

East Point, Georgia
10:45am

Ameera left the apartment and walked down the block to the warehouse where the lab was located. She punched in the ten-digit code on the keypad and the door opened with a loud "click."

Through the protective glass, she looked into the large lab. She saw that the refrigerated truck was running, with the exhaust vented through a window. The truck was backed up to the door of the large walk-in freezer. Yamani, Ali, and Nasser were wearing full biohazard suits with oxygen tanks. They were carefully transporting the jerry cans full of botulinum from the walk-in freezer into the back of the truck. Under Dr. Saad's supervision, who also wore a hazmat suit, they carefully transferred the liquid chemical into a stainless steel tank inside the refrigerated section of the truck's cargo area. They carried the empty jerry cans back into the freezer.

When they were finished, the men walked through a sterile room where they rinsed their biohazard suits under a decontamination shower.

Finally, the four men emerged into the office area. They were exhausted but excited about the last stage of their daring plan.

Ameera silently prayed for courage. "Father, I need to talk to you privately."

Dr. Saad led her into his small office and said, "What is it, Princess? We don't have much time before we drive to Greensboro."

She barged into her complaint, "I am really concerned about this plan."

Dr. Saad sighed. "It's a fool-proof plan. We've been over it dozens of times. Today is the day we've lived for since the devils killed your mother and brother."

"I know, Papa," Ameera said, using the term she used as a child. "But I'm having second thoughts. Why are we killing thousands of innocent people?"

Dr. Saad looked at his daughter incredulously. "How can you ask a stupid question like that?"

Ameera continued, "I'm just asking why we are killing all these people. All of a sudden, it doesn't make any sense to me. Murdering these people won't bring Mama or Akmed back."

Dr. Saad's face was turning red. "This isn't murder! It's war! And we didn't start it. The arrogant Americans came to our home and destroyed our family. Since that day, I've had nothing to live for."

For the first time in her life, Ameera was frightened of what her father might say or do to her. "Papa, you still have *me*. We're still a family. But for the last two years, you've been so consumed with revenge that you haven't treated me like your daughter. I've just been a fellow soldier. Vengeance is destroying you from the inside."

Dr. Saad's frustration and anger came boiling to the surface. "What's gotten into you? Why are you talking like this?"

Ameera hesitated, but then the story came flooding out of her heart. "I had several dreams where I saw Isa. Jesus spoke to me and told me he loved me. I've heard that other Muslims have had similar dreams. I've been praying to him."

Her testimony was met with stony silence. Tears streaming down her cheeks, she continued. "I've been reading the Bible, Father, and it teaches that we should be willing to forgive those who have hurt us."

Something changed in Dr. Saad's eyes, like he had made a split-second decision. He looked at Ameera as if he didn't recognize her. Then to her surprise he said, "Will you show me what you've been reading?"

"Sure, Father!" Ameera said. She turned to the desktop computer in the office to access BibleGateway.

With a few clicks, she found the website and logged onto the Gospel according to Matthew. "Let me read you this," Ameera said as she twirled around in the desk chair to show it to her father.

Suddenly, she saw that Yamani and Ali had joined him. Yamani had an automatic pistol in his hand. He was pointing it at her face.

Dr. Saad said, "My daughter is dead. I don't know who this devil is, but she is no longer my daughter."

With that, he turned and walked out of the office.

"You dirty traitor!" Yamani yelled. Spit flew from his mouth and she dodged her head to avoid it. He stepped forward and drew the pistol back before violently swinging it toward her head. Ameera tried to avoid the blow by ducking, but she was too slow. The pistol struck her above the right temple.

Stars exploded in front of her eyes. Then the pain came. She lost her balance and crumpled from the chair to the floor. She could feel the wet, sticky blood begin to pool from her head. She was barely conscious.

"Take her into the storeroom and tie her up!" Yamani said.

Ameera felt rough hands grabbing her by the arms. She tried to resist but didn't have any strength.

Ali dragged her across the floor and out into the warehouse.

The concrete floor scratched her legs and she was vaguely aware that she had lost her shoes because she could feel the cold. She heard a door open as they moved her into a storeroom.

"Use the duct tape on her hands and feet. Cover her mouth as well!" Yamani shouted. "But don't cover her eyes. I want her to see me put a bullet into her."

Ali grabbed the roll of silver duct tape. He roughly threw her onto her stomach and wrenched her arms behind her. Sitting on her back, he wrapped several layers of the thick duct tape around her wrists. It was so tight that her hands began to tingle from the loss of blood flow.

He turned around and grabbed her legs, pulling them straight out. Keeping her ankles together, he wrapped several layers of tape around them and threw her bare feet back on the floor, crushing her toes.

Then he grabbed her left shoulder and flipped her over like

a rag doll. The back of her head smacked on the hard concrete.

"Pull her up so she can see me," Yamani ordered.

Ali pulled her to a sitting position and leaned her against a storage shelf. He pulled off another strip of duct tape and applied it to her mouth.

Ameera was struggling to breathe. The blood from her left temple had gotten into her eye when she had been lying face down on the floor. Her vision in that eye was blurred. Still, she could see the hatred in Yamani's face.

In a moment of clarity, she thought how ironic it was that she had been so close to this team during the planning of this mission. They had been comrades. But hate and jihad were the things that bound them together. When the hate left her heart, so did her desire to kill. Her father didn't recognize her because she had changed. She realized that before a few days ago she had been exactly like these two men. If she died today, she was glad that she had experienced this new life for a few days.

Yamani walked over to her and kicked her in the ribs. Ameera coughed in pain and felt certain that her ribs had cracked. She had to fight even harder to breathe.

"Filthy swine!" Yamani yelled. This time she couldn't avoid the spit that flew from his mouth.

"I should put a bullet between your eyes, but an instant death would be too merciful for you."

He began to wave the pistol toward different parts of her body, teasing her.

Instead of being afraid, a sense of calm and peace filled her mind. She prayed silently, "Lord Jesus, give me strength to die well for you."

"I've got it," Yamani said. "A gut shot. You'll live for a few minutes, but then you'll die in agonizing misery."

He pointed the gun at her torso and fired.

Ameera's eyes were closed, but she jumped at the sound of the pistol discharging in a small room. She felt a fiery, hot pain in her abdomen, but she didn't lose consciousness.

"Allah Akbar!" Yamani shouted. "We have killed our first infidel today! But it won't be our last!"

Yamani and Ali turned and left the storage room, slamming the door.

Ameera was alone in total darkness. But she felt herself sliding toward a bright light.

45

East Point, Georgia
11:32am

Ameera groaned as she regained consciousness. She felt as if half of her torso was on fire. She never imagined how much pain a tiny bullet could cause. With her hands taped behind her back, she couldn't feel her stomach, but she could tell that her lap and hips were covered with blood—her blood. And there was nothing she could do except to die a slow death.

She prayed silently, "Please, God, I don't ask you to save me. Take me into your arms. But please give me the strength to save the people who are being attacked today."

She had always been limber, and she wondered if she could move her hands under her feet and bring them back in front of her body. Carefully easing herself down on her right side, she curled her knees up toward her chest as tight as she could. Every movement sent hot, searing pain into her side. Then she maneuvered her hands toward her feet until they were behind her ankles. She realized that she would have to jerk her legs up at the same time she pushed her hands under her heels. She was out of strength and fading fast. But she willed the effort to make the motion.

She heard a voice scream. Then she realized it was hers. But it had worked. Her hands were in front of her. She lay on her side panting. The floor was slick from her blood. She looked down for the first time and noticed that the blood was seeping from a wound between her navel and side. Yamani's aim was a little off—or else she would be dead now. But that didn't matter because she would soon bleed out anyway.

Using both her hands to push herself up, she sat on her knees and looked around. A dirty window at the top of the storage room admitted a faint light. She looked around but saw nothing that she could use. The shelves were stacked with cardboard boxes containing lab supplies.

"God, I can't do this without you," she sobbed. "Please help me."

Then she caught a glimpse of something that had fallen under one of the metal shelves. It was just across the room. Using her hands as leverage, she crawled across the floor on her knees. Each motion only intensified the pain, and by the time she had covered eight feet, she was nauseous from the effort.

Now back down on her side, she looked under the shelf and saw the answer to her prayer. A box cutter with a razor sharp blade had fallen under the shelf.

"Thank you, God," she cried.

She moved her hands under it and started sliding out the knife inch by inch. Even though her hands were taped together, she was able to pick up the box cutter with her right hand. Holding the blade toward her, she started a sawing motion. She knew that if she missed she would cut her wrists, but what did it matter now? She was dying anyway.

The razor blade sliced through the duct tape, but there were too many layers. Her hand began to cramp from the tedious back and forth motion with the box cutter. She changed hands and started sawing the tape with her left hand. Finally, there was enough of an opening that when she pried her hands apart, the remaining tape broke.

Ameera ripped the duct tape off her mouth and gulped a fresh lungful of air. She bent over in pain from the effort. She was getting weak, and her vision was blurry. She just wanted to lie down and go to sleep.

Shaking off the new spasm of pain, she cut the duct tape around her ankles. Every movement took her full concentration. She was free now, but what could she do? She was too weak to stand, so she crawled to the door and tried the knob. She assumed it would be locked, but the door opened.

She glanced up and saw a wireless phone on the desk across the office. If only she could reach it. But then the dizziness took over and Ameera slumped to the floor. Her last conscious thought was that she would wake up in heaven.

46

April 12

FBI Regional Office
2635 Century Parkway N.E.
Atlanta, Georgia
11:42am

C.I.A. Director Tony Parker had never visited the Atlanta FBI office before.

After landing at Hartsfield International in the Agency's Gulfstream, Parker and his aides were met by a U.S. Army UH-60 Black Hawk helicopter from Fort McPherson. After boarding, it took less than 15 minutes to reach the helipad behind the FBI office in northeast Atlanta.

As he rode the chrome and glass elevator in the modern office building, he turned to his two aides and said, "I suspected the FBI has a larger office budget than we do. Look at this place."

The elevator arrived at the fourth floor and the group exited into a large reception area. It was appointed with burl wood and furnishings that looked as if they belonged in a prosperous law firm.

A field agent was waiting. "Director Parker? I'm Agent

Kapa. I'm the Agent in Charge for this office. This way, please. Director Cagle is waiting for you in my office."

AIC Kapa led the group straight through a large room filled with cubicles. Inside each cubicle, field agents were either talking on their phones or working feverishly on their laptops—many of them were doing both. Tony noticed that everyone was formally dressed—coats and ties for the men. Dark slacks or skirts with matching jackets for the female agents.

Director Bridgeman Cagle was waiting for them outside Kapa's office. He extended his hand to Parker and nodded at his two aides. "Gentlemen, please come in."

Kapa's office filled half the entire fourth floor with its own reception area where three assistants were busy at desks. They stood when the group arrived and followed them into the office. Parker noticed floor-to-ceiling windows spanning two full walls. He detected the slight refraction of the light, which indicated that these were mirrored glass—and bulletproof as well.

"Have a seat," Director Cagle said as he indicated a large conference table set to the side of the room. The Director took the head seat and Parker sat to his right. Kapa sat to his left. The other agents took their seats and immediately pulled out their laptops to provide updated Intel on the operation.

Director Cagle said, "Agent Kapa, please bring Director Parker up to speed on what you've gotten so far."

"It isn't much. We've supplied the picture of Dr. Saad to all the local law enforcement agencies. They have a BOLO alert for him. But nobody has seen him."

Kapa continued, "We contacted all the medical lab

equipment suppliers in the area. We asked about any unusual orders. We think we got a hit. Six weeks ago, there was an unusual order for six, large, sterile storage tanks and three molecular multipliers. However, the customer's company name and address turned out to be bogus."

"That had to cost a lot of money. Can't you trace the credit card or check used for payment?" Director Cagle asked.

"Yes, sir. The total bill was a little over $62,000, but it was paid for by a debit card from a local bank."

"Whose bank account is it?" Director Cagle asked.

"Again, the name and address on the account turned out to be bogus," Kapa said. "We interviewed an employee of the bank who remembers that a woman with a French accent opened the account. It's not every day that someone opens an account with $80,000 cash."

"Cash?" Parker asked. "Aren't banks required to report any cash transaction over $10,000 to the government?"

"That's for withdrawals, but not deposits," Kapa explained.

"What else did the teller remember about the woman?" Director Cagle inquired.

Kapa replied, "As I said, she spoke broken English with a French accent. She had short, blonde hair and wore a hat and large sunglasses. Here's the video from the surveillance camera at the bank. But as you can see, she keeps her head down."

"Has there been any other activity on the account?"

"No sir. We're monitoring the account. If the credit card is used again, we'll be notified. We have a SWAT team standing by to respond by chopper."

Director Cagle had a reputation for having a volcanic

temper, and it was getting close to erupting. Biting off every word to maintain a measure of calmness, he demanded, "Is that all you have for me? Don't tell me I brought the Director of the C.I.A. all the way down here to tell him we don't have a single lead."

"There's more, sir," Kapa said apologetically. He pointed to a tall man standing behind the group. "This is our chemical weapons expert, Dr. Richard Handley. He believes that the most probable way a chemical or biological weapon would be deployed would be through a water system. Terrorists have attempted it before and failed. We have divided our agents and law enforcement teams into groups watching the water delivery systems for every community within 100 miles of Atlanta."

"How many water systems are we talking about?" Parker asked.

Kapa looked at one of the assistants for the answer. "Eighty-six water systems for communities with a population of over 5,000."

"That sounds like a waste of manpower to me," Parker remarked. "We don't even know if Dr. Saad is in the Atlanta area. And we're not certain when he has planned an attack. This kind of plan is going to chew up dollars in a blink of an eye."

Director Cagle slammed his fist on the table. "The President has authorized us to use any and all means necessary to uncover and prevent such an attack. He told me to spend whatever it takes to get it done."

Parker didn't say it, but he thought it was dangerous to give any government agency a blank check. "It's a good thing our government can print more money," he said and stood to his feet to leave. His assistants obediently trailed behind him.

As he left, Parker wondered if Solly had uncovered any more Intel on this threat. But he had no clue about how to contact him. He would just have to hope that Solly would call him again—and soon.

47

East Point, Georgia
12:44pm

Ameera was singing her favorite childhood song in Arabic. She was playing with her family in a beautiful park. She saw the faces of her mother and her brother smiling at her. But when she looked at her father, his face was full of anger and hatred. Ameera wondered, *How can this be Paradise if I'm afraid of my father?*

The dream slowly dissolved and she regained consciousness. She tried to move. The biting pain in her left side reassured her that she wasn't in Paradise. Then she remembered she was still in the warehouse where her father had manufactured enough botulinum to kill tens of thousands of people. She was bleeding. She knew she was dying. What could she do? The phone.

Ameera began to crawl across the office. The desk was only six feet away, but it might as well have been twenty. She didn't think she could make it.

God help me, she prayed. She crawled another step and prayed again, *God, help me.*

She was losing perspective of time. It seemed as if she had

been crawling for hours when it had only been a few seconds. She felt her head bump into the office chair. Her life was slowly seeping out with her blood, but she knew she had to do something. She was finding it extremely hard to concentrate.

"Come on! What am I trying to do?" she cried.

Then she remembered. She pulled herself up beside the desk and grabbed the phone. As she did, she collapsed onto her side again but managed to keep her grip on the handset. But she had no idea who to call. Then she punched in a number from her memory and prayed that it would work.

48

3310 Foxtrot
Alpharetta, Georgia
12:50pm

Regan's cell phone rang and she glanced at the screen. She didn't recognize the number, but the area code indicated it was from the Atlanta area. She started to reject the call and send it to voice mail, but something inside her made her answer.

"Hello?" Regan said.

There was no reply. She was about to hang up when she heard a faint voice say, "Regan...it's me."

"Who is this?" Regan asked urgently.

"It's...Bridget."

Regan wondered at first if this was a cruel prank. But who else besides the three of them in the room knew that Bridget was Ameera?

"Bridget!" Regan said. "Where are you?" Solly and Ty snapped to attention.

Ameera spoke in a voice that was barely above a whisper. "I'm dying. Please listen. Jesus came to me in dreams. I love Him. My father had me shot."

"What are you talking about?" Regan said.

"No time. Listen. Botulinum...sprayed on people at golf game...today. They plan to steal airplane from the green airport."

"I don't understand what you're talking about. Where are you now?"

The voice on the phone was barely intelligible now. "Regan...I am sorry for hurting you in Paris... Forgive me."

Regan heard a loud crack as if the receiver had been dropped on the floor.

Silence.

"Bridget! Ameera! Talk to me. Where are you?" Regan demanded.

Silence.

"Are you there? We can send someone to help you!" Regan shouted into the receiver.

Nothing. Regan ended the call and turned to Solly and Ty.

"That was Ameera. She sounded crazy. Like she was out of her head. She claimed that her father had shot her. She said something about seeing Jesus. It didn't make much sense to me. She asked me to forgive her. Then it sounded like she dropped the phone."

Solly said, "What else did she say? Try to remember her exact words."

Regan closed her eyes. "She said something about botulinum sprayed on a golf game today. Then she said something about a green airport."

The color drained out of Solly's face. "If they have botulinum toxin in their possession, this scenario just got a thousand times worse. Botulinum is more deadly than anthrax and sarin combined. It's the most lethal substance on the planet."

"The Masters tournament," Ty said softly. "That's the premier sporting event in the world this weekend. Did she say when they were planning the attack?"

"Today!" Regan said.

"We've got to warn the people at Augusta immediately!" Ty shouted as he pulled out his cell phone. "It's time to call the authorities and notify them."

"Not so fast, Ty," Solly said. "There are all kinds of crazies who call in threats to major sporting events. If you called them, they would come after you. Have you considered that this might be a ploy? Ameera could have been calling to provide misinformation. She might have been trying to get us to go in the wrong direction while they strike somewhere else. We need more proof."

Turning to Regan, Solly asked, "What did she say about a green airport?"

"She said something about stealing an airplane," Regan said.

Ty said, "If she was telling the truth, they may be planning to hijack a crop duster. And one of the airports we called that has a crop duster is Greene County."

Solly spoke up, "I called that airport this morning and left a message."

Ty rushed over to the aviation sectional chart for Atlanta and ran his finger eastward from Atlanta. "Here it is. It's outside of Greensboro, which is exactly halfway between Atlanta and Augusta. Let me call them again."

Solly looked at his list and gave Ty the number. It rang six times and then a recorded voice came on that said, "You've reached Hap Potter with Potter Crop Dusting. I can't talk right now. Leave a message and I'll get back to you as soon as I can."

Ty hung up.

"What should we do now?" Regan asked. "We can't just sit here."

"You're right. Ty, how fast do you think you can drive us to Greensboro?" Solly asked.

"Faster than you could, old man," Ty said. "Let's go."

They grabbed their bags and equipment. Solly handed Ty a heavy black bag that he had taken off the private jet.

"What's in here?" Ty asked.

"Enough firepower to stop some terrorists," Solly said.

49

APRIL 12

Greene County Airport
Greensboro, Georgia
2:05pm

Hap had used his tractor to pull his AT-602 up to the chemical tanks. His newest customer, Max Phillips, had called to say that they would deliver the chemical by 1:30pm. They were late and it was a slow day at the airport. The grounds were deserted except for him, Jeanette the FBO receptionist, and Pete, a local CFI hoping for a student.

Hap mindlessly scratched his whiskers and thought about a message he had gotten on his voice mail earlier that morning. It was someone asking if he had encountered any strange characters inquiring about crop dusting jobs. He'd laughed it off because the guy's voice had sounded like he was from Australia. He wondered if it was one of his pilot buddies just playing a prank on him. But this new Max customer was certainly a little strange. He checked his watch. Where was he anyway?

He looked up at the sky. At least he had a fine spring day to fly. The wind could be really strong, but after a cold front had barreled through a couple of nights ago, there was low humidity and light winds.

He saw the old minivan pull up into the parking lot. A large refrigerated truck was following it and waited at the gate that led to the airport ramp. Hap started toward the office just as three men walked in the front door. He recognized two of them as Max and his son. He started to greet them, but then to his horror, one of them raised a pistol and fired two shots, hitting Jeannette between the eyes. Pete came running out of the flight planning room and was gunned downed by another man who had produced an AK-47.

With the sound of gunfire and the smell of cordite heavy in the air, Hap pivoted to run back outside onto the ramp. If he could somehow make it to his hangar he could retrieve his Sig Saur pistol to defend himself. But he was too slow.

Yamani screamed, "Stop, you devil! One more step and I'll shoot you in the back!"

Hap stopped. His brain was working feverishly trying to think about how to call for help.

"Put your hands up and turn around."

Hap raised his hands and turned. Dr. Saad and Ali searched the offices of the FBO and came back shouting in a language that Hap didn't understand.

Dr. Saad said, "I need the key to unlock the gate to allow my truck onto the ramp. Give it to me."

Hap was too stunned to speak. He shuffled over to the main counter. He shuddered when he saw the body of Jeannette twisted on the floor where she had fallen from the gunshot to her head. A dark pool of blood was spreading on the tile floor.

Hap reached under the counter and pulled out a key on a large wooden key ring. He held it up. "This is the key to the gate."

Yamani said, "And now, please be so good as to open the gate so we can deliver the chemical to your plane."

Hap turned and looked his adversary in the eye. He said, "Think again, you fool. I don't know who you are or what you're doing. But I know one thing. I'm not flying for you today. You can kill me, but I'm not going to be involved in any of this wicked business."

"I expected you to say something like that. I don't need you to fly. I'll be flying your airplane. And, inshallah, after today you and your plane will be famous—or at least infamous," Yamani said with a wicked grin.

He squeezed the trigger. Hap was dead before he hit the floor. As he fell, his last thought was about seeing his Dorothy in heaven soon.

50

INTERSTATE 20

55 miles east of Atlanta
2:25pm

Ty had been driving his Chevy Tahoe well above the speed limit since leaving the Atlanta area. He had kept his eyes open for State Troopers. The last thing he needed now was to be pulled over for speeding. As always, Interstate 20 was packed with cars, and most of them were going well above the posted speed limit.

"Pull over at this next rest area," Solly instructed from the back seat where he and Regan sat.

"What's wrong? You need to take a bathroom break?" Ty asked.

"No. We need to get some of our weapons out of the back."

They pulled off the exit and parked away from other vehicles. Ty raised the tailgate and Solly unzipped the long, black bag.

Ty whistled. "You didn't tell me you were bringing *all* your toys."

"You never know what you're going to face, and you only get one chance to be outgunned in a firefight. What would you like?"

"I'll start with the Uzi pistol," Ty said. "What is that you have?"

"It's a Heckler and Koch UMP9," Solly said. "It fires a 9x19mm hollow point cartridge. It will stop an elephant—and any other living creature." Solly grabbed the short assault weapon and added three curved magazines to his jacket pocket. He tossed three Uzi magazines to Ty. "Let's go."

When they were back on the highway, Regan was checking their location on the GPS on her iPhone. "The Greensboro exit is coming up in about 15 miles. The airport is a couple of miles northeast of the town."

Ty pressed down on the accelerator.

51

GREENE COUNTRY AIRPORT
Greensboro, Georgia
2:35pm

Yamani took the key that had fallen out of Hap's hand and walked out toward the fence. He unlocked the large padlock and rolled the gate open. He motioned for Nasser to drive the truck onto the ramp behind the flight office. Yamani walked slowly in front of the truck directing Nasser to back up near the chemical tanks in front of the airplane.

Once the truck was stopped, Yamani rolled up the back door and pulled a heavy chest from the floor of the truck. He dropped it to the ground and opened it, pulling out two of the hazmat suits with their oxygen tanks and masks.

Ali and Nasser donned the suits and made sure the oxygen system was operating. Then they climbed up into the back of the truck and opened the lock that led to the refrigerated section. Cold air blew out from the compartment containing the stainless steel tank that held the deadly toxin. Ali picked up a long rubber hose and attached one end to the top of the tank. When he was sure the seal was tight, he carried the hose to the door of the truck, unwinding it carefully. He handed the hose to Nasser who unwound it as he carried it toward the plane parked on the ramp.

When he reached the plane, he opened the tank to the hopper beneath the fuselage. Once the end of the hose was coupled with the airtight nozzle going into the hopper, he turned and gave a thumbs-up sign to Yamani and Dr. Saad who were standing behind the flight office.

"We are ready, Dr. Saad," Yamani said.

Dr. Saad was holding a scientific calculator. "Wait, let me check something."

The current air temperature at ground level was 19 degrees Celsius, but the chemical temperature was minus 2 degrees in the tank. Dr. Saad thought aloud, "The ideal temperature for the best dispersion of the droplets will be about 10 degrees Celsius. The warming rate of botulinum in an outside temperature of 19 degrees is two degrees every twelve minutes." He continued to input numbers into his calculator. "What did you say your flying time to the golf course would be?"

"Once I get airborne, it will take me only about 35 minutes to be over Augusta," Yamani said.

"Excellent," Dr. Saad replied. "Start transferring the chemical. But delay your takeoff for 20 more minutes."

Yamani turned toward Nasser and circled his finger to signal that the transfer could begin.

Inside the back of the truck, Ali pushed a button on the side of the stainless steel tank. An electric pump began whirring, and he monitored the transfer of 500 gallons of the most toxic substance on earth into the hopper of the crop duster.

52

Greensboro, Georgia
2:55pm

Ty had taken the exit into the sleepy town of Greensboro. It was a Saturday afternoon, but the downtown area was almost deserted. Regan, still studying her GPS, was providing directions to the airport.

"Take highway 278 out of town and the airport should be on the left."

In a few minutes, Ty saw a green sign with an outline of an airplane and an arrow pointing left. He roared down the airport access highway.

"What are we going to say to the people at the airport?" Regan asked.

"We'll just ask them if they've seen any unusual characters around the airport today," Solly said. "But keep your eyes open for anything out of the ordinary."

"You do know that this is rural Georgia?" Regan said. "We have plenty of strange characters who have lived here all their lives."

"I want to talk to Hap Potter, the owner," Ty said.

As they pulled up in the parking lot in front of the FBO, they saw a couple of old pickup trucks, a beat up Chevy Impala, and a Ford mini-van that had seen its best days.

"You guys stay in the car," Ty said.

He stuffed the Uzi under his shirt in the back of his jeans and got out of the SUV. He walked through the front doors and looked around the office. There was nobody in sight.

"Hello," he said, "Anybody here?"

He walked over to the counter and saw the body of the receptionist where she had fallen. His instincts kicked in immediately. He pulled the Uzi out and held it with both hands. He walked quietly toward the doors leading out to the ramp. As he turned the corner, he saw the body of Hap Potter collapsed in a pool of crimson. Through the glass doors, he observed two men standing on the ramp. They were watching a third man wearing a hazmat suit disconnect a hose from the underbelly of a bright yellow crop duster.

Ty glanced at the older of the first two men. He couldn't see all of his face, but from the side he appeared to resemble Dr. Hakeem Saad.

Ty turned and walked quietly back out through the flight office to the parking lot, out of sight of the three men. He put a finger to his lips to indicate that Solly and Regan should keep quiet. He motioned them to the back of the Tahoe.

Ty whispered, "There are three dead bodies in the flight office. Maybe more. A truck is loading chemicals into a crop duster now. Two men are watching from the ramp and I think one of them is Dr. Saad."

Solly took charge and said, "Our first priority is stopping

that plane. Our next priority is capturing or neutralizing the enemy. Did you see any other people?"

"The back of the truck is open, so there could be others," Ty said. "What's the plan?"

Solly said, "First, Regan, you're going to get in this truck and drive back toward town. When you are out of danger, call 911 and say there's an emergency at the Greene County Airport. Tell them there's a bomb or a plane has crashed or something. I don't want you in harm's way."

Regan was fuming. "You call 911. I'm not leaving you. This started with me, and I'm going to see it to the end—whatever that may be."

Solly conceded. "Okay, you can stay. Here's a Beretta with a full clip. Just pull back on this slide on top to load it. Keep your head down and keep your phone handy. If things go wrong, call 911 immediately."

At that moment, things went wrong.

Without warning, the truck came barreling around the corner of the flight office. When Nasser saw the three of them holding guns, he jammed on the accelerator and aimed the vehicle toward them.

"Get down!" Solly shouted as he shoved Regan to the ground beside the Tahoe.

Ty ran across the parking lot, hoping to divert the truck away from Solly and Regan. He started pouring rounds into the windshield. The truck didn't slow down but veered toward Solly and Regan who were crouched behind the SUV. The driver held an automatic pistol out the window, shattering the windows of the Tahoe with dozens of rounds.

Pointing his weapon toward the front doors of the FBO, Solly fired two short bursts and blew out the glass. Then he grabbed Regan by the shoulder and almost lifted her off her feet. "Quick! Into the flight office!" Still crouching, they ran through what was left of the doors and fell in a heap on the floor.

From the other side of the parking lot, Ty inhaled slowly and took a bead on the head of the driver. As he exhaled, he gently squeezed the trigger. He saw the driver's head explode and watched in horror as the truck slammed into the back of his Tahoe, igniting the fuel tank. A massive explosion blew glass and metal in every direction. He ducked away from the debris and screamed, thinking Solly and Regan were still beside the truck.

***

Out on the ramp, Yamani had started running toward the plane at the first sound of gunfire. Shielded by the flight office, Dr. Saad and Yamani had no idea who was firing. Then they heard a huge explosion as a black cloud of smoke and flames arose from the parking area.

"Take off immediately! May Allah bless your effort, my son!" Dr. Saad shouted. "Don't let anything stop you from your mission!"

Dr. Saad and Ali took up defensive positions behind a concrete partition near the taxiway and aimed their guns at the back door of the FBO. They waited for soldiers or policemen to emerge, but there was no movement.

Yamani reached the crop duster and climbed the rungs on the side of the fuselage into the one-man cockpit. He pulled the cockpit cover downward and latched it into place. There was a noise-attenuating headset on the seat and he placed it over his head, making sure it was plugged in.

With practiced ease, he turned the booster pump on and then the ignition switch. The familiar whine of the booster pump did little to calm his nerves. He watched the ITT gauge climb to the proper temperature and switched off the ignition. Once the four-bladed prop was spinning freely, he pushed the power level forward. The 1,000 horsepower engine roared as he fed it more power.

He released the brake and started taxiing forward just enough to get some momentum to turn his tail wheel. He stomped hard on the left rudder and the plane swung in an arc toward the single taxiway. As he taxied, he glanced at the windsock to determine the direction of the wind. He quickly dialed in 800 feet AGL on the altimeter. Then he switched on the avionics master switch and clicked the frequency to 128.1 to monitor Atlanta Center ATC chatter.

How did they find us? Who has come to stop us? Yamani wondered. If it was the U.S. Military, he knew he would never make it off the ground. At any moment, he expected a missile from a military chopper to slam into his cockpit.

Dr. Saad had told him that even if he were shot down while airborne, the toxin would spread and cause casualties—especially if he was over a populated area. Yamani was ready to die as a martyr for Allah.

***

Out in the parking lot, Ty's ears were ringing from the sound of the explosion. But he then heard another sound that alarmed him. He could detect the distinctive whine of a turbo-prop engine revving up. That could only mean one thing. The crop duster was taking off. He had to stop him somehow.

Resigning himself to the fate of Regan and Solly, Ty sprinted around the side of the FBO building where the truck had emerged. At the corner, he cautiously glanced out onto the ramp. He saw the bright yellow crop duster taxiing toward the single runway.

Without thinking, Ty broke in a run for the taxiway. He started firing his Uzi at the plane, although at this range he had little hope of hitting it. He hadn't run more than a dozen steps when the ground around him exploded from shots being fired at him. He glanced to the right and saw two men firing from behind a partition. He dove for cover near the chemical tank stand. The thin metal bars didn't offer much protection, and he crouched as low as he could. He was trapped with bullets pinging off the metal and kicking up pavement around him. All alone, he was outnumbered and outgunned.

53

Greene County Airport
3:05 pm

Still shaken from the explosion, Solly rolled off Regan and asked, "Are you okay?"

Regan said, "My ears are hurting. But I think I'm okay." Then she laughed nervously. "Sorry, you have glass and concrete dust in your beard."

Ignoring the debris, Solly said, "Let's go. We've got to stop that plane." They carefully made their way across the lobby toward the back doors leading to the ramp. Regan recoiled when she saw Hap's body. Solly knelt and placed a finger on his neck. "He's dead."

They knelt near the glass doors and saw the crop duster taxiing toward the runway. They heard gunfire. To the right, they could see two men behind a barrier firing at Ty.

Solly led Regan to a side door exiting the office, hoping to sneak up behind the two men and surprise them.

Ali kept firing at the figure they had pinned down across the ramp. They had expected an army, or a SWAT team; instead, there was only one man. Dr. Saad watched as Yamani taxied the crop duster to the runway and turned left. He taxied so fast that his tail wheel was off the ground. It appeared for a moment that he was trying to take off. But as the plane approached the end of the asphalt strip, it slowed and then turned completely around.

Yamani jammed the power lever forward and the engine roared to life. He pointed the nose down runway 7 and kept the nose wheel centered on the middle. He breathed a little easier when the tail wheel came off the ground and he had rudder control. He glanced at the airspeed indicator monitor. When the indicator touched 80 knots, he pulled back on the yoke and climbed into the sky. Yamani always loved the way this airplane climbed like a homesick angel. He realized it would be the last time he would ever take off. This was his day to die for the cause of jihad.

Dr. Saad gave silent praise to Allah as he watched the crop duster soar steeply in the sky and bank right toward Augusta. He and Ali continued to fire toward the figure still trapped near the chemical tanks. They were so focused on Ty that they hadn't even noticed Solly and Regan creep up behind them.

"Hands up!" Solly shouted.

Without hesitation, Ali turned and raised his weapon to fire. Before he could complete his turn, Solly cut him down with a burst from his UMP9.

"Dr. Saad, I suggest you show more wisdom than your young friend here. Throw down your weapon and put your hands up!"

Dr. Saad turned around slowly with his weapon in his hands. But he didn't raise his gun. "And just who are you?" he asked.

"Who I am doesn't matter," Solly said. "What matters is that we know who you are and what you're trying to do."

"There's nothing you can do to stop us. Allah will smile today because we will strike a blow against the Great Satan. I've already won. You'll never take me alive. Either I am going to kill you, or you will kill me. And if you kill me, I will go to Paradise and be rewarded as a great martyr!"

Dr. Saad raised his weapon toward Solly.

Solly aimed lower and with a burst of fire blew out Dr. Saad's left kneecap. He screamed in agony and fell to the ground, dropping his assault weapon.

"You aren't going to Paradise—you're just going to prison for a long time."

Solly stepped over to him and kicked his weapon away. He checked to make sure the other terrorist was dead. Then he searched Dr. Saad's pockets and removed his cell phone. He threw it as far away as he could. Then he picked up the AK-47 and handed it to Regan who held it awkwardly in her arms.

He knelt down beside Dr. Saad who was writhing in pain. Solly said, "I'll call someone to come and collect what's left of you and take you to a prison hospital. Meanwhile, we've got a plane to stop."

About that time, Ty came running across the ramp yelling, "You're alive! We don't have any time to waste. We've got to stop that plane!"

"Great thinking, Sherlock," Solly said and pointed across the ramp to a twin-engine turboprop. "Can you fly that King Air?"

Ty said, "I can fly anything with two wings. You and Regan untie the ropes from the wings and the tail and I'll go inside to look for the key."

Solly and Regan ran toward the King Air while Ty dashed

into the flight office. He ran into the inner office and saw a board with various keys hanging on hooks. He searched until he found the one with "Beechcraft King Air" on the key ring. He grabbed it and ran back out to the ramp.

Sprinting to the left side of the aircraft, he unlocked the door and pulled down the air stairs. "Climb in and pull the door closed behind you. Regan, join me in the cockpit. We'll let Solly ride in the back so he'll have a better shot."

Regan ducked her head to follow Ty toward the cockpit. Her impression was that this was an old aircraft, and it smelled stale from sitting closed up for a long time. Ty jumped in the left seat and pointed to the right seat for Regan. He buckled his seat belt and shoulder harness. He looked around until he found a booklet containing the aircraft checklist. "Sit down here beside me and grab that headset in the seat. Buckle your seat belt and your shoulder harness."

"Have you ever flown an airplane like this before?" Regan asked.

"Well, not exactly like this, but all planes are basically the same. You pull the yoke toward you and the trees get smaller. You push the yoke forward and the trees get bigger. It's simple. Now take this and read me the engine start checklist."

54

Greene County Airport
3:22 pm

Ty handed the well-worn notebook with laminated pages to Regan. She flipped it open to the pre-start checklist. "You mean you don't even know how to *start* this plane? I'm getting out!" Regan protested.

Solly was sitting in the back, watching their interaction with growing impatience.

Ty put his hand on Regan's arm and said, "Regan, calm down. I've flown many kinds of aircraft. But each one is a little different to start. Once the props are spooling, it's a piece of cake. Now start reading the checklist. And if you believe in prayer, then pray that this battery is charged."

Regan opened the booklet and said, "Okay. So here's the pre-start check-list."

"We don't have time for that one. Just read me the engine start checklist." Ty said. Ty put his headset on, inserted the key and pushed the master switch to "on."

He pointed to her headset and said, "Put on your headset and speak into the microphone. It's voice activated, so I'll be able to hear you. Read as fast as you can."

"Right ignition on."

Ty flipped a switch. "Check."

"Check illuminated stable N1 greater than 12%. What does that mean?"

The right prop of the King Air started spinning slowly and then picked up speed.

"Don't comment, just read faster."

"Condition lever low idle."

Ty moved the fuel flow lever in the console forward a little. "Check."

"Monitor ITT and N1 1090 degrees Celsius max...rise in 10 seconds."

He looked at the instrument panel and put his finger on a gauge. "Check."

"Right oil pressure."

"Check. Coming up."

"Condition lever high idle."

Ty advanced the condition lever forward. "Check."

By now, the right propeller was spinning fast and making a lot of noise.

"N1 past 51% right ignition off."

Ty said, "It's coming. It'll be there in a few more seconds. There. Right ignition off."

"Right generator on."

Ty flipped another switch. "Check."

"Charge battery."

Ty stared at a gauge and after about 20 seconds he said, "Done. What's next?"

"Right generator off."

"Check."

"Left engine ignition, on."

Ty said, "Okay, I've got it from here." Ty quickly repeated the steps for the left engine that he had just followed. "Stand by. We'll be taxiing soon."

In less than a minute, both props were spinning fast and roaring loudly.

Regan was glad she had the headset on.

"Read me the after start check list," Ty barked.

"Transfer pumps on."

Ty was relieved to see that the King Air's fuel tanks were full. "Check."

"Crossfeed auto."

"Done. I've got it now. Thanks, Regan. You make a great first officer."

Ty released the parking brake and advanced the power levers. The King Air started rolling forward. He pushed the left rudder and the aircraft turned and started toward the taxiway. He switched on the avionics master and twisted the frequency control to set 122.8 and pushed the propeller levers to the maximum speed level.

He then depressed a small button on the left side of his yoke and said, "Green County Unicom. King Air..." He paused to look for the registration that was printed on the instrument panel. "...King Air 9497 Whiskey taxiing onto runway seven. Any other reported traffic near Green County, please respond."

He released the button and said over the intercom, "We're supposed to do a full run-up, but under the circumstances, we're going to skip it. We've got a bad guy to catch."

Ty turned and yelled to Solly, "See if you can find another headset and plug it in beside one of the cabin seats. I hope to get you close enough to open the cabin door and take some shots at that crop duster."

Regan cinched her seat belt tighter and swallowed hard.

Ty taxied out quickly toward the runway, glancing at the windsock. It favored a takeoff from left to right down runway 7, the same direction the crop duster had departed. He estimated that the airstrip was at least 4,000 feet long. Under ordinary conditions, he would taxi all the way to the end of runway 7 in order to have the benefit of the entire length. But he was running out of time. That would take another three minutes. He estimated that the King Air was about 50 knots faster than the AT-602, but he didn't have any time to waste.

He turned right. "Hang on. We're going to do a short-field takeoff."

Regan stared ahead and said, "There isn't enough room to take off!"

Ty said, "Trust me. I know what I'm doing."

By now, Solly had found a third headset. "Remember, Ty, this isn't like those fighter jets you used to fly. Are you sure we can make it?"

"No, I'm not sure. But I'm sure that if we waste any more time we won't catch up with the crop duster."

He pointed the nose of the King Air down the runway. As he lowered the flaps, he instructed Regan to look to the left of her yoke for an airspeed indicator.

"Do you see it?"

"Yes!" she said.

"When we start rolling, tell me when the needle hits 90 knots."

With the brakes engaged, Ty slowly pushed the power levers forward until the engines were roaring and the entire aircraft was shaking. Then when it seemed that the aircraft couldn't withstand the vibration a second longer, he released the brakes and the King Air shot down the runway like a slingshot.

"Read off the airspeed to me."

"It's not moving yet!" Regan exclaimed.

"It will. Any second now," Ty said calmly.

"Okay. Here it comes. Sixty... seventy... eighty..." Regan glanced up through the windshield and saw the end of the runway approaching and the tall trees rushing toward them. "We're not going to make it!" she screamed.

Ty pulled back hard on the yoke and a moment later retracted the gear. The King Air cleared the runway lights at the end by a mere two feet. But he was flying. Glancing at a chart on the left of the instrument panel, he saw that his best angle of climb was 100 knots. He set the airspeed needle there and started climbing. When he had reached 1,000 feet, he retracted the flaps.

Ty spoke over the intercom, "A King Air performs best up at higher altitudes, but we don't have that luxury today. I'm going to climb up to 5,500 feet as we head toward Augusta. I can just follow I-20 below us."

Ty leveled off and trimmed the airplane for straight and level flight. He kept the power levers at maximum to milk every knot he could out of the twin PT6A-28 turboprops.

Regan could finally breathe again because she realized that Ty did actually know how to fly this airplane. She looked at the cars and trucks below.

"The best kind of IFR is I Follow Roads," Ty said with a grin. "Keep your eyes open for that bright yellow crop duster. He had about a ten-minute lead on us. He is probably flying very low, and I estimate that we're about 50 knots faster than him, so we should be catching him in about five more minutes."

Solly said, "You guys keep looking. I've got a phone call to make." He pulled out his satellite phone and hit a speed dial number.

55

APRIL 12
Augusta National Golf Club
Augusta, Georgia
3:45pm

A gentle breeze teased the tops of the majestic pines. The brilliant hues of the massive azalea bushes provided a vivid background for the most breathtaking golf course in the world. Amateur golfer James Gillen looked around and smiled. He caught a faint whiff of the honeysuckle vines winding around many of the pine trees. For at least the hundredth time, he whispered, "Thank you, God, for letting me play in the Masters."

On the PGA tour, Saturday is known as "moving day." You can't win the tournament on Saturday, but you can certainly lose it. Saturday is the day that the PGA pros want to move up to a position near the lead so that they can have a chance to win on Sunday, the final round.

An invitation to play in the Masters is the most coveted prize in the golfing world. Those invited include all the winners of the previous Masters, the winners of the previous five U.S. Opens, British Opens, and PGA Championships. The top 50 professional golfers in official world rankings are invited as well, including winners of all the PGA tournaments during the previous 12 months.

As a nod to the tournament creator, Bobby Jones, the Masters has a tradition of honoring amateur golf by inviting the winners of the most prestigious amateur tournaments in the world. The current U.S. Amateur champion always plays in the same group as the defending Masters champion for the first two days of the tournament. The winner of the U.S. Mid-Amateur is also invited to tee it up with the pros.

The USGA specifically designed the Mid-Am as a championship for post-college golfers who were not pursuing golf as a career. The Mid-Am was a response to the fact that most older golfers found themselves disadvantaged in competing against college golfers who typically play much more often. The requirements to compete in the Mid-Am were that a golfer had to be over 25 years old and have a handicap of 3.4 or lower.

James Gillen had won the Mid-Am the previous year, and he had to pinch himself repeatedly as a reminder that he was really competing in the Masters Tournament.

As a forty-five-year-old attorney, golf was one of his passions but not his business. He had surprised everyone by being the only amateur in the field to make the cut on Friday.

As he stood on the 10th tee of his third round, he glanced over at the leader board and could hardly believe his eyes. On the front nine, he had been in "the zone." He had hit every green in regulation and made four birdies. He was currently tied with

Phil Mickelson for the lead of the Masters.

Over 35,000 patrons on the course were cheering for him. Everyone had expected any of the several big-name pros to charge into the lead. But the headline story was about James Gillen. An amateur golfer had never won the Masters. Ken Venturi came close in 1956 only to lose to Jack Burke, Jr. by one stroke. Could this be the year that an amateur golfer won?

James' caddy was his friend, Barney, and they were having the week of their lives. Every morning, they drove up through the famed Magnolia Lane and parked in the reserved spots for Masters contestants. They had full access to the clubhouse and the locker room.

They were almost too distracted by the history and tradition to concentrate on golf. But James had played inspired golf and had shot 70 on Thursday and 69 on Friday. And today, every shot was flying on line.

James gazed down the 10th fairway, which sloped sharply downhill and turned left. He asked Barney to hand him his driver. He teed his ball up on the right side of the tee box. As he took a couple of practice swings, he reminded himself to swing "inward to outward" and create the draw needed for this fairway. Gripping the club lightly, he took a smooth backswing and released the club head down. At the last moment, he rotated his right wrist over his left. The result was a perfect towering hook that bounded down the sloped fairway. His ball came to rest only 160 yards from the green.

The patrons lining the tee box applauded enthusiastically amid shouts of "You can do it, James!" "Win it for all of us!"

James waited for his playing partner, Ricky Fowler, to hit

his drive. As he walked down the fairway, he tipped his cap and smiled to the patrons.

It was a beautiful day. The sun was shining and the humidity was low, which is rare for Georgia. It was one of those magical moments. As he and Barney walked down the fairway, James said, "Barney, this is the best day of my life—except for the day I met the Lord, the day I married my wife, and the days my kids were born!"

Barney laughed and said, "At least you have your priorities in order!"

Neither of them had any idea that there was a crazed terrorist intent on making this the last day of their lives. Five hundred gallons of lethal poison were only a few minutes away from spoiling their dreams.

56

APRIL 12

FBI Regional Office
2635 Century Parkway N.E.
Atlanta, Georgia
3:48pm

Tony Parker felt his phone vibrate. He started to ignore it because he was busy leaning over a map of central Georgia. He was pointing out locations where there were water supply systems.

Following a hunch, he pulled out his phone, saw, "blocked" on the screen and took the call. "Who is this?" he said.

"I think you know you who I am. Where are you?"

"Solly, I was beginning to think I wouldn't hear from you. I'm in Atlanta at the FBI office. Where are you?"

Solly said, "Listen carefully. I don't have time to repeat any of this. We're in a King Air and we've just taken off from the Greene County Airport near Greensboro, Georgia. We're in pursuit of a bright yellow crop duster that we believe is carrying botulinum toxin to spray on the Masters golf tournament. It should reach Augusta in about 20 minutes."

There was silence on the other end of the phone.

"Please tell me you're kidding me," Parker said.

"This is the real deal, Tony. We could use your help."

"Why in the world haven't you called me sooner?" Parker demanded. "If this attack succeeds, I'm arresting you for obstruction of justice and you'll never see the light of day."

"Tony, calm down and put me on speaker phone. We were simply following a lead. There was no way we could know it is legitimate. If you'll send your people to the Greene County Airport, you'll find one Dr. Hakeem Saad on the ground beside the flight office. He'll need a new knee, but he should live. Don't let him get away. Meanwhile, have your bio-terror expert there tell us how we can bring this crop duster down without killing thousands of people."

Parker said, "Okay, you're on speaker phone. We'll send S.W.A.T. teams by chopper to the Greene County Airport to retrieve Dr. Saad. Our chemical weapons expert is here. I'll let him speak to you."

A voice came over the phone. "I'm Dr. Richard Handley, what's your situation?"

"We were told by Dr. Saad's daughter that they have botulinum toxin in the tank of a crop duster, and they're planning on spraying it over the golf course at Augusta. I've got firepower and I think I can bring the crop duster down when we get close enough. What do you suggest?"

Dr. Handley said, "We were guessing the chemical agent was anthrax or ricin. Botulinum toxin dispersed as an aerosol is another matter. It's much more dangerous. If the terrorist successfully delivers it, everyone in Augusta who breathes just a miniscule amount could potentially die in less than an hour."

Solly said, "I don't need the worst-case scenario. I need to know how to stop him. Can we shoot him down?"

Dr. Handley paused to think for a few seconds.

"Are you there?" Solly asked impatiently. "We're running out of time here."

"I've got him in sight!" Regan shouted from the cockpit. "There, off to our right, flying low!"

Solly said, "I need some directions. We've just spotted the crop duster."

Dr. Handley said, "I can't be certain because we don't have any protocols for this scenario. But I assume the botulinum is in a cooled liquid state in order to be stored in the tank. If you shoot down the airplane, the results could still be catastrophic. When the plane hits the ground and breaks apart, the botulinum will be dispersed. As it reacts to the warm air temperature, it will convert to a gaseous state. It will be invisible, odorless, and tasteless and very lethal. It could be dangerous to anyone within a radius of five miles of the crash site—maybe more, depending on the wind direction."

"So we can't shoot him down?" Solly said. "What can we do then?"

"If your aim is off and you happen to shoot a hole in the tank containing the botulinum, it could still be released into the air and become toxic," Dr. Handley explained.

"Are you telling me we don't have any way of stopping this madman without killing people?" Solly said. "There's got to be a better answer. Get your heads together with some of your fellow nerds and come up with something—and do it fast because we're almost out of time."

Solly unstrapped his seat belt and leaned into the cockpit. "Head toward the crop duster and hold. The bioweapons expert said we can't shoot it down without releasing the poison gas. They're working on plan B now."

"What if there's no plan B?" Regan asked, her voice shaking.

"There's always a plan B," Solly said.

Ty descended and maneuvered the King Air directly behind the AT-602 so that the pilot couldn't see him. As Ty approached, he retarded the power levers and slowed the aircraft by applying left rudder and right aileron to crab the King Air almost sideways. He applied a few degrees of flaps and raised the nose, and soon they were matching the crop duster's speed and flying only 100 feet behind him.

"You're sure he can't see us?" Regan asked.

"I'm sure," Ty said. "There aren't any rearview mirrors on airplanes. And besides, the back of his canopy is solid."

"What are we going to do?" Regan asked.

"Solly, what are your experts saying?" Ty asked. "We need a plan because I can see Augusta coming up at twelve o'clock and about ten miles."

Solly said, "I'll check." He lifted his satellite phone to his ear. "What's your plan, gentlemen?"

"Water," Dr. Handley said.

57

5,500 feet AGL
Inside the King Air C-90
Over rural Georgia
3:46pm

Solly blinked rapidly as he took in Dr. Handley's instructions. "We all agree that if you can somehow bring the plane down in a body of water without rupturing the tank in the air, then the liquid botulinum toxin should be diluted in the water. Since the water temp is cooler than the air, the chemical agent should theoretically retain its liquid state."

"I never like the word 'theoretically.' Will it work or not?" Solly asked.

"A theory is all we have. This is a scenario we've never encountered before."

"Will there be any deaths if we can put him down in water?"

"Any fish or waterfowl will certainly perish. And the water source should be quarantined and not used for drinking purposes."

"Great. We'll try. And don't even think about calling and asking PETA for their permission. I'm sure Air Traffic Control has us on radar since I called you. If we can pull this off, make sure you have plenty of EPA geeks there to secure the body of water, wherever that may be."

"Roger. We're on it." Parker was back on the line. "Anything else?"

"Start praying now. This may be a one-in-a-million shot," Solly said.

Solly quickly disconnected and replaced his headset. "We need to put that sucker down into water. But the tank containing the poison gas has to be intact. So we can't shoot him down. You're the hotshot Marine pilot. Any ideas?"

Ty was thinking quickly as he began looking for bodies of water along their flight path. He said, "I've been looking at his tail section. It looks pretty flimsy. If I can destroy his elevator and rudder, he won't have any control over the airplane and it will spiral straight down."

"How are you going to destroy his tail?" Solly asked.

"If I come from the side and swipe him with the tip of my wing, I can take off his tail and hopefully I'll only damage a small portion of our wing. We should be able to stay airborne."

"*Should be*?" Regan asked. "That sounds dangerous to me."

"Do you have any other suggestion?" Ty said.

"Why don't we call the Air Force to shoot him down?"

"The bioweapons expert said that if the aircraft is destroyed in the air, the toxin will be released," Solly explained.

"There," Ty said as he pointed ahead. "See that large lake in the distance? We'll be over it in a few minutes. Let's do it."

Ty banked hard to the left and pushed the power levers forward. He retracted the flaps and his speed increased. As he banked the King Air in a steep 60-degree turn, Regan grabbed the top of the instrument panel and screamed.

"Hold on, I'll level off in a second," Ty assured her.

After performing a 270-degree turn, he leveled the wings. He was now flying on a perpendicular vector toward the crop duster. Keeping the tail section of the yellow plane at the same spot in his windshield, he glanced to the left to see that they were approaching the lake.

"Regan, move back into the passenger cabin with Solly. You've got a better chance of surviving a crash back there!" he shouted. "I've never been in a mid-air collision before. So I can't guarantee we'll make it. Solly, make sure both of you are strapped in."

Regan released her shoulder harness and scrambled back into the passenger cabin.

58

Inside the AT-602
500 feet above ground level
3:55pm

Yamani was sweating profusely as he glanced ahead at Augusta, Georgia. He had made this flight many times using Microsoft Flight Simulator software. He was surprised at how realistic the computer animation had been. But this wasn't a virtual flight using a computer. The vibration of the thundering engine reminded him that this was real. He had been glancing left and right for other aircraft, but the sky was empty. The chatter on the Atlanta Center Radar had been normal communications between aircraft and ATC. There had been no indication that they even knew he was in the air.

The flight from Greene County had been problem-free. The only issue was fighting the occasional bursts of turbulence. But that was common when flying so close to the ground. He had to work to maintain his altitude of only 500 feet.

He estimated that he would be over the city of Augusta in less than ten minutes. He would make one pass over the city then bank around to the right and descend to about 100 feet, flying low over the golf course. He checked and rechecked the chemical level in the hopper. He ensured that the sprayer dial was set to "fine." Then he reviewed the process of engaging the sprayer switch.

He was ready.

He had been training for jihad for the past five years. This had been the assignment given to him by Al-Qaeda. Could he actually do it? Could he really give his life for Allah? He was inspired by the memory of the heroes of 9/11. If they could fly airliners full of passengers into buildings, surely he could fly this aircraft over a golf course and crash into a single building. With fresh resolve, he practiced his final declaration, "Allahu Akbar!"

59

Greensboro Fire Department
Greensboro, Georgia
3:48pm

Mike Parks had been the Chief of the Greensboro Volunteer Fire Department for 15 years. It was a part-time job, so he supplemented his income by working as Fire Marshall for Greene County.

Both were good jobs and Parks enjoyed his hobby of singing in a local band specializing in 60s music. They were called the Mud Dogs. The drummer loved mudding on his four-wheeler, and when he suggested the name, nobody else in the group had come up with a better one. So, like mud, it stuck to the group.

The Mud Dogs kept their amplifiers and sound system at the fire station, which was fine with the Fire Chief—and the Fire Marshall. Mike was there this afternoon getting ready to load up their trailer for a gig in Madison, Georgia. The phone rang and Mike rolled his eyes. He was hoping it was not another brush fire or an animal that needed rescuing. He was looking forward to the cash he would make with the Mud Dogs tonight.

Parks answered, "Chief Parks here."

It was the Emergency Operations Center dispatcher. She said, "Chief, we just got a 911 call from a passing motorist. He said there's a huge fire at the airport. He thinks a plane might have crashed into the building there. We have EMS on the way."

Mike sighed as he saw his Saturday night cash flying away. "Thanks. I'm on it."

He jogged outside the Fire Department and glanced toward the northeast. He could see a thick, black cloud of smoke spiraling into the afternoon sky.

He pulled out his cell phone and hit a speed dial button. It would summon the volunteer firemen in Greensboro to the station. These guys were pretty good about showing up within ten or fifteen minutes of getting his call. Sometimes that wasn't fast enough to prevent a structure from burning to the ground. But at least they could keep a fire from spreading to other structures. And the city just couldn't afford to pay any full-time firemen.

Mike suited up in his gear and waited. He called EMS and they connected him to Harvey Rowe, one of the EMTs for Greene County.

Harvey said, "We're five minutes out from the airport."

Mike said, "Call me back and give me a report when you arrive. We'll be there in ten to fifteen."

Over the next ten minutes, four volunteer firemen roared up in their pickups. Screeching to a halt, they jumped out and ran into the firehouse. Once they had donned their gear, Mike gave the signal to leave.

He jumped behind the wheel of the fire truck and pulled out into the street. Turning left toward the airport, he switched on the siren and floored the accelerator. The diesel engine growled in protest as the fire truck sped toward the smoke.

Mike's phone rang and without taking his eyes off the road he said, "Speak to me."

Harvey said, "The fire looks like it was caused by a truck that collided with an SUV in the parking lot. They are still burning. The flight office is on fire, too. We don't see any people, but we're just starting to search."

"Roger that," Mike said. "We'll be there in five."

60

Greene County Airport
3:55pm

Dr. Saad was delirious with pain. He had watched as the infidels had taken off in pursuit of Yamani. He had prayed to Allah that they wouldn't be in time to stop him from his mission.

He had tried to drag himself away from the airport office, but he was in agony. Every movement caused fiery darts of pain to shoot through his left leg. He was losing blood at an alarming rate. He knew that the entire airport office would soon be engulfed in flames.

Then he heard the sirens. He didn't know if they were policemen or ambulances. But a plan began to take shape in his agile mind.

In a few minutes, he saw two EMTs walk around the side of the burning building. They were both carrying large cases.

Dr. Saad raised himself to lean on his left arm and waved his hand. "Help me, please!"

The EMTs broke into a trot and ran to him.

"What happened here?" Harvey asked as he glanced over at the bloody body of Ali.

"It was a terrorist attack!" Dr. Saad said in his best American accent. "I'm Dr. Max Phillips. I'm a professor at Georgia Tech. I was out here to take flying lessons when some terrorists came onto the field. We tried to run away, but they shot my flight instructor here. Then they shot me. I played dead, and they left. Please check on my friend and see if he's okay."

The other EMT checked for a pulse on Ali and shook his head.

Dr. Saad continued, "You've got to stop them. They are in a twin-engine aircraft and they are heading for Atlanta. They are going to crash it into the CNN Center. Please call the authorities!"

Harvey said, "Settle down, Dr. Phillips. We'll let the authorities know. But we've got to take care of you."

Meanwhile, the other EMT called 911 and reported the terrorist threat to Atlanta. Then he said, "Wait here, and we'll get a stretcher for you. We've got to get you to the hospital."

Within minutes, Harvey had applied a compress to Dr. Saad's leg. He had hooked up an IV and loaded him onto the ambulance.

As they were pulling away, the Greensboro Fire Department truck came skidding into the parking lot. Harvey waved his hand at Mike as he passed him on his way to the hospital.

61

Inside the King Air C90
500 feet AGL
3:56pm

Ty kept the crop duster in the same relative position in his windscreen. That meant he was on a perfect collision point. His plan was simple. They were approaching the large lake beneath and just ahead. He was closing fast, approaching the crop duster from behind and left. Keeping his nose lined up with the tail of the other plane, at the last second he would step on his right rudder. The nose of the King Air should swing right and miss the tail. His left wing should then contact the tail section and rip it off.

On second thought, it was not a simple plan. It was dangerous. It was foolhardy to attempt a mid-air collision and survive. There was little room for error, and he knew that if his aim was even a little off, the King Air could go tumbling to earth. If that happened, there was no chance for any of them.

Maybe he should just veer away and let the madman complete his mission of terror. Was it worth risking his life and the life of his friend? Was it worth risking the life of the woman he was coming to care for? In that moment, Ty realized that he really did care for Regan. A great deal. But would he ever be able to tell her?

He was only a few seconds away from impacting the smaller plane. He concentrated on his angle to approach. *There! Punch the rudder!* Just as he started the maneuver, a fresh gust of turbulence lifted the King Air. As he sped past, he guessed that his left wing had missed the tail of the crop duster by only a few inches. But he had missed.

Without hesitation, he banked hard to the right. This time, he put the King Air in a 90-degree bank. He heard Regan screaming over the intercom. With one wing pointed toward the sky and one to the ground, he pulled back on the yoke to prevent the King Air from succumbing to an accelerated stall. Within seconds, he leveled his wings and was lined up behind the crop duster again. He was gaining on the slower flying aircraft. They were nearing the center of the lake now. Ty realized that he didn't have enough time to swing wide and attempt another approach from the side. The city of Augusta was not far beyond the lake. He had less than a minute to bring it down.

He could think of only one other way that might work, but it was a long shot. He could fly directly into the tail section of the crop duster. Using one of his props, he could rip the tail assembly to shreds. But that risky maneuver would mean he would lose at least one engine. And he could damage the King Air so much that it could no longer fly. His entire wing could be ripped from the fuselage. If that happened, they would tumble to the earth for sure.

As he gradually gained on the other plane, Ty banked gently

to his left so that his right prop was lined up with the rudder and elevator of the crop duster. He knew that there could be shrapnel from the engine and prop when it disintegrated. He didn't want to use the left engine since it was spinning close to his head. *I already have a hole in my head for trying this bonehead trick*, he thought. He smiled at his own sick humor.

For all of his career as a pilot, Ty had focused his energies and skill on not crashing. Now, he had to resist that intuitive instinct and crash a perfectly good aircraft into another one. He glanced to his right. The prop was spinning only a couple of feet from the tail section of the crop duster. He was looking ahead at the left wing of the yellow plane and suddenly worried that the nose of the King Air might impact it before his prop shredded the tail.

"Hang on!" he shouted.

There was a terrible grinding noise as the four-bladed prop tore into the thin aluminum of the other plane's tail assembly. Jagged pieces of metal and cable exploded into the right side of his windscreen, cracking the glass. The aircraft was shaking and Ty could smell the acrid stench of burning metal.

Then the King Air pitched violently to the right as the left engine continued to spin while the right engine was tearing apart. Ty kicked the left rudder pedal and pulled back on the yoke to pitch the King Air to avoid crashing into the crop duster. But he was no longer flying as much as he was limping through the air. He quickly pulled the fire suppression lever for the right engine and feathered what was left of the grinding propellers on the right engine. Alarms were still sounding, tones were ringing, and lights were flashing that Ty had no clue how to stop.

He remembered his first flight instructor's advice, "When something goes wrong, fly the airplane!"

He twisted a knob beneath the center console to crank in rudder trim enough for him to release the pressure on his left foot. He could barely maintain enough speed to keep from stalling. Even with full left aileron, the aircraft was still banking to the right. He finally mustered enough courage to assess the damage to his right wing and was alarmed by what he saw.

62

Inside the AT-602
300 feet and descending
4:00pm

Without warning, Yamani's body was thrown violently against his shoulder harness. He heard a deafening grinding noise from behind him. The nose of the crop duster then pitched violently down toward the lake beneath him. He was spinning to the right out of control. He quickly reacted by pulling back on the yoke, but there was no response. The lack of pressure on the stick confirmed that the cable connecting it to the elevator was severed. He pressed the left rudder pedal to correct the spiral, but there was no response there either. The surface of the lake was approaching at an alarming rate.

What had gone wrong? Had a missile been fired at him? But there had been no explosion. He had gotten so close to his goal. Had Allah forsaken him? As Yamani realized his mission was a failure, he cried, "Inshallah!"

Then he remembered the sprayer switch. Perhaps he could release at least some of the poison before he crashed. It was hard to move his hands with the aircraft spinning, but he reached out his left hand toward the sprayer switch. Just as he touched it, there was a massive shock as the crippled plane splashed into the lake.

The plane floated for a second, then the heavy engine pulled the nose under the water and it began to sink. The force of the impact had rendered Yamani unconscious. But even if he had been awake, he wouldn't have had time to unleash his harness before the heavily loaded crop duster sank to the bottom.

63

Inside the King Air C-90
600 feet and descending
4:02pm

Through the cracked windscreen, Ty could barely make out the damaged right engine. Most of the top of the engine cowling had been ripped back and was flapping violently in the airflow. It was acting like a giant airbrake to slow down the right wing. That's why he couldn't control the bank.

He had no idea whether his plan had worked to bring down the crop duster. But he had other worries now.

Ty yelled over the intercom, "Solly, look out the right window and tell me what you see."

Solly said, "Your right engine is almost ripped off. There's a large piece of metal from the other airplane stuck in the engine cowling. It's flapping like it might tear off at any second."

Fighting the controls, Ty shouted, "Pray! We're going down if it doesn't tear off."

Ty suddenly felt less pressure on the yoke.

"There it goes!" Solly said. "Your prayer worked!"

Ty hadn't had time to pray. He was still fighting to keep the crippled plane in the air. "What else do you see?"

Solly said, "There's fuel spewing out of the top of the wing where it has ripped open. And...uh oh. It looks like the end of the right wing is missing! And there's another part dangling like it's going to separate any second."

Ty said, "We've got to try to gain some altitude! We're too low."

Ty pressed on the left power lever trying to get more altitude, but it was already at full position. The aircraft was wobbling through the air on the edge of a stall. He couldn't stop their descent and the aircraft had started into a right turn again.

Ty glanced through the windshield. The Augusta airport was only about four miles away, but it might as well have been a thousand. They weren't going to make it.

Ty turned the com to 121.5, the emergency frequency. He said with more calmness than he felt, "Mayday, mayday, mayday. King Air 9497 Whiskey is four west of Augusta. Declaring an emergency. We are damaged from a midair. Crop duster down in lake northwest of Augusta. We are going down also."

They were down to about 200 feet and Ty had little lateral control. As they were banking gently right, Ty saw a short pasture coming into view. That was his spot. He lowered the flaps to slow the aircraft and heard a grinding sound from the right wing. He thought, "Great. Damaged right wing. No flaps today. Who needs 'em?"

He kept the gear retracted since it would only dig into the ground. This would be his very first gear-up landing. And maybe his last landing ever.

He yelled over the intercom, "You guys brace for a crash

landing! It's going to be rough!"

As he approached the short pasture, he gradually reduced power on the left engine. Then he started sinking too fast, so he added back a little more power. He was over the fence and just a few feet above the ground. There were trees at the end of the pasture. If they landed near there, they had little hope.

Ty pushed the yoke gently downward and pulled the power lever all the way back. The belly of the King Air plowed into the ground and immediately started sliding violently sideways. Gradually, the speed of the slide began to slow. *I've made it!* he thought.

Just then the left wingtip dug into a mound of dirt and the King Air flipped over on its back. Ty could hear agonized screams coming from the passenger cabin.

The aircraft continued to slide, crumpling the top of the cabin. It slid into a stand of tall pine trees. Both wings were torn off before the crumbled cabin came to rest upside down in a ravine.

When the King Air flipped over, Ty's body slammed against the yoke, crushing his chest. His last thought before he gave in to the darkness was, *Now comes the fire.*

64

EMT ambulance
Thirty miles west of Augusta
4:15pm

"How are you feeling, Dr. Phillips?" Harvey asked.

They were rocking side-to-side in the back of the ambulance as they sped toward the nearest trauma-certified ER hospital in Augusta.

"I'm doing better. The pain medication helped," Dr. Saad said with a grimace. "Where are you taking me?"

"We're going to the emergency room at University Hospital in Augusta. They are the closest facility certified to treat a GSW," Harvey replied.

"GSW?" Dr. Saad asked.

"Gunshot wound." Harvey checked the monitor connected to Dr. Saad's chest. "We're required by law to report all GSWs."

"Of course," Dr. Saad replied. "And I hope they will be able to prevent the attack on Atlanta."

"We reported it. That's all we can do."

"How much longer until we arrive at the hospital?"

"Ordinarily, it would take us about thirty minutes, but there's a big golf tournament in town, so the traffic is pretty thick. We should make it in about 40 minutes."

"I wonder if you would loan me your cell phone so I can call my wife. She is going to be desperately worried about me."

Harvey thought for a second. "Well, it's against company policy. But I'm a Georgia Tech fan, so I'll make an exception for you."

Harvey dug his cell phone out from his pocket and handed it to him.

Dr. Saad dialed a number he had memorized. He was calling another member of an Al-Qaeda cell imbedded in Georgia. When a voice answered, he spoke a code phrase that indicated that he needed an emergency extraction.

"Edith, it's me, Max. Don't be upset. But when I went to the airport for my lesson, there were some criminals there. I got shot in the leg. But I'm okay. Please call Dr. Saad and let him know I won't be at our meeting tomorrow."

He paused for a few minutes as he imagined how a worried wife might respond.

"Now, don't worry, sweetheart. I'm going to be fine. They're taking me to the emergency room at Augusta General Hospital. We're on Interstate 20 now, and we'll be at the hospital in about 30 minutes. Can you meet me there?"

He paused again.

"Yes, dear. And please bring our boys with you. I want them to drive you."

He paused.

"I love you, too. Goodbye."

He handed the phone to Harvey and said, "Thank you,

young man. I appreciate your kindness."

As they sped toward the hospital, Dr. Saad thought, "It's too bad that this will be the day that you die."

65

Greene Country Airport
4:15pm

The Greensboro Volunteer Fire Department had been joined by the Union Point Fire Department. These committed volunteers had been working hard the past fifteen minutes directing powerful streams of high-pressure water at the source of the flames. The fire from the collision of the two vehicles had spread to the flight office and the other parked cars. These fires had been extinguished until they were smoking hulks of blackened metal. The pungent smell of burning rubber filled the air.

Mike Parks had repositioned his truck and team behind the flight office. They were finally bringing that fire under control. His worst fear was that the fire would spread to the underground fuel tanks or to the aircraft tied down on the ramp. He smiled and gave a thumbs-up sign to his assistant, Bubba. There had been a lot of damage, but this fire wasn't spreading any further.

Another EMT team had arrived by then and had checked the condition of the man lying beside the concrete bunker. Mike noticed that they had covered him with a white sheet.

He felt the vibration in the air before he heard the sound. He glanced up to see three Black Hawk military helicopters descending toward the field. The backwash from their powerful rotors stirred the thick smoke into twisting ribbons.

As soon as the Blackhawks settled, the doors flew open and Special Forces soldiers poured out onto the grass. Ducking to avoid the props, they ran toward the burning flight office with their weapons ready.

Mike wondered if this was some kind of military exercise. If it was, the county should have been notified beforehand.

An officer in full battle gear approached him and asked, "Who's in charge here?"

Mike said, "Well, since you have the guns, you can be in charge. I'm Mike Parks, the Fire Chief for Greensboro. We were called out here to fight a fire that started in the parking lot."

The officer said, "I'm Captain Greg Smith, Special Forces. There has been a report of possible terrorist activity here. Have you discovered any bodies?"

Mike pointed to the body beside the flight office covered with a sheet. "There's one corpse there. Died from gunshots—lots of them from the looks of it. There was a survivor, and he's been transported to an Emergency Room by our EMS squad."

Captain Smith and Mike walked over to the body and pulled back the sheet. He compared the face of the man with a small picture he pulled out of his pocket. He shook his head.

He handed the picture of Dr. Saad to Mike and said, "We're looking for a terror suspect who looks like this. Could this have been the survivor who was taken to the hospital?"

"I don't know," Mike said, "The ambulance was leaving just

as we arrived. I didn't see his face. I can call the EMT in the ambulance. Name's Harvey. He's a buddy of mine."

Captain Smith said, "Give him a call, but tell him not to be alarmed. This is a really bad dude. We were sent here to secure him. When you call your friend, just describe the picture to him over the phone and ask him to confirm or deny that this is their patient. If he confirms, then tell your friend that he should be considered dangerous. We need to get law enforcement to their location."

Mike pulled out his cell phone and called up his "favorites" screen. He punched Harvey's name and listened for the ring. It rang several times and went to Harvey's voice mail.

"Hey, Harvey. It's Mike. The guy in your ambulance may be a terrorist. I've got his picture here." Mike described him. "If that's the guy you've got, treat him as a dangerous criminal. Call me back when you get this message."

Mike said, "That's weird. Harvey always takes my calls, even if he's on another line. Well, maybe he's busy."

Captain Smith asked, "Where would they have taken the patient?"

"Probably to University Hospital in Augusta. It's the nearest facility with a level 1 trauma unit."

Captain Smith spoke into the com in his helmet, "Red Unit Three. On me, back at the chopper. We're out of here in three. Red Unit One and Two, remain and secure the area. Now move!"

Mike watched as the troops ran back to the Black Hawk. As soon as the last man had jumped in, the rotors sped up and the helicopter shot away from the airport on a line toward Augusta.

He wondered what in the world was going on, but he had a sneaking suspicion that The Mud Dogs weren't going to make their gig tonight.

66

Augusta National Golf Club
11ᵗʰ Fairway
4:15pm

There was an electric buzz generated by the thousands of patrons watching the leader boards. An amateur golfer was actually leading the Masters. It was the lead story for all the sportscasters and sportswriters in their specially equipped media tent. If an amateur golfer could win the Masters, it would be the biggest news in the world of sports for the entire year—perhaps for a decade.

There would be thousands of references to how Bobby Jones must certainly be smiling in golfing heaven. It was breaking news on all the sports channels.

And James Gillen was in the center of it all.

On the previous hole, he had hit a perfect seven iron that drew toward the back left pin placement on the 10ᵗʰ Green. His putt was 22 feet and he was trying to lag it up for a tap-in par. But the ball kept rolling and fell into the cup for another birdie. The patrons roared their approval, and their cheers could be heard all over the golf course.

James had pumped his fist in triumph as the ball rolled into the cup.

On the 11th tee box, James had pounded his best drive of the day down the left center of the fairway. The 11th hole was the first challenge of the famed "Amen Corner" that encompassed holes 11, 12, and 13.

Every hole at Augusta has a name, and the 11th is aptly named White Dogwood. Dozens of dogwood trees grew among the pines to the left of the fairway. Their white blossoms exploded like fireworks among the shade of the pines. James and Barney arrived at his ball.

"Man, this is a long hole!" James said. "I crushed that drive, and I still have 195 yards to the green."

He glanced over to his playing partner's drive, which was 20 yards farther down the fairway. "That Ricky Fowler must be on steroids or something, can you believe how far he hits it?"

"Don't pay any attention to him. You're not playing against Fowler. You're playing against the course," Barney advised. "You have 195 yards to the pin." Then he picked up a sprig of mowed grass and tossed it into the air to check the wind. "But it's downhill and the wind is helping. I think you need to hit a 180-yard shot."

"I think you're right. Hand me a five iron," James said.

"Now keep it right. If you go left into the lake, you're dead," Barney warned.

James took a couple of practice swings. He was full of adrenaline, and he was striking every shot perfectly. He looked at the pin and decided to take dead aim. He stood behind the ball and visualized a high, soft draw starting out toward the 12th tee box and curling left toward the pin on the green.

He took his stance and tried to relax over the ball. His backswing was smooth. But his downswing was a little too fast. The moment he hit the ball, he knew it was wet. He looked up to see the ball start toward the middle of the green and curve left into the small lake to the left of the green.

When the ball splashed in the lake, the crowd cried in unison, "Ahhhh!"

James was angry with himself for making such a poor swing. Barney was trying to keep him upbeat. "It's okay, buddy. We can drop it by the lake and you can still get up and down for bogey."

But the wind had gone from James' sails. Because the ball had entered so far into the lake, his drop was still across the lake from the green. He took his drop beside the water and proceeded to chunk his chip back into the water.

Again the crowd commiserated, "Ohhhh!"

Now, James was embarrassed. He dropped again. He wasn't going to chunk another chip. As if on cue, he hit this chip thin and his ball shot across the green and down the other side into the rough.

By now, the golf-savvy patrons refrained from making any noise. The silence was their polite acknowledgement that this hole was becoming a disaster.

Barney was silent as they walked to the other side of the green.

When they reached the ball, they saw that it had settled down into the rough. "Hand me a pitching wedge," James said.

Barney handed him the club and bowed his head to hide his disappointment.

James chipped up to within 12 feet. The crowd politely applauded this effort.

As James lined up his putt, he counted his strokes. One in the fairway; two in the water. Out in three. In the water again for four. Drop again for five. Across the green laying six. Up in seven.

If he could make this putt, he could escape with an eight. *Pro golfers had survived one disaster hole and gone on to win*, he thought lamely.

He stroked the putt and looked up to see it kiss the edge of the hole and spin out to the left. Again the crowd groaned.

James tapped in for nine to a smattering of inappropriate applause from the patrons.

James' poor play continued over the next few holes, and he never got close to the lead again in this Masters. He would always remember that Saturday as the day that he led at the greatest golf tournament in the world for a few minutes.

Barney and James would joke many times about the disaster at the 11th hole. But neither they, nor the thousands of patron there that afternoon, would ever realize how close they had come to being a part of a real disaster.

The Masters always provides the headlines in the Sports Section. But had Yamani succeeded, this tournament would have been the bold front-page headline of every newspaper and magazine in the world.

67

Four miles west of the Augusta Airport
4:15pm

"Ty, can you hear me?" Solly yelled.

Ty heard something, but the buzzing in his head was overpowering any other sound.

"Ty, are you okay?" Solly yelled again.

Solly and Regan had sustained minor injuries in the rear of the King Air when it had flipped over. They had managed to unbuckle their restraints in the upside down cabin and crawl out on the ceiling through a large hole in the side of the fuselage. They couldn't get into the cockpit because the access doorway had been crushed.

Ty hadn't replied to Solly's calls. There was the smell of jet fuel in the air, but no sign of a fire yet.

Solly assessed their injuries. His shoulder seemed to be out of joint, and his head had struck one of the seats in the cabin. Blood covered his face, but the wound didn't seem to be that deep.

Regan was in shock and shivering. The crash had broken her ankle. But apart from a few scrapes, Solly didn't see other significant lacerations or wounds. He put his arm around her and led her to a safe distance away from the plane. He sat her on the pine straw and placed his thin coat around her shoulders.

Solly quickly returned to the front of the airplane. The nose cone was gone, and the cockpit windshield was demolished. He could see Ty hanging there upside down, but there was no motion. There was no way he could get to him.

Dear God, please let him be alive, Solly silently prayed.

He yelled into the crushed cockpit, "Hold on, Ty, we're going to get you some help." He returned to Regan to see if his satellite phone was still in the pocket of his jacket. But it was gone. It must have fallen out when they crashed.

Then Solly heard the distinctive sound of helicopter blades beating the air coming their way. Ty's radio call declaring an emergency had apparently worked. Help was on the way. Solly just prayed it wasn't too late.

68

APRIL 13

**Dwight D. Eisenhower Army Medical Center
Augusta, Georgia
7:45am**

Ty was in the middle of a nightmare. He was in an unfamiliar airplane and it was spinning out of control. He was trying to reach out to take the yoke to regain control, but when he grabbed it, it came off in his hand. He was frustrated and confused. Was this real? Was this a dream?

He felt a hand on his shoulder. Then he heard a distant voice, "Settle down there, soldier. You're going to be alright."

He blinked his eyes and grimaced from the pain of the effort. It was easier to keep them closed. As his mind slowly started functioning, he struggled to remember what had happened.

He vaguely remembered the crash landing. If he was here, he figured he must be alive. That was a good thing.

He slowly opened his eyes and saw that he was in a sterile white hospital ICU unit. Every part of his body was hurting.

"Owww," he managed to groan.

"No need to speak, buddy," Solly said. "You've just come

through three emergency surgeries last night. You had internal injuries, broken ribs, and a punctured lung. But the docs fixed you up. They say that you should be as good as new in a few weeks."

"Owww," was all he could manage again.

Solly smiled. "Feeling pain is a good thing. Don't talk. Just listen. Now I don't want you to get a big head, but that was quite a job of piloting you did. You sent the crop duster into the lake, and then you were able to put us on the ground almost in one piece."

"Regan...okay?" Ty managed to groan.

"She's fine. She has a few cuts and a broken ankle. She's getting some rest now."

"Did we get the bad guys?" Ty asked.

"The crop duster went down in the lake and the pilot died. The chemical was dispersed into the lake. There aren't many fish alive in that lake, and EPA has quarantined it for the foreseeable future, but the greater disaster was averted. He was just a few minutes from releasing the toxin over the crowd. There could have been thousands of casualties."

"Will any of this hit the news?" Ty asked.

"Not on your life," Solly said. "The Feds are embarrassed it got this close to happening. They are going to cover up this story and take care of the damage, of course. They don't want to scare the American people needlessly."

Solly continued, "My friend, the CIA Director, threatened to arrest us for obstruction of justice. I told him to go ahead. I'd be glad to call a press conference and bring to light the events of the past few weeks."

"So it's over?" Ty asked.

"Not exactly. An ambulance was taking Dr. Saad to University Hospital here in Augusta. Three miles outside Augusta, the ambulance was attacked. The two EMTs are dead—bullet holes in their heads. Dr. Saad is gone without a trace. I should have killed him when I had the chance."

EPILOGUE

ONE MONTH LATER

May 12
Alpharetta, Georgia
6:30pm

Regan's doorbell rang. She looked at her reflection in the mirror and smiled as she put the finishing touches on her hair. She wanted to make sure everything looked just perfect.

Solly had returned to Israel. They had promised to stay in close contact. Regan had gotten out of her cast a couple of weeks ago and had found another townhome in Alpharetta. She had expected her job at GWA to be gone when she returned. But instead, she received a promotion. Solly must have certainly had some strong connections.

Regan no longer had to shuttle between Paris and Atlanta. She had a corner office at GWA's new cutting edge technology center in Gwinnett County.

After waiting an appropriate amount of time to irritate Ty, she opened the door. Ty stood there with a smile on his face and some flowers in his hand.

"For me?" Regan asked.

"Yes, ma'am," Ty said. "These flowers may lose their aroma, but you, my lady, will smell forever."

Regan couldn't help but laugh at Ty's corny humor. "Stop it! Do you ever turn it off?"

"If you mean my boyish charm or my sparkling wit, never," Ty replied.

"Let me put these in water," Regan said. "I need to grab my raincoat, too. The forecast is for storms later tonight."

As she removed a vase and filled it with water she said, "I miss Solly."

Ty said, "He called me today."

Regan carefully arranged the flowers in the vase. "What did he want?"

"He wanted to know how you were doing," Ty said.

"Me? He didn't want to know how you were doing?" Regan asked.

"That too. He also said that I should bring you over to Israel sometime to join him on one of his digs."

Regan opened the closet and slipped into her London Fog raincoat. "Who knows? That sounds like fun."

"It's more work than fun. Trust me," Ty said, helping her with her coat.

"I'm ready. Where are we going tonight?" Regan asked.

"I dunno. Let's just hop in my new pickup and see where it takes us."

They stepped outside and the air was thick with humidity. Thunder rumbled in the west and a freshening wind whipped through the tops of the pine trees. The night sky was already spitting a few sprinkles.

Walking to the curb, Ty grabbed Regan's hand and launched into his best raspy Ray Charles imitation of *It's a Rainy Night in Georgia*.

As they reached the curb, Regan was laughing. "That was awful! But if you're Ray Charles, you better give me the keys. Besides, I haven't driven your new Chevy Silverado."

Ty handed her the key fob and said, "You always like to be in control, don't you?"

Without replying, Regan unlocked the doors and Ty jumped into the passenger side. After she adjusted the seat to her height and checked the mirrors, she cranked the engine and the smooth 6.2 Liter V-8 rumbled to life. Regan pulled the gear stick into drive.

Then she turned to Ty and said with a grin, "Yes, I do."

AUTHOR NOTES

Although I have written about a dozen non-fiction books, this was my first attempt at a novel. I wrote the entire novel in about 100 days. I was pleasantly surprised at how quickly these fictional characters came to life.

Although this is purely a work of fiction, there is a powerful thread of truth woven into the plot. The Dead Sea Scrolls were composed, hidden, and discovered at Qumran in Israel. While the two prophecies in this novel are conjecture, there are those in the academic community who insist that the Israeli Antiquities Authority hasn't released all of the Dead Sea Scrolls to the public. That's not my fight, so I will let the academicians debate that point.

I first visited Qumran as a college student in 1974 when I was in Israel as part of a month-long archaeological class. There was evidence of the residual effects of the recent Yom Kippur War throughout the country. Israel was a nation under attack.

I specifically recall visiting an El Al Airline office in Jerusalem to submit a claim about my luggage, which had been damaged by the airline on the flight to Tel Aviv. The El Al employee listened to my complaint and dismissed me by saying, "Can't you see we're at war now? Come back and see me when the war is over." I never went back to the El Al office.

Since then, it has been my joy to visit Israel about 25 times, and every time I visit I feel as if I'm going home. I see the hand of God moving there in the miraculous restoration of the nation.

Yahweh spoke this promise through the prophet Amos:

*"I will bring back my exiled people Israel. They will rebuild the ruined cities and live in them. They will plant vineyards and drink their wine; they will make gardens and eat their fruit. I will plant Israel in their own land **never again to be uprooted** from the land I have given them," says the Lord your God."* (Amos 9:14-15)

Before 1948, the only interpretation of that prophecy was that it related to the return of the Jews from the Babylonian exile. Israel did return from Babylon, but the Romans uprooted them again in 70 A.D. when they destroyed the Temple in Jerusalem. I believe we are just now seeing the fulfillment of this and many other prophecies about the restoration of Israel.

I want to express my gratitude to my friend, Reuven Solomon, who has guided most of my trips in Israel. Reuven is a smart, kind-hearted, funny guy. I'm biased, but I think he's the most knowledgeable guide in Israel.

Thanks also to my daughter and son-in-law, Drs. Jason and Jenni Holman. Their medical knowledge about the fatal effects of botulinum toxin was invaluable to me. I just hope the Homeland Security folks weren't monitoring our Google history on bioterrorism!

I've been a private pilot since 1975 and have over a thousand hours of flying time. Before I stopped flying a few years ago, I held a multi-engine license and an instrument rating. I've always been fascinated with aviation. I'm grateful to my friend Toby

Cline, who flies a Boeing 747 for Cathay Pacific. Thanks, Toby, for reviewing the aviation sections and for describing to me what an intentional mid-air collision would look like. Hopefully, neither of us will ever have to put that knowledge to use!

I want to express my appreciation to my editor, Mary Ann Lackland, CEO of Fluency, Inc., for reading the manuscript and making helpful suggestions on my first fiction novel.

I also want to thank my friend, Jim Denison, for his insights into radical Islam. Jim is a top-notch scholar and theologian. His book, *Radical Islam: What you Need to Know*, is a powerful exposé of the serious threat that radical Muslims present to America. And Ameera's dream is not farfetched. More Muslims have come to Christ over the past 15 years than in the previous 15 centuries, many after seeing visions and dreams of Jesus. For verification of this phenomenon, read Tom Doyle's excellent book, *Dreams and Visions: Is Jesus Awakening the Muslim World?*

Finally, I want to thank author Joel Rosenberg for giving me the inspiration to write this novel. I've enjoyed reading all of Joel's novels, and he taught me that it is possible to combine an exciting plot with the absolute truth found in the Bible.

June 2013
David Orlo
Tyler, Texas